Praise for Holly Schindler

playing
h u r t

"[An] excellent second novel. Clint and Chelsea, two ex-athletes . . . explore the sometimes painful, sometimes passionate road to healing. Schindler does not sugarcoat the agonies and heartbreaks of first loves, first losses, and first disappointments. Anyone who says 'kids today have it so easy' should pick up a copy of *Playing Hurt*."

—Brian Katcher,
author of *Playing with Matches* and *Almost Perfect*

"If you're a fan of romance, good luck putting this one down. *Playing Hurt* is a delicious, tantalizing love story that will captivate you until the final, satisfying sigh. Holly Schindler's lyrical writing is an absolute delight to read."

—Kristin Walker,
author of *A Match Made in High School*

a blue so dark
~

★ "Breathtakingly, gut-wrenchingly authentic ... A haunting, realistic view of the melding of art, creativity, and mental illness and their collective impact on a young person's life."

—*Booklist*, starred review

playing
h u r t

playing
h u r t

HOLLY
SCHINDLER

flux
™
Woodbury, Minnesota

First Edition
Second Printing, 2011

Cover design by Ellen Lawson
Cover image © iStockphoto.com/Daniel Laflor

Flux, an imprint of Llewellyn Worldwide Ltd.

This is a work of fiction. Names, characters, places, and incidents are either the product of the author's imagination or are used fictitiously, and any resemblance to actual persons (living or dead), business establishments, events, or locales is entirely coincidental.

Cover models used for illustrative purposes only and may not endorse or represent the book's subject.

Library of Congress Cataloging-in-Publication Data
Schindler, Holly, 1977–
    Playing hurt / Holly Schindler.—1st ed.
        p. cm.
    Summary: Chelsea Keyes, a high school basketball star whose promising career has been cut short by a terrible accident on the court, and Clint Morgan, a nineteen-year-old ex-hockey player who gave up his sport following a game-related tragedy, meet at a Minnesota lake resort and find themselves drawn together by the losses they have suffered.
    ISBN 978-0-7387-2287-0
    [1. Loss (Psychology)—Fiction. 2. Love—Fiction. 3. Resorts—Fiction. 4. Minnesota—Fiction.] I. Title.
    PZ7.S34634Pl 2011
    [Fic]—dc22

                                                          2010044173

Flux
Llewellyn Worldwide Ltd.
2143 Wooddale Drive
Woodbury, MN 55125-2989
www.fluxnow.com

Printed in the United States of America

Acknowledgments

Thanks, as always, to the fantastic crew at Flux, particularly my editors, Brian Farrey and Sandy Sullivan.

And to Team Schindler—Mom (world's best first reader and sounding board), and especially John, my brother, for unwavering support throughout a long journey and for always being at all my author events, camera in hand.

And to the incredible bloggers and readers I've met online—whose enthusiasm is priceless—you make each release an absolute blast.

Thank you, thank you, thank you…

Chelsea
end line

Acamera winks at me from high in the bleachers like
we're sharing a secret. Fans in the home section of the
Fair Grove High gym smile in envy as I hurry toward the
bench, wishing some winking camera had ever, in their
entire lives, shared a secret with *them*.

Other cameras follow suit, flashes popping at me from
all over as I jog the last few steps to the huddle. Each step
sends fiery sparks through my hips—sparks I've been trying to ignore during practice for the last week and a half.

I fight a grimace and tell myself I'm doing a good job
covering up the pain. But when I glance up at the bleachers, I realize my little brother's squinting at me from
behind his thick glasses. He lowers his camcorder, wrinkles
his face into a worried frown.

I try to turn my attention back toward Coach Tindell, but my eyes bounce from the dried-up apple-doll face of my next-door neighbor, Mrs. Williams, to my second-grade teacher (who's wearing an absurdly large pair of papier-mâché basketball-shaped earrings), then to our mail carrier, to the boy who kissed me on the playground on the last day of the fourth grade, to two distant cousins, to Mack, owner of the Quick Mart down the block from my house (who constantly brags about patching the front tire on my cherry-red Camaro last spring the same way he might brag about patching up Brad Pitt's ride). My Camaro is now parked in the Fair Grove High lot, slathered in well-wishes from my boyfriend, Gabe, who is as sweet as a box of Valentine's Day candy hearts. *Go Chelsea!* he's written with windshield markers. *#23!* And, *Nitro!* which is the only thing the rest of the team calls me anymore.

"Doesn't *look* like a ball player," I hear trickle from the crowd. The sentence has been following me everywhere, flopping around like an untied shoelace ever since I was profiled by *USA WEEKEND* Magazine, since I was pictured on the cover of their issue highlighting the best female high school athletes in the country. My airbrushed, ultra-flattering portrait revealed that I was toned but not body-builder enormous; that unlike the stereotypical female basketball player, I also have most-definitely girly addictions—to strawberry-tinted lip gloss, waterproof mascara, and my straightening iron.

Doesn't look like a ball player. As that sentence floats, I get the urge to say something like, "Get real—women were playing basketball at Smith College in 1892," or, "Wasn't Title IX forty freaking years ago?" or, "I certainly *hope* we're past making jokes about butch girl jocks." Or, "How many more *times*, as women, are we going to have to prove that *feminine* and *powerful* can, in fact, be synonyms?"

"...thousand shots a day...set shots, lay-ups, free throws," I hear drifting from the crowd. "Five-mile run, an hour at the weight bench." They all know my daily work-out routine. They all talk big about it, beam the way most people do when talking about their kids.

As I glance up at the bleachers, I see a couple of poster-board signs hovering above the heads of the crowd, the hand-painted messages screaming *Chelsea Keyes—Pride of Fair Grove!*

I wipe my sweaty forehead with my fingertips. The humidity in the gym hangs in the air like a soaking wet sheet on a clothesline. But the rest of the team is still smooth-skinned. Almost powdery. Not a single sweat-shine on any of their cheeks.

"Work ethic powered by nitroglycerin," someone says from the front row of the bleachers. It should rev me, the way the Fair Grove fans are talking me up, thinking I'm like the active ingredient in dynamite. It should inspire me far more than Tindell's quickie pep talk. Instead, the words sit heavy across my shoulders like a barbell. Like some-thing I need to lift.

Our team breaks from the huddle; when I turn back toward the court, though, somebody's got their hand around my wrist.

"Do you need to sit this out?" Brandon hisses. He's standing up, right there in the front row of the bleachers, the entire town of Fair Grove watching him. I glance down at the camcorder, which he's lowered but hasn't turned off. The power light flashes as it records my every move.

I try to wrench my arm away, but he just grips me tighter. "You're not hurt, are you?" he asks.

"Don't be such a twerpy, jealous little sib," I snap, far more nastily than I'd intended.

I jog back toward the center of the court, my hips firing bullets with each step.

———

"I don't know why you torture yourself," Brandon says. I jump, slam my finger down on the remote's *pause* button. What should have been the first game of my last season as a Fair Grove High Lady Eagle freezes on my TV screen. *Should* have been. Things just didn't work out that way, though.

I relax my shoulders inside my worn-out Mizzou Tigers T-shirt, trying to act completely blasé as Brandon leans against my doorjamb in his rumpled pajama bottoms.

"It's *not* torture," I insist, flashing a smile. Brandon doesn't buy it; he tosses a disgusted look at me, his braces gleaming in the TV glow.

I try to look away, but my eyes land on the old trophies that pose triumphantly on my bookshelves, all those tiny little brass sculptures of athletes dunking their metallic balls or going for victorious lay-ups. But they don't really make me feel good anymore. Not proud. Just … furious at myself. I smile at Brandon, pretend this isn't the case. "I'm just *watching* it," I tell him. "Like some old movie on cable, you know?"

"Sure," Brandon grumbles, rolling his eyes behind the lenses of his glasses, which shine, tonight, like two circles of moonlight on his face. "And that's exactly why you only watch it in the dead of night, alone in your room. If it was all that innocent, you wouldn't have to hide."

I narrow my eyes, cross my arms over my shirt. Raise my eyebrow in a way that shows him I don't intend to put the remote down. Or turn my TV off.

"I'm right next door, Chelse," he informs me. "I can hear what you're doing in here. Watching your last game over and over. Do you even *sleep* anymore?" He clings to the doorway, waiting for an answer.

Attempting to ignore his very existence, I push *play*. The court at Fair Grove High bursts back onto the screen. Our state-of-the-art glossy floor shines under the gym lights like skin coated with baby oil. The regulation markings—black paint indicating the half-court and free throw areas—are still as familiar to me as the lines on my face.

I lean forward on the edge of my bed and squint at the screen, at the former me, marveling at the way my player's concentration has sharpened my senses; I'm just like a *real* eagle swooping in to tear the flesh from its unsuspecting kill. Which is exactly what I'd planned to do to the Aurora

Lady Houn' Dawgs, who'd come to *my* home court. Tear the juicy flesh from their vulnerable little puppy bones.

The cheerleaders along the sidelines are screaming their ridiculous fight song. The rhyme sounds awkward to me even now, watching it all unfold again for what must be the five-hundredth time.

Eagles, Eagles, we're so regal. Rule the court like queens!

The camera lens swivels away from the court, zooms in on a pair of tan thighs bouncing beneath the violet hem of a pleated skirt. My entire TV screen fills with tight muscle.

"*Brand*," Gabe moans from somewhere off-camera. "The game. Shoot the *game*."

The screen blurs as Brandon swivels again, clears as the view settles on Gabe's beautiful face.

"Come on," Gabe moans. "Help me out here." He shakes his head, a few blond curls tumbling down toward eyes so green you'd think for sure, at first, they're dabs of paint. Or contacts. They're *yeah, right* green—only, it's the kind of *yeah, right* that really does turn out to be true after all, the same way the rolling landscapes of the Emerald Isle turn out to be reality, not just something Photoshopped by an advertising exec for the tourism industry.

Gabe purses his full lips in distaste. "You could be a *little* proud of your sister, you know."

The screen jiggles as Brandon turns back to the cheerleaders, three of whom are staring not *at* the camera, but just to the side of it. At my Gabe. Three of them wave with their fingertips. Giggle and shove their chests out, displaying their figures the way models on *The Price is Right* point out items up for bid.

"I just don't get you," Brandon says. "When you could have *that*..."

Gabe chuckles while the camera zeroes in on his left earlobe, then pulls back in a jerky motion. "Your sister's more interesting," he says. "'Cause I had to convince her."

Gabe's words pick me up like a Wilson game ball, toss me back into my junior year when the King of the Ladies-Pay-All Dance kept popping up at my locker door, winking at me in the hallways. Texting me during bus rides to away games. I can still hear the team razzing me like Gabe had cooties, their elbows in my ribs, because jealousy behaves that way sometimes. *You don't want that, do you,* people say, pointing at the chocolate chip cookie you've got your hand on, wrinkling their nose, because the minute you agree, *No, I really don't,* they can swoop in and pop the entire cookie into their mouth, making their cheeks bulge out like Dizzy Gillespie.

But even when I said it about Gabe—*No, you're right, he's so not my type*—he wouldn't give up. Wouldn't let himself be swooped up by anyone else. Not one of my teammates or the cheerleaders or the tennis girls in their short skirts or the debate captain or the salutatorian. He kept chasing *me,* telling me he just wanted to spend a little time bathed in the glow of my star. Nobody'd ever talked to me like that. And when I finally agreed to go out with him, the entire female population of FGH stomped their feet on the tile floor of the hallways. I swear, it felt like the Big

Quake—the one that seismologists have long predicted for Missouri's New Madrid Fault—had finally hit.

"I wish I'd never brought the stupid camcorder to that game," Brandon says from my doorway.

"*You* didn't bring the camcorder, Gabe did," I remind him. "You were just shooting while Gabe took notes for the paper." Because, in addition to recapping the Eagles' wins and losses for *The Eagle Eye*, our school-wide Monday-morning newscast, Gabe Ross's mug shot showed up every week at the top of his sports column for the *Fair Grove High Bulletin*.

"I know what you're doing," Brandon tells me. He slathers me with such a disapproving look that I almost think, for a minute, we've traded our ages like baseball cards. Like suddenly *I'm* the one who's two years younger. "You're watching that last game to figure out where your big mistake was, right? FYI—there's no *mistake* here, Chelse. It was an *accident*. And there's no way to redo it, either. It *happened*."

I stare at the edge of the bench, visible at the bottom of the TV screen, wishing like hell I'd been sitting on it. *Just a game or two,* I catch myself thinking. *If I'd just sat a couple of games out…*

"I'm serious, Chelse. Watching this crap is self-imposed torture. All it's going to get you is hurt all over again," Brandon warns. "I know it—just like I knew you were hurt that day at the game."

"I'd been hurt a million times before," I remind him in a near-shout. "Jammed fingers and pulled hamstrings and sprained ankles. *Every* athlete gets hurt. The best players just suck it up and push through it." But my hip was different. I knew that—I should have *known* to sit it out. I start kicking myself internally all over again.

"Getting loud in there," Dad says, with the same warmth as a corrections officer. He steps into view in my doorway, beside Brandon, a glass of water in his hand. The moonlight bleeds through my venetian blinds, casting horizontal shadows on Dad's face the way the crossbars of a cell might.

I hit *stop*, so that my final game disappears and the screen fills with a late-night infomercial for a juicer.

Scratches, the gray tomcat Dad brought home for my eighth birthday, mews from my bedroom doorway and swirls his body between Dad's legs. He slithers across the floor, then launches himself up onto my antique iron bed.

I'd bet that, for Scratches, the distance between the carpet and the top of my fluffy white comforter is practically the same as the distance between the gym floor and the rim once was for me. And Scratches is *ten*—a senior cat—but he can still make the leap. Here I am, young enough that an entire career in college basketball should be spread out before me. But I'm done. It's over. Time has run out. Basketball is an hourglass with a whole pyramid of sand on the bottom.

Scratches climbs into my lap, then instantly starts purring and working his paws against my stomach. Okay, it's not like I've completely let myself go. So my stomach's still flat. But now that it's not rock hard, it just seems—

doughy to me. Especially when Scratches starts kneading like this.

"You've got finals tomorrow," Dad barks at me. "Last finals of your senior year. Got those grades to think about."

Right, I think. Grades are especially important now that I've blown my chances at an athletic scholarship. Grades are *all* Dad thinks about. But I don't know what kind of an academic scholarship he thinks I'll get at this point. It's May already, and graduation is looming so close that my cap and gown are hanging on the closet door.

"We were just watching TV," Brandon says.

When Dad turns toward him, his face softens. "Just keep it down a little, 'kay, bud? Don't wake your mom."

Brandon nods.

"*Bud,*" I sneer when Dad disappears. "Of course."

"Chelse, he just doesn't—"

I push *play* again.

"You don't exactly make it easy on him, you know," Brandon insists.

"Gimme a break."

As we stare each other down, I notice the cowlick that frays out from the crooked part in Brandon's unruly hair. He tries to gel it into something like order during the day, but by evening, it's always worked its way loose. Reminds me of the times when he was little, when it always stuck out in about three hundred directions; Mom could never get it to lie down. I think for a minute that if I could just stare long enough, Brandon's cowlick might actually make him look seven years old again. Which would make me nine—a girl who'd only just begun to peel back her talent. A girl at the beginning of her story.

But the scruff on his chin and the silver hoops in his ears, which he wears even when he sleeps, won't let me play make-believe. Won't let me fantasize that I'm not a has-been who gets her only exercise at the Springfield YMCA pool, swimming laps in a lane marked by ropes and floaters while the white-haired AARP geezers do water aerobics nearby. That I'm not the girl those geezers bestow their wrinkly smiles upon while they wave, flapping their floppy triceps, like I'm one of them. Part of their fragile group.

Which I am. Which is why I haven't stepped onto a basketball court in more than six months. Which is why I'm reduced to watching old footage of myself like a washed-up, middle-aged used-to-be with zero prospects.

"Forget it," Brandon says finally, turning away. "You're hopeless."

I turn the volume up just to spite both Brandon and Dad. "Shut the door on your way out," I call.

On the TV, Gabe scribbles something in his notebook just as a chant erupts. Hearing it, Gabe flashes that killer smile of his; on cue, my belly turns into a wobbly wad of strawberry preserves.

Gabe drops his pen onto the notebook on his lap and starts clapping, his angelic tenor providing harmony to the deep baritone just one row behind. The camera swivels until Brandon zooms in on Dad, whose face is flushed with excitement and happiness and even... the idea is as distant as my first day of kindergarten, but there it is just the same: pride.

"Take it to the key," Dad and Gabe and Brandon start to repeat in unison, like they're singing the chorus of their favorite song. "Take it to the *key*." I swear, Dad's so worked up that the fringe of his pepper-gray hair is even sweaty.

"She decide on Tennessee or UConn yet?" the father of my elementary school best friend shouts, tapping Dad on the shoulder.

And Dad—maybe not exactly an All-American himself, but a former ball player who used to put his daughter on his enormous ex-jock shoulders so she could dunk her first basket, who let her stand up in his lap so she could see the court when he took her to watch her first college game, who bought her that first pair of high-tops—turns toward him and grins. "Neither, yet. I'm voting for Tennessee, though. Closer to home."

Take it to the key.

Everyone's chanting it. Everyone sitting in the home section, anyway. "Take it to the key." Only that's not really what they're saying. They're not really talking about the tongue formed by the boundaries of the foul lane, the free throw line, the end line. They're talking about *me*. Chelsea Keyes. A clever pun.

"Come on, Chel-*sea*!" Dad shouts, just before he sticks his fingers in his mouth and whistles.

Take it to the Keyes. It's like I'm still in that gym, the way those words knock on my eardrums. And I swear, I can still feel the beat of frenzied, stomping feet pouring off the bleachers, straight into my chest. *Take it to the Keyes.*

"... the hometown crowd goes wild for the number twenty-three shooting guard, Chelsea Keyes, a dominating force for the Fair Grove Lady Eagles," Fred Richards, sportscaster for the local KY3 news team, is saying. "Keyes averaged an astounding twenty-four points per game her junior year, and it looks like she's on track to keep or *better* her average this season."

Richards's booming announcer-voice is just as recognizable (to anyone living within a hundred miles of his station) as, say, the color orange. Gabe always snagged a seat behind Richards and his cameraman, allowing Fred's voice to narrate the footage he shot for *The Eagle Eye.*

"... a rebound by Keyes," Fred continues as I snag the ball, then launch into a lay-up. "Shoots and ... *scores* for Fair Grove, giving the Lady Eagles a solid ten-point lead."

On the screen, I jog away from the basket, chasing the ball with the rest of the team toward the far end of the court. Sweat soaks my jersey and the roots of my hair—not from physical exertion but from searing pain. Every time I watch this footage, I relive it all. And I know that at this point in the game, with less than five minutes to go in the third quarter, the me on TV is in such anguish that I've resorted to marking time like some fatty on a treadmill ten minutes into her New Year's resolution.

The ref blows his whistle, waving his arms as he calls a foul on my team. Boos ooze from the crowd like thick black tar.

When Beth Hardy, number sixteen, point guard for the Aurora Lady Houns, steps up to take her free throw, the me on TV closes my eyes. No one knows it, but I'm visualizing that two Lady Houns are causing the pain radiating from my very core. I'm trying to picture them standing on either side of me, taking turns tugging on a dual-handled, old-fashioned lumberjack saw that's slicing through me. In an attempt to turn my pain into anger at the enemy, at the opposition, I try to imagine they're cutting me in half.

Take it to the Keyes. My heart starts to go haywire as Hardy misses and I turn and charge down the court. Theresa, our point guard, has snagged the rebound and dribbles down the court behind me, her long yellow French braid bouncing against her shoulder blades as fiercely as the ball against the floor.

Take it to the Keyes.

Like they always do at this point in the game, my eyes dart away from myself, away from the ball, and land on two boys arguing—front row, far corner of the bleachers, just feet from the hoop. Pushing. Shoving. Not angrily, not like they're really having a horrible disagreement, more like two brothers toying with each other. Which is exactly what they are—the Highful twins, Levi and Tucker, elbowing each other, eyes hidden by their filthy ball caps. Even though Brandon's camera angle only shows their profiles, their stupid grins still leap out like name tags. Dopes, both of them. Morons in Fair Grove FFA T-shirts.

Elbow, elbow, nudge, push.

Levi's holding an enormous soda. And every time Tucker nudges him, Levi spills a little more on the knee of his jeans. *Stop*, Levi mouths, and Tucker throws his head back. His shoulders ripple with laughter. Levi punches him in the arm.

But the Chelsea playing basketball doesn't notice their horseplay. Now that her feet have landed inside the key, right beneath the basket, she pins her eyes on the ball as Theresa passes it. She opens her hands; when the ball hits her palms, *I* can feel it—the me sitting on the edge of my bed, I mean. Months after the game, I can still feel the skin of the ball, rough and bumpy as a hedge-apple. It smacks my palms so hard, my skin burns.

Shaking pom-poms, stomping feet on the bleachers. A frenzy explodes, our small town gymnasium transforming into an enormous outdoor arena the moment before some legendary, world-renowned band bursts onto the stage.

"... a pass to Keyes..." Fred announces, his voice high-pitched, the sound of pure adrenaline.

Nitro, Nitro, Nitro... the crowd chants.

But powered by explosives is the last thing in the world I feel. The Chelsea on the TV screen is being pulverized by spinning metal teeth in a blender. Her hips are being twisted and cracked. And Beth Hardy is no puppy—she's a rabid dog, out to attack. Her defense is so mean, it has claws and blood-stained canine teeth.

As the crowd screams, chants, stomps, I turn my crackling, fire-consumed body away from Hardy and I launch myself into a jump hook. But I know, even before I release the ball, that the shot's all whopper-jawed. I've jumped too high to get the most power, and my body's rotated all wrong.

"... Keyes shoots and ..." Fred Richards narrates happily. But I wonder, as I always do at this point, how he ever could have thought my air ball, soaring wildly, would have landed anywhere near the hoop. How he ever could have expected to end his sentence with "... *scores!*"

In the bleachers, Tucker mouths an *ow* and reels his arm back to punch his twin. Levi tries to lean out of Tucker's reach; as he twists to the side, Tucker's hand makes contact with the plastic soda cup, knocking it out of Levi's fingers. The cup flies toward the court, hits the floor near the end line, tumbles. The soda spills beneath the basket. The brown, bubbly shadow creeps across the glossy gym floor, spreading across the key.

I hit *pause* on the remote while Chelsea is still in the air. At this moment, I have yet to come down from my crazy, desperate jump. My feet have yet to hit the puddle of Levi's spilled drink. I have yet to lose my balance and slide through the sloppy soda. My legs have yet to shoot out in opposite directions like a Fair Grove cheerleader doing the splits. My body has yet to slam against the brick-hard surface of the court.

The me on TV has yet to be rushed to the emergency room, where a doctor will let his eyebrows crash together as he points to my X-rays, at the fracture that slices through my hip bone and makes me look like a cracked teacup. That doctor has yet to shake his head when I finally come clean about the pelvic ache, saying, *Your hip was surely already weakened by a stress fracture, Chelsea. Overuse. You should have told someone you were hurting.* I have yet to be sent for hip surgery, yet to be termed *out of commission.* I have yet to see my dreams of college ball ripped to the kind of violent, life-altering shreds that usually fill a trailer park after a tornado.

I stare at myself, wishing I could have paused my *life* here. Wishing I could have dangled in the air forever, and never had to endure the excruciating pain that followed.

Clint
minor penalty

C all me crazy," says Earl, owner of Lake of the Woods fishing resort, from behind the check-in counter. "I happen to think that a man on vacation wants ... a vacation."

I instantly feel deflated. I glance back up at the poster I've just thumbtacked to the wall of the lobby. It's not a *bad* poster. In fact, I personally think the collage I've put together of the northern Minnesota landscape looks enticing. Whitewater rapids, kayaks on clear rivers, brown fingers of hiking trails—what could be better? *Give me a week, I'll give you the tools for the best body of your life!* my poster promises. *Lake of the Woods Boot Camp!*

"It's a good idea," I say, trying to defend myself. But my words hesitate far too much to convey any real confidence. I clear my throat and decide to be more assertive. "It's not like I'm forcing people into the gym. It's intense outdoor activities—hiking, swimming, rowing—surrounded by our incredible scenery. Isn't that why people come up here in the first place? For the scenery? You don't vacation in Minnesota to be *inside*."

"I dunno," Earl mumbles. "Most people like a little leisure with their time off. Hikes are strolls here, Clint. Kayak trips are sight-seeing adventures, not races. Swimming amounts to floating on an inner tube near the dock. *Vacation*, son. Rest. Relaxation. That's what folks come here for. You should know that by now. The men fish. The women make eyes at the tour guides."

"They don't 'make eyes' at me," I say, as the door to the dining room flops open.

"It's all right, Clint," Todd says around an enormous bite of a sandwich that reeks of vinegar. "Not everybody can be the stuff of fantasy. Just a select few of us." He's not really joking all that much. Here we are, on our first day of summer work back at the resort, and already he's walking around in a Lake of the Woods T-shirt that's too small for him, displaying all those hours at the weight bench for the girls on vacation. Usually, we don't get too many eighteen- or nineteen-year-olds here at the resort, mostly families with younger kids. But Todd's obviously hoping for the best.

He wipes his mouth with the back of his wrist and lets out a moan when he sees my poster. "What is *that*? What's wrong with you?"

19

"It's just an idea," I say.

Todd shakes his head. "No, no, no—no more ideas. You're blowing everything."

"Blowing what? I told you, it's just an idea."

"No, no, no," Todd mumbles, finally swallows. "Look. I can understand you working hard senior year. Making up for lost time, maybe. Okay, sure. But last year—you, me, and Greg, away at school. Didn't even have to deal with being in a dorm—we had our *own place*. No parents. The perfect opportunity. And you *studied*. For God's sake, who works so hard, freshman year of college? Huh? Do *you* know?" he asks, turning to Earl.

Earl just tugs on his steel wool beard, trying not to laugh.

"Really—who *studies* like that?" Todd shouts again, like I'm deaf or something. "You take—gym—you take—James Bond Movies 101—you take—freshman comp. Did you go to a single party *all year*, Morgan?"

I just stare at him. He knows I didn't.

"You blew it. The freebie, gimme year. You *blew* it. And now, at the very beginning of the summer, when everybody takes a little breather, you've got *three* jobs?"

"I don't have three—"

"Tour guide here at the resort," Todd interrupts, holding up his index finger. "Working at Pike's Perch," he says, holding up his middle finger when referring to my parents' restaurant. "And now," he finishes, holding up a ring finger slathered in mayo from his sandwich, "*that*." He points at the poster, then shoves the rest of his sandwich in his mouth.

"Maybe you're spreading yourself a little thin," Earl adds.

"It's not like my folks pay me or anything," I protest. "Working at Pike's is just kind of like helping around the house. And some extra cash on the side would really help with tuition next year. Not to mention geology textbooks—those things aren't exactly cheap. Maybe you guys could sign up for my boot camp. Help a guy out."

"No way," Todd says, shaking his head. "Huh-uh. I'm not contributing to this *working* craziness. Working, studying, *jeez*. And another thing—if your parents don't stop bragging about your A's to everybody at Pike's, I'm gonna kill you. My parents eat in there."

"What about you?" I ask Earl.

Earl grimaces. "I'd rather get a whoopin'."

"I'll get somebody," I insist, laughing now. "You just watch."

"Speaking of watches," Earl says, nodding once at the old wristband I wear. Old-fashioned, I guess, but I've never been into cell phones, which seem to be the only way anybody keeps track of the time anymore. Besides, around here, cells never really work all that great. Shoddy reception at best. "Think you've got a hiking tour waitin' on you," Earl finishes.

I glance at my wrist, slam my box of stick pins onto the counter. "Bet you *both* a free dinner at Pike's I get somebody before the week's out," I say as I rush for the door.

"Your folks sure aren't gonna like you givin' away their food," Earl warns.

Todd laughs as he leans against the front counter, waiting, just like he always does, until the very last millisecond before heading out to his fishing tour. Which is just Todd's style—he's pretty much last-second about everything. Not that he's some irresponsible moron; Earl wouldn't let him get close to one of his launches if he couldn't trust him. Todd's just never been in a hurry in his life.

I'd shout some smart-ass stinger back at the two of them, but I'm already too far out the door for either of them to hear me.

Outside smells kind of swampy, earthy. It's familiar, like I guess it should be; Pop started taking me here to fish and hike when I was barely out of second grade.

A white launch putters across the lake, leaving a trail of ripples behind it. Greg is onboard, entertaining a load of noisy tourists, baiting lines and telling wild stories of fish caught by other vacationers. "God, it was big as a whale!" I think I hear him shout. He's really worked up today, probably just excited to be back at the resort, his voice carrying across the stillness of the water. He's really putting on the works, priming his first group of tourists for their own *Old Man and the Sea* adventure.

Greg and Todd and this resort: my three oldest friends. Their faces fill Mom's family albums, in photos of Fourth of July picnics and birthday parties. But everything changes. We're not here just to play anymore. Greg and Todd and I have all passed every requirement and certification known to man (or known to Earl, anyway) so that we could work as the fishing guides. So that we could steer groups of tourists out into a lake that spreads itself so wide, it sometimes seems as big as the Atlantic. And while Todd and Greg only want to work on the boats, I'm what Earl calls the floater. I take up the slack wherever it shows up. Fish, sure, but also take the tourists out birding, or hunting wildflowers. We go canoeing. Ride ATVs.

It's the second summer Earl's given us these jobs. Sometimes I just can't believe my luck. Little does Earl know, I'd pay *him* to work here.

"Come on, guys," I say, waving at a clump of tourists gathered near the path behind the main lodge. They stop chattering long enough to look at my T-shirt, see the Lake of the Woods fishing resort logo embroidered across my left shoulder. They smile, one after another, realizing I'm the one they've been waiting on.

"Hope you guys all brought your cameras," I say, holding the digital I've borrowed toward the sun. These people and I don't know each other by our first names yet, not on this first hike of the summer. But we will. Soon they'll be calling *Clint!* as they point out red blooms along the edge of the path, asking me what they're called. By the time they leave, they'll know all the Minnesota wildflowers by their first names, too.

My calves go warm as I start up the incline of the dirt path. The late May sun beats especially hot on the back of my head, making me feel wet behind the ears for leaving my Lake of the Woods ball cap in the lodge.

I pay close attention to my pace, making sure a chubby lady dressed in bright orange pants at the back of the group doesn't fall too far behind. With every step, my old compass bangs against my leg, rattling around in the pocket of my shorts. Almost sounds like a giggle, the way the metal parts jiggle against themselves. Like the compass is teasing me—*think you're gonna to get lost on the same path you've hiked every summer for the past decade, Clint?*

But the truth is, a weird sense of peace washed over me last week when I found my old Boy Scout compass.

"Come *on*," Todd had shouted from the top of the stairs that led to my parents' basement. "You *said* you knew where the tent was."

I'd muttered under my breath as I picked up a dusty box. The cardboard flaps opened, letting Boy Scout relics—including my compass—fall onto a pile of family quilts.

I stared at it, turning it over in my hand, not really understanding the calm sensation that filled me just from holding it.

"Morgan!" Todd had shouted. "Come on! Losin' daylight. Are we going camping or what?"

I'd dropped the compass into the pocket of my shorts before tossing the box aside. "This'll go a lot faster if you two losers'd come down and help me *look*."

The compass has weighed down the pockets of my hiking shorts every day since.

I take a deep breath of sweet summer air. Birds in the branches above me chatter small talk; ducks follow their mother down to the lake, single file. The clucking ducks remind me, a little, of the tourists trailing mindlessly behind me. They chatter to each other, none of them paying enough attention to their feet; I can hear their sneakers stumble off the edge of the trail every once in a while.

I glance over my shoulder at the first two people in line behind me. A father and daughter, obviously. I peg the dad for a runner. His daughter's about twelve, wearing an awful pink *Girl Power* T-shirt and clutching her phone like it's somehow going to save her from dying out here in the woods. She smells like grape bubblegum and the comfort of a childhood bedroom. She blushes when she catches my eye.

Even though I've tried to deny it, Earl was right about the *making eyes* junk. Every single summer, younger girls like this one get crushes. Blush at one guide, then another. Twirl hair around fingers, get all giggly.

Frankly, a crush from a twelve-year-old is just plain embarrassing. Especially with her father watching. But the occasional older girls who come to the resort have a tendency to get a little goofy, too. And I wonder, sometimes, what good a summer fling really does the girls who are old enough to have them. What *good* is something so short-lived it's practically disposable? Throw-away love. Maybe it's okay for Todd or Greg, but I don't get the point.

I've just started to hope, with everything I have, that Little Miss Girl Power won't spend her entire vacation traipsing around after me, when she glances at the trail ahead of us and gasps.

"*Look*," she says, pointing at the tattooed tree. At least, that's what we've always called it here at the resort. And that's exactly the way it looks—like the body of some old heavy metal rocker. Covered in hearts and letters. Some painted. Some carved with pocket knives. Every summer romance that's ever played out at Lake of the Woods has been etched into the skin of the tree.

She's just the right age to be infatuated with the idea of love. To maybe even be infatuated with the idea of heartbreak. I think that sometimes, heartbreak looks adult to little girls like this one. Same as lipstick or high heels.

I look at the tree even though I really don't want to. And I find it, instantly, like I always do every time my eyes hit the bark: *Clint & Rose*. At the bottom, near the thick, gnarly roots that poke up out of the ground. As I stare, I can still feel the tiny glass bottle of red model paint I'd held in my hand while crouching to paint our names down there. God, I was younger even than Girl Power back then.

Rosie, Rosie, Rosie. I miss you...

"You all right?"

When I turn, I realize the girl's dad, the runner, is staring at me, eyes filled with worry. Kind of rattles me, makes me remember the time when *everybody* was flashing me that look.

Two years ago. Hard to believe days can stack up so fast, but there it is, just the same: the accident was a little over two *years* ago.

Suddenly I'm thinking about Rosie's room, and the paperbacks she'd leave open on her bed, spines cracked and broken so they'd lie flat. I'm thinking about her singing at Pike's during the dinner rush, with the half-assed "band" she'd formed with Todd and Greg. I'm thinking about the little white Miata she drove too fast. I'm thinking about the way she wore her black hair in braids even when she was too old for pigtails. I'm thinking about how fantastic it was just to hold her hand.

I'm thinking about the funeral, too. About the way Greg followed me across the snow-covered cemetery, all the way to my truck. Watched me swat away every *I'm so sorry* that came my way. Watched as I told my parents I wasn't going right home.

"*What?*" I snapped at Greg as I unlocked my driver side door. We were both still in our black overcoats. Uptight wool things our moms had bought, insisting we'd need them for special occasions, that we were getting to the right age for them. We kind of looked stupid though, not really even like ourselves.

"You think I'm gonna *crack* or something?" I shouted at him.

Greg shrugged, his hands hidden in his pockets. "I dunno, man. I wouldn't blame you if you did."

"Yeah, well, I'm not. Okay?"

"It's okay to—"

"To *what?*" I yelled, the driver side door of my truck screeching open in the cold.

"To—I don't know—want to—scream—or something. I'm just saying—if you want to scream—"

"I gotta go to work."

"You can't be serious."

"Work," I said again. "Inventory. Pike's."

"We just *buried* your *girlfriend*," Greg said. "You can't tell me your parents—"

"I gotta go," I said, climbing into the cab.

I flicked the radio on and drove through the winter streets until I hit Baudette. When I got to Pike's, I parked two spaces over from my usual spot and unlocked the front door of the restaurant, even though I always used to come in through the back. And I tossed my coat onto the first table inside, even though I always used to keep it on the hook in Pop's office. And I swore that everything would be different. Where I put my shoes. What I ate for breakfast. Where I went every weekend.

Because if I changed every single thing I did, wouldn't that mean I had a different life? Wouldn't that mean that I'd *feel* different, too? I wouldn't hurt so bad anymore?

I'd work. I'd work like I never had before. Starting with counting the jars of mustard in Pike's.

"Sure you're okay?" the twelve-year-old's dad says again.

I pull myself back to the hiking trail. Everybody's looking at me with that awful worried look.

Suck it up, I tell myself.

"Of course," I answer, smiling at the entire group. "Fine." By now, I've said it so many times over the past two years it's practically a mantra. *What's done is done.*

I hate that being here, remembering, has suddenly made me as tattooed as that tree. I figure I've got disaster and heartache written all over my face.

"Just feeling for the poor tree, you know?" I say.

"Yeah," the dad agrees, snorting a chuckle as he glances back to the carved-up trunk.

His daughter cocks her head at me. When she catches my eye, she blushes again. Her thumbs jab her phone. She lets out a squeal of frustration when she realizes her reception sucks. I cringe as I lead the group up the hill.

We press forward. The sun shines down on us like she's completely oblivious that anything bad could ever happen on the beautiful planet she lights every single morning.

Chelsea
air pass

The entire senior class is packed into Hill Toppers'
Pizza, which, in Fair Grove, is pretty much the only
place to celebrate commencement. Like every single year
on graduation night, one of the pretty corn-fed girls in
camisoles and tight jeans (sitting on the laps of the more-
than-willing boys) will turn up pregnant. One of the football players who passes a bottle of Wild Turkey under their
table and spikes their Cokes will be rushed to a Springfield
hospital to get his stomach pumped. And five or so kids
from the honor roll, who were never so much as tardy to
a single class, will find themselves suddenly aching for a
splash of wildness and decide to take a cue from the name
of the town's only pizzeria; they will, in fact, go hilltop-

ping after midnight, cars racing eighty miles an hour down some rolling back road.

We're at a table in the back, me and Gabe and the team, orange smears of grease making abstract art of our empty plates. Everyone has gotten so rowdy at this point that the radio might as well be dead. And Hank, the sweaty-faced owner of the pizzeria, keeps glancing up from the pale circles of dough he smears with blood-red sauce, anxious about what all this screaming and toasting and carrying on will mean for him.

"Better not be a bottle out there," he shouts, wiping his wet forehead with the back of a hand. Which makes laughter roar out with the force and volume of a V-8 engine revving to life.

At my table, Theresa and Megan, our starting point guard and power forward, are acting out a scene from last season. Lily, our small forward, whose skinny frame has always made her look like a tetherball pole no matter how many all-you-can-eat rib dinners she's consumed, joins in, shooting an imaginary basketball the same way Brandon plays air bass to his favorite songs on the radio. Hannah, our center, who's built like a highway billboard, launches into belly laughter so fierce her chestnut hair starts to work loose from its ponytail.

While the rest of the team rehashes all the highlights of the season, my eyes zip across the newspaper articles pasted on the Hill Toppers' walls. I stop when I find the picture of me, number twenty-three, fists pumping the air victoriously after a game back in the spring of my junior year.

As I stare at the bold black print of the title that hangs above my picture *(FINAL FOUR, HERE WE COME!)*, I swear I can *feel* my Tin Man metal plate and screws scraping against my hipbone.

The team could have gone this year, too, without me. But for all their laughing and joyous recapping tonight, we all know it was the worst season in eighteen years of FGH Lady Eagles basketball. And it didn't matter how many pep talks Tindell barked out in the locker room; the team ran onto the court defeated. Without their star player, they visualized losses rather than wins. They weren't even *present* during the last game of the season; Lily pulled a history study sheet out of her gym bag, and Hannah put an iPod bud in one ear. Theresa and Megan wore glassy, distant looks—the kind of expression that usually fills classrooms during long lectures on osmosis.

As I stare at the walls, I realize that my picture is actually starting to yellow a little around the edges.

On the other side of the pizzeria, Bobby Wilcox, yearbook editor and honor roll president, stands up, swaying on his feet. His face turns about as green as the peppers on Hank's pies as he raises his cup like he's about to toast the entire class. But before he can get out a single word, his eyes go all doorknob and he turns to the side, gagging and puking up about six slices of pepperoni.

The cheerleading squad screams in disgust. Three of them actually climb up onto their chairs, as if Bobby's vomit has feet and can scurry across the floor and climb their bare legs.

What I notice—what makes me grimace—is the cup. Bobby's dropped his cup, and it's rolled across the floor. The brown bubbly puddle, polka-dotted with crushed ice, makes my skin squirm far more than the sight of his half-digested dinner does. I stare at it, keeping watch, thinking that maybe Hank should get some yellow crime scene tape, mark off the area. After all, anyone who was at my last game should know that spilled soda is just as dangerous as knives or bullets or a car with no brakes.

Staring at the puddle, my head pulses with the memory of the ref's frantic whistle. I hear, once again, the shocked gasp that rose from the crowd. And I remember my own terrified shriek, which overwhelmed the scream of the whistle and the collective groan of the fans; my screech was so violent it practically diced up my throat like a Ginsu knife.

"That puke better not smell like booze, Wilcox," Hank yells, just like he does every year, smashing a different last name onto the end of the sentence. He stomps out from the kitchen, his face flushed and dripping with sweat.

The football team moans and points; a chorus of *I didn't bring a bottle, not me, no way,* climbs into the air; chairs scrape; the bell on the entrance starts jingling. The Wild Turkey is carried out tucked under a football player's enormous biceps. My own table is emptying, too, as Gabe nudges me, sticks his nose against my ear. "Come on," he murmurs, his breath warming my neck. "Let's go."

We step outside, stop in a clump just beyond the enormous slice of pepperoni painted on the plate glass window.

The front door of Hill Toppers' does an excellent imitation of a playground swing, flying open and shut again in rhythmic bursts. We—the former Lady Eagles—linger on the sidewalk, awkwardly toeing pebbles with our sandals, as they—the former Fair Grove High seniors—start piling into the cars lining the curb, ready for the hilltopping and stomach-pumping and baby-making portions of the night to officially begin.

We stare at each other, knowing there's no way to change a scoreboard after the final buzzer. So we finally start exchanging hugs, plastering on smiles and pretending to be overjoyed that high school is over. Pretending we all don't wish we could hit some magical *rewind* button and start again.

Especially me. Only I'd need to go back a little farther than the team; I'd start with those driveway practice sessions, those daily runs, the pounding, the stress, the overuse. Because Gabe and I are *still* going to college together, as we'd planned since the start of our senior year—now, though, it's nowhere exotic. Just Missouri State University in Springfield, a mere fifteen miles from my front door, just like Gabe's older brother and three-fourths of the college-bound Fair Grove High seniors, Gabe to become a journalist, as he'd always planned, and me to ... *what?*

A scream peals through the night, like the squeal of a balloon with a leak. A few jokesters are already crammed into the cab of a pickup. Sean Greyson, pitcher for our baseball team and photographer for the *Fair Grove Bulletin*, who'd tallied every last vote for "Best Smile" and

"Class Clown," who'd shouted, "Gabe, stop drooling over her long enough to just *look* at the camera" when we'd posed for the "Class Couple" photo last month, has actually pulled his entire torso out of the passenger side window and is waving at me.

"Here! Chelsea! Catch!" he shouts, launching something right at me. Instinctively, I lean forward, open my hands like I'm receiving a pass.

The truck careens down the street, the screams of joyous freedom growing faint as I turn the object over in my hands. A box of Trojans.

My face flames as the team starts to back away, down the street, shouting ridiculous *woo-hoo*s and *ooh-la-la*s. I want to yell at them to stop, to come back, because this isn't how I want to say good-bye, not like this, me standing there like a moron, so mortified I probably look like exactly what I am: a virgin.

The word itself scrapes me raw. *Virgin.* It sounds so babyish, so pathetic and old-fashioned. My head fills with the image of a grainy black-and-white video from the 1950s, a bunch of girls in crinolines and bobby socks sitting around listening to *How to Protect Your Chastity.*

"Better leave you two alone," Theresa teases, while Megan and Hannah and Lily chime in with "I'd wish you good luck, but you don't need it" and "*We* know when we're not wanted."

I open my mouth, but nothing comes. They—the team, already a *they*—become the back pockets of four pairs of denim capris, four pairs of flip-flops smacking against heels, four swishing ponytails.

The condoms in my hand are getting screams and *yeahs* and *a'rights* from the seniors on the street. So I shove the box in my purse, tug at my own ponytail.

Gabe slips his hand into mine. His skin is cool against the fire of my embarrassment, sort of like a bed sheet you slide your body onto in the midst of a summer heat wave.

"Don't let them get to you," he murmurs in my ear. "If you hadn't been hurt, you'd have had the wildest locker room stories of all."

The tough athlete in me bristles—as it always does, even though I should be used to this by now, six months after Gabe officially took the job of knight in shining armor. The old me would have punched Gabe in the face for trying to take care of me; *I can take care of myself,* she would have said. But Gabe winks, and the new me allows my heart to melt into gooey caramel. *He knows—he always knows,* she thinks. One look at my face and he can see what's racing through my head; we don't have to practically *blah, blah, blah* each other to slow and painful death with some horrific and soul-wrenching conversation. That's a good thing, right?

Under the yellow haze of streetlights, we walk quietly down Old Mill Road, passing the post office and heading for the entrance of White Sugar, my family's bakery. A giant *Congrats, Fair Grove Seniors!* sign hangs across the plate glass, obscuring part of the view of the store's interior. I've logged so many hours inside, though, that the darkness and the sign don't keep me from seeing the cream puffs in the display case, the cheesecake under glass—the one with *Yay, Gabe!* written in cherry swirls across the top. I can see, too, the metal backs of the stools that line the counter and flank the small table in the corner. The wall behind the cash register, where a framed copy of *USA WEEKEND* Magazine still hangs, the one with my mug on the cover. The cracked "$" button on the cash register that I push every weekend while customers smile at me, politely, but not with admiration. Not anymore. Just smile like they're all telling me, *Egg timer went off on that fifteen minutes. That fame a' yours is over.*

I jingle my keys out of my pocket, slam them into the door. When we step inside, the place still smells faintly like the tantalizing mixture of icing and fresh bread.

I flick half the lights on, in order to give the counter area a soft glow while the area closest to the entrance stays as dark as a shut-tight closet (don't want to give anyone the idea that we're open). But I've barely lifted my hand from the switch when a gasp rattles its way out of my throat.

"Gabe," I whisper, my fingers flying to my face as I survey the store, "this was supposed to be a graduation gift for *you*." Instead, Gabe obviously used his Mrs. Keyes Seal of Approval to gain access to the bakery hours before we'd tossed our mortar boards into the sky. Bouquets of tulips (my favorite flower) pop from the counter. Iridescent streamers cascade from the ceiling, along with glow-in-the-dark stars on glitter-infused string. A stool that's been pulled out into the center of the floor cradles my gift, which is wrapped in white tissue and tied with a silver ribbon that shines like a chrome bumper.

"It just wouldn't be like me if I didn't outdo you in the gift department, would it?" he asks, locking the door behind us.

Of course it wouldn't. The birthday poetry in my dresser memento box, the framed ticket stub from our first movie (given to me last Valentine's Day), and the anniversary, sepia-toned photo of our two hands intertwined proves that Gabe Ross definitely outshines his girlfriend in the romance department.

"Just wait until your birthday," I say, wagging a finger at him.

"Think you can take me?" he asks, then snares my gift box from the stool before I can start shredding the white tissue. "Uh-ah," he says. "Not yet. This takes a certain ... unveiling."

I put on a fake pout as I slip behind the front counter. "*Your* graduation gift, kind sir," I say, hoisting the heavy glass lid off Gabe's cheesecake. "Made by yours truly. I only have to work seventy-three-thousand indentured servant hours to make up for all the cream cheese I blew on my first attempts. No crummy cracked top for *you*."

Gabe chuckles as he folds his arms across the counter. Leans in to get a good look at my—okay, slightly slanted—creation. "Forget the fork. I'll eat it with a spatula."

He's still leaning over the counter when he raises his grass-green eyes. The way he looks at me, it's like his stare has fingers—it pokes its way into my eyes, then my head, and starts rifling around in the contents of my soul. It's way too intense, but I can't quit staring at him. I lean to meet him halfway across the counter; his lips barely graze my own. He pulls back slightly, still close enough for his breath to warm my cheek, but his mouth just half an inch out of reach.

"*Tease*," I snap.

I start the espresso machine up as he slides onto a stool. Every once in a while, a half-drunken senior's shout filters into the shop. But this is life, as it's been for nearly a year—me and Gabe closed in, huddled together, while the rest of the world passes by, their shouts muffled, distant. This is life as it has been ever since I peeled open my post-surgery eyes to see Gabe at my bedside, his face clear while the rest of the room looked blurry. This is life, as it's been since I'd first returned to school after the accident, the rest of our classmates speeding by us in the hallways while Gabe carried my books and held my hand and murmured as I plodded along, babying my hip, *Just take your time.*

Now, though, in the relative quiet, all I can think of is that box in my purse, the one with the stupid warrior on the cover. And the blinds on the front window, which could easily twist shut. And knocking the tulips to the floor while Gabe and I stretch out on the counter, and running my fingers through Gabe's curls and ripping his shirt right in two ...

"I'm going to miss you when you're in Minnesota," he mumbles, making me jump high enough to practically take flight.

I glance over my shoulder. He's picked up one of the hundred or so Lake of the Woods brochures Mom pummeled me with last Friday, after I'd taken my very last Fair Grove High final exam. "Up there almost to Canada," I say, mimicking Mom's high-pitched, breathless excitement. "An outdoor adventure before you head off to college!"

"You have to promise me you'll be careful up there," Gabe says. "I mean, hiking, rafting..." He keeps talking, flipping through the slick pages of the brochure. But all I can think about is the blond hair down his forearms, the tan on the back of his neck, the way it would feel if he pole-vaulted over this stupid counter, grabbed me, and backed me into the kitchen. What it would be like if, blinded by sheer passion, we tumbled in a whirl against the shelves, knocking confectioner's sugar all over our naked bodies, our mouths leaving sweet, sticky trails behind as we kissed each other's...

"*Chelse.*"

This time, when I jump and turn toward Gabe, he's got his arms crossed over his chest and his green eyes look like combination locks—closed up tight. "No," is all he says.

"No, *what?*"

"No, not tonight. Not now. Not in your parents' place. Not rushed through and not on the night before you leave for your summer vacation. *No.*"

I frown, shake my head like he hasn't just gotten all ESP on me, reading my mind like that.

"Don't deny it. You keep staring at your purse, where

you tossed those condoms," he says, grinning. "Look," he goes on, standing up from his stool and slipping behind the counter. "The guys around here, it's terrible to say it, but a lot of them go through girls like Kleenex—it doesn't matter that you've used one, because another will just pop up in its place. That's not *us*. Even without your accident, that wouldn't be us. We've been together a long time now," Gabe goes on. "And yes, I want you. You know I do. But I didn't want to make love to you for the first time on somebody else's schedule. You know that, right?"

My insides are knotted tighter than a chain net on a basketball hoop. *Make love to you?* The phrase makes me squeamish. Does it have to be so formal? And why is Gabe aiming for perfection *now?* As everyone in the entire gossipy senior class probably knows, he already lost his virginity—the summer before we met, at a journalism camp.

"I mean, I didn't say anything about it on prom night because sex at prom is a real cliché, right?"

"The prom," I sigh. Prom had been a night of pumpkin chariots, slow dancing in a strapless, ocean-blue Vera Wang, feeling glitzy and perfect next to Gabe, until we were in his 'Stang and we were on the highway, driving and not sure where to, just the two of us, no need for parties, and we could have owned the entirety of the world that night, the top down, wind destroying my up-do, but who cared, because there had never been anyone as free, all the way to Kimberling City, a good seventy miles from home, to stand at the edge of Table Rock Lake while the sun dyed the water the same color as orange childhood lollipops, and Gabe started tracing a pattern on my bare shoulders. *Know what it is?* he'd asked. *The infinity symbol. Just like us...*

"How's the Carlyle sound?" he whispers now, into my ear.

"The Carlyle," I repeat, as Gabe wraps his arms around my waist.

"I was going to surprise you when you got back from Minnesota. But I figure, it'll give you something to look forward to ... "

"The Carlyle," I say again, like these are suddenly the only two words I know in the entirety of the English language.

"I've already put a deposit down on a room. A night of our own, on our *own* time."

My head becomes a carousel on warp speed. "Swankiest hotel around," I mumble. "Guess—that's—the perks of snagging a summer job at a prestigious law firm in Springfield."

"I'm the grunt under the paralegal, Chelse. That's all. No capital murder cases this year. But it beats flipping burgers. Besides," Gabe goes on, a mischievous glint sparkling in his eye. "I'll spend whatever I want on what should be one of the most important nights of your life. Of *our* lives."

I roll my eyes at him, wordlessly reminding him that the gossip about FGH's gorgeous sports editor and a mystery journalist from a rival school had spread through the girls' locker room long before he'd started dogging me in the hallways, flirting shamelessly with me.

Gabe shakes his head insistently, whispers, "I've never been with somebody I *love*. And you deserve much more than the Carlyle, Chelse. I'd fly you to Paris if I could."

The espresso I've made for Gabe has drizzled down from the coffeemaker into a tiny white cup. But we just stand there, arms wrapped around each other's waists. I can feel Gabe's pulse racing through every inch of his skin, even through his shirt. I know I ought to do something—say something—utterly romantic. But I'm no poet. I'm an ex-ball player with zero experience in the bedroom. And I'm too tall even to put my head on Gabe's chest.

Suddenly, now that it's upon me, now that it's going to be real, my fantasy's taking a detour. I see Gabe and me in some lush bedroom, tangled in the heat of passion ... but when Gabe puts the weight of his beautiful body on top of mine, the room fills with the sound of metal crunching. *What is that?* Gabe asks, lifting himself off me. But it's too late—the metal plate in my hip (every time I think of it, I always picture the rusted metal roofing that tops outbuildings in and near Fair Grove) has crunched in on itself, and my leg is stuck, bent so that my knee is practically up in my ear. *Stop laughing,* I'm screaming, but Gabe can't quit ...

"Come with me," Gabe says, erasing my disturbing daydream. "Just for a minute. The cake'll wait. I want to give you *your* graduation gift."

I start to reach for the white box, but he swats my fingers away.

"Don't need that," he says, grinning and dragging me toward the door. Confusion wrinkles my face.

I get the keys back out of my pocket, make sure White Sugar's locked up tight while we're gone—not that it really matters in Fair Grove, home of Lady Eagles *and* honest souls. "Should I have turned the espresso machine off?" I ask.

Weekend nights, Gabe's vintage Mustang can always be found just beyond the White Sugar entrance, at the ready in case we decide to drive to nearby Springfield for a movie or a dinner that's more than just a slice of pepperoni. So I assume that's where we're headed now—to Springfield—as I hurry over to his car. I'm careful to keep my legs, greasy with rose-scented lotion, a good three feet from the car's grill; I've learned that if there's one thing you never do to Gabe Ross, it's lean against his '65 'Stang. Or fog up the glass with your breath. Or toss a gum wrapper on the floorboards. Or put your shoes on the leather seats. Or, for that matter, try to tease him that he's just a little bit guard-at-the-museum uptight about his car.

"We're not *driving* anywhere. Won't be gone that long," Gabe says, holding his hand out.

Instead of taking it, I let my eyes rove toward the giant antique clock that hangs just below one of the street lights. At a quarter past nine, the breath of the humid Missouri night swirls warm over my bare arms. Forget frying eggs— at this rate, by the time August shows up, we'll be able to bake White Sugar's chocolate chip cookies on the pavement.

"It's almost tomorrow," I say, pointing at the clock. "The day I leave for Minnesota."

"We've still got lots of time," Gabe insists, wiggling his fingers at me.

I slide my hand into his cool grip and we walk toward the ancient mill that serves, even now, as the cornerstone for the entire town. Sure, mill business is as dead as the dried flowers the craftier women in town use for handmade door wreaths. But the historic landmark's still the prime location for Fourth of July picnics, ice cream socials, heritage festivals brimming with bluegrass music.

We make our way through the grass while a scattering of early summer fireflies dance over the blades. Bittersweet vines are already curling themselves around the base of trees, and when we get close enough, I'm sure we'll see its purple flowers popping up around the corners of the mill. Halfway across the field, though, Gabe stops and points to the black sky. I look up.

"The Chelsea Keyes Star," he says. "I bought it from the International Star Registry and named it after you. All the papers are wrapped up in that box at White Sugar, but I don't need a map to find it. I'd know it anywhere. Sparkles brighter than any other star in the sky. Just like you."

I don't say anything, but the fact is, his gift instantly starts rubbing me like sandpaper. And I'm not even sure why—isn't this just a romantic Gabe Ross gesture?

"You bought me—a star," I mumble. "Thank—thank

you." I hope that somehow, in his ears, this doesn't sound quite like the awkward gratitude you give your clueless great aunt for the gym sneakers she's bought you, complete with Velcro—*Velcro*—of all the ridiculously awful things.

"It's kind of like how the sailors used to use the stars as a map. Or a compass, right?" Gabe goes on. "Only way I could think of to show you that I think the heart is a compass, and that *my* heart always leads me right to *you*."

I blink away the tingles that spring to my eyes. *You're an ass, Chelsea,* I think. *An ass. Gabe's not belittling you, for God's sake.*

"It's beautiful," I say, staring up at the sky. But the words sound kind of hollow to me—exactly like the lie they are.

"Listen," Gabe says, making his voice go husky, "I'm not going to let you have a bite of my graduation cake unless you give me twenty-one kisses. One for every night you'll be in Minnesota."

I close my eyes just as our lips meet. I open my mouth, strengthening my lips against his, stretching our kiss from one moment to another, another.

"At this rate," I say when we finally do come up for air, "it'll take all night to get to twenty-one."

"That's just fine with me," Gabe whispers.

As Gabe kisses me again, my eye wanders up to the sky. Our kiss cools as I realize that the Chelsea Keyes Star doesn't look one bit brighter than any other star out tonight.

Clint
goaltending

You want to know what heaven is?" Kenzie asks as she comes banging out the kitchen door. She pauses to dim the lights in the dining room. She's starting up right where she left off last summer. Even though I'd hoped that nine months apart would have cooled the ridiculous crush she developed last Fourth of July.

Her big hiking boots clomp against the floor as she sashays across the dining room of the lodge, which is empty by now except for the two of us. Candlelight and her hope wash over the walls. When she approaches the table where I'm sitting, her hips start working overtime, swiveling like seesaws.

I'm afraid of her question, but I don't want to hurt

her feelings, either. So I decide to play along. "Heaven … a never-ending line of pine trees on the horizon."

"No," she says, her voice all singsong.

"What, then?" I ask, folding my hands behind my head.

"Fried morel mushrooms, of course." She plops a plate down on the table. "Handpicked by yours truly this afternoon. The chilled bottle of Coke is compliments of Chef Charlie, who has just retired for the evening."

I nod, staring into the candle that flickers in the center of the table. We really are alone, then. Me and Kenzie, whose wavy chestnut hair is going all crazy down her chest, making arrows that point directly at her breasts.

Okay, Kenzie. I get it. I notice. I just choose not to do anything about it.

She slips into the chair on the opposite side of my table, props her elbows on the tablecloth, leans forward.

I push the camera she's loaned me across the table. "There you go," I say. I tell myself to pretend not to notice her little seduction scene. "Wildflowers and sunsets galore—black silhouettes of pine trees."

"*Postcards* galore," Kenzie corrects me with a smile, an adoring twinkle springing into her eye. "You always take the best shots around here. I swear, you single-handedly keep the gift shop in the black. Don't know what we'd do without you."

"Yeah—you poor helpless techie," I say. "Updating the resort's website, keeping all the vacationers from blowing their tops by maintaining their Wi-Fi connection." I cringe, just like I always do when I think about Earl's great Wi-Fi-In-Every-Cabin idea. If you ask me, it kind of spoils things a bit. "You'd never be able to take a few pictures with a digital camera."

Kenzie sticks her tongue out at me, clutching onto the fact that I've teased her, that I'm playing. I know she's decided to take it as an indication that I'm interested, and I instantly regret it. "Takes an artistic eye," she insists. "Techies aren't born with one."

Her adoring stare is giving me the willies. I pick up the soda and guzzle about half of it all at once, to keep from having to say anything.

"Go on," she says, pushing the plate of morels closer to me. "You get the first bite."

I stare at the triangle-shaped slices that've been fried a perfect golden brown. "Heaven," I mumble. My mouth waters. But I know if I take one, I'll just be egging her on. I stare at her, wondering what my excuse is going to be this year. Last summer, I'd thwarted her advances with a shrug and a *thanks for asking, Kenz, but I've just got too much to get done before I head down to the U.* This summer? She'll never buy it.

But it's late in the day—I'm too tired to fight her. So I finally put one of the morel slices on my tongue.

"Good?" Kenzie says, the first of a whole round of questions she already knows the answers to. "Way to a man's heart, right? Through his stomach? One of those clichés that really does turn out to be true?" She pops a morel into her mouth, her smile curling up from the edges while she chews.

Her voice hangs in the air above us. I don't want to hurt Kenzie. But at this point, it's painfully obvious she'll never get bored with my disinterest. I'm beginning to wonder if she's got a thing for the unobtainable. Or maybe, I think, Little Miss Computer Science just sees me as some problem nagging at her, sees my heart as some complex equation she's sure she can solve if she just keeps at it long enough.

But the whole thing's starting to annoy me; she's just as bad as that little twelve-year-old I met a couple days ago. Only Kenzie is no twelve-year-old. The girl's a *twenty-one-year-old* Northwestern student who comes home to Minnesota every summer to put aside a little extra money for college by staying with her folks and working at the resort. Shouldn't she be *past* this crush stuff by now? Shouldn't she have learned that sometimes, a guy just really isn't interested?

Problem is, I've known Kenzie since she was as young as that twelve-year-old. I hate that it's getting harder to thwart her advances without showing irritation, and I know my annoyance would only stomp on her heart. I take another slug of my Coke, the bubbles sharp as they travel down my throat.

"There's nobody in here." Todd's voice explodes out of the kitchen, into the dining room. "You said he'd be here."

"That's what he told me. He just had to drop a camera off," Greg says. He flicks on the overhead lights that Kenzie's dimmed. The room fills with a harsh glow, and Kenzie leans away from me.

They stand in the kitchen doorway, looking mortified.

"You want us to leave?" Greg asks.

"No," I shout.

Kenzie slumps into her chair, making a face.

"Hey, Kenzie," Todd says, flashing a goofy grin as he pulls a chair up to our table. He practically sits on *top* of Kenzie, he's so close. Quite a different reaction to her than he used to have, when we were kids and Kenzie was a computer geek with thick glasses, the nerdy girl a couple of years ahead of us in school. Now that she looks like a contestant for Miss Minnesota, Todd slobbers all down the front of his T-shirt every time he sees her.

And the T-shirt he's wearing right now is already pretty nasty. He's got about six tons of fish guts all over it. Kenzie notices right off, wrinkling her nose.

"Come on, man, join us," I tell Greg. I reach for the closest chair and pull it toward the table.

Greg plops himself down next to me, his shirt and shorts still smelling like fabric softener. He's the exact opposite of Todd—a slim runner instead of a beefy weight lifter, a neat-freak instead of a slob, dark-headed instead of blond. And he's far more in tune with what's going on with other people than Todd could ever be.

Greg raises his eyebrow. I know he thinks maybe he's interrupted something here. Or is starting to *hope* he's interrupted something. *How many girls did he try to introduce me to last year?* "If you don't want to go to Pike's tonight—" he begins.

"*None* of us have to go to Pike's," Todd says, smiling at Kenzie.

"You two could go," Kenzie suggests, pointing at Todd and Greg.

"No—*I'm* going," I insist, not wanting to be alone with her all night.

"You could come with us," Todd tells Kenzie.

She stares across the table, right at me. Her eyes dart back and forth across my face as she waits for me to invite her. To tell her to come with us.

Greg elbows my rib. He thinks I should ask her, too.

"Going to be—a—great summer, huh, Kenz?" Todd asks stupidly.

She glances at him, then turns back to me. "Like Independence Day last year," she says softly. "Remember? You, me, a couple of beers? Sitting on a dock, listening to the Baudette fireworks? Sounded like some distant battlefield. And cheering when a firecracker got high enough over the pines for us to see? Remember?"

Do I. I hadn't thought a thing about it at the time, the two of us hanging out on the Fourth. Kenzie, though—she took it as me telling her I was ready to date again. But it doesn't happen twice. Not like it happened with Rosie. And any relationship I might ever have again will feel so empty by comparison—like some dumb old summer fling.

Empty's the last thing I want.

Greg elbows my rib again—harder this time. Yeah, Kenzie's beautiful. She's smart. But she makes me nervous when she turns it on full blast. As soon as she tries to cross that friendship line, I get antsy. Weirded out. *Why doesn't she go after someone else?* I wonder. *She could have anybody.*

"Clint!" Earl shouts, bursting into the dining room. He grabs a chair and drags it up to our increasingly crowded table. Todd takes this as an opportunity to scoot his own chair closer to Kenzie's.

Earl gobbles up half the morels before Kenzie can let out a syllable of protest. Takes up my bottle of Coke and gulps the remainder of it, letting out a satisfied "Ahhhhh" and smoothing his gray beard.

"About that boot camp of yours," Earl starts.

"People would be lining up in droves if they knew about your hockey experience," Kenzie says innocently.

"*No,*" I shout. "No hockey."

Greg and Todd both frown at me while Kenzie flinches, touches her chest. "I just thought—you were *great,*" she says. "And there are so many old pictures of you on the ice around here. Even hanging up in the back of Pike's. I could scan one into the computer, paste it into your posters—"

"Were, was, woulda'," I snap. "Nobody cares about something I *used* to do. I don't do team sports, all right? None. Especially not *hockey.* You know that. Can't believe you'd even bring it up."

The silence stretches. My anger throbs. Kenzie's eyes turn wet and she shrinks a little, but Earl just clears his throat and puts his hand on my shoulder. Smiles as though my outburst never happened.

"I'm not gonna get that free meal," Earl says. Before I can ask him what he means by that, he explains. "Guy called the lodge this afternoon to confirm the reservation for his family vacation. One of his kids is off to college next year and he and his wife bought her the vacation as a graduation gift. He started talkin' this kid up, askin' 'bout activities here at the resort. And I thought, seems like a perfect fit, even though I guess you probably won't be able to push the kid as hard as you really had in mind for the boot camp, but this guy's willing to pay well, and—"

"I think you lost me," I say.

"Special case," Earl finally explains. "Former basketball player, broke her hip. Lost her chance at an athletic scholarship, big career, the whole enchilada, but she's healed, and when this guy started askin' which activities around here would be a good place to start her out, I mentioned the boot camp. He really got interested in you workin' with her one-on-one."

"She?" Kenzie asks. "The basketball player's a *she?*"

Earl nods. Shrugs. "Sounds like a case a' once bitten, twice shy. Like this guy's mostly afraid his kid mighta lost some a' her confidence. What do you say?" he asks me. "Gets here tomorrow."

"Jeez, Earl," I moan. "Way to give me the heads up."

It's stupid to get mad at him. I mean, I *asked* for this. But I was envisioning some out-of-shape vacationers. A former athlete's a different story. Kind of kicks me in the gut, the idea of working with a ball player.

"Been lookin' for you all afternoon," Earl says. "Didn't know about her situation till today. And I thought—"

"You already told her dad I would?" It sounds like

some sort of accusation, the way I've put it. Like I've found out that Earl has just set me up for the fall of a lifetime—a tumble from a cliff. And I already get the feeling, for some reason, that he really has.

"Don't bust his balls about it, Clint," Kenzie says, which makes me cringe. Kenzie doesn't usually talk so rough. I can tell Todd likes it, though, the way he gives her a half-nod.

"Maybe the ball player will even get you to have a little fun," Kenzie says.

"I have fun," I say defensively. "Loads of it."

"Mmm-hmm," Kenzie mumbles, crossing her arms over her chest. I can feel Greg staring at me, gearing up to weigh what I'm about to say. Like my answer's going to mean something. I don't need him trying to decode my every move. So I shrug, act like it's no big deal.

"Sure, I'll do it," I say. "One reconditioned ball player, coming up."

"Yeah," Kenzie says, flashing a glare my way. "We all know how easy it is to get broken-down jocks back in the game."

Which is my cue to leave.

Chelsea
technical foul

Brandon's our finisher, the last runner in a relay who can sprint like nobody's business. Without saying so out loud, we've planned it this way, letting Brandon be the last driver in our excruciatingly long car ride.

After all, a full day on a highway that snakes through three different states can turn even the most spacious SUV into the world's tiniest jail. And Brandon's sick of it, too, like we knew he would be. He forces our Explorer on faster, practically tilting the vehicle onto two wheels as he careens off an interstate and onto an exit ramp. The SUV bounces down a gravel road like a rubber ball.

"Brandon," Mom scolds from the back, gripping the headrest on the passenger's seat behind me.

"It's under control," Brandon moans.

"You'll miss our turnoff to the resort," she warns. But Brandon just reaches for the volume dial on the radio. Music sharpens him, gives him the kind of focus that will tune out everything but the land the headlights lick. He forces the Explorer on even faster.

Over my shoulder, I catch Dad staring out the window, calm washing his face. He trusts Brandon. Completely. But Mom looks ready to climb into the driver's seat and grab the emergency brake herself. When I stop staring into the back seat long enough to look through the windshield, my hands fly forward and my nails dig deep into the dashboard, anchoring themselves like camping stakes. "Brand? The tree!"

Brandon swerves, sending our luggage sliding across the back of the Explorer. A stack of duffle bags falls, landing with a hard thump. His finger jabs the volume. "What was that?" he asks, suddenly worried. "Annie's okay, isn't she?"

"Annie?" I ask. "Annie's here?"

Annie. The name he'd wailed last month, curled up in his bed. "Annie," he'd grieved, mumbling her name as he moped, slumped into the couch in his pajamas until noon. "Annie," he'd doodled in his notebooks at the kitchen table, instead of doing his homework. "Annie," as though it was a girlfriend who'd dumped him, not the name he'd given his Fender bass, which had been taken in for a repair to the bridge. "Aaaaa-nnnn-ieeee," he'd wailed, even though the repair ticket said she'd be back in two days tops.

"What do you think you're going to do with a bass you can't plug in?" I ask.

"I brought the Marshall, too," he says.

"The *Marshall*?" I repeat. "That stupid bass amp's heavier than the entire rack of free weights at the Y."

"So?" He frowns, his braces catching the moonlight.

"So, you can't go three lousy weeks without trying to smash our eardrums?"

"Oh, don't get after him too much, Chelse," Mom says, turning her wiry little body around in the seat so that she can examine our fallen piles of luggage. "You'll make me feel guilty for bringing my Cuisinarts."

"Your—you brought *food processors* and *muffin trays*?" I ask.

"Still got to tweak a few recipes," Mom replies joyfully. "If I don't keep at it, we'll never get this year's book done on time."

"The book," I mumble. The White Sugar annual cookbook—a simple, spiral-bound collection of holiday baking ideas that Mom prints up every fall, then stacks on the checkout counter shortly after Halloween. The book that always sells out before Thanksgiving.

"What's the point of even *going* on vacation?" I snap. "We could still be home for this."

"Now, now, now," Mom says, her voice muffled as she pushes herself deeper toward the back of the SUV, arms flailing about, undoing zippers and checking on the contents of the bags in a kind of clumsy, too-fast way. The way she bangs against the car walls kind of reminds me of a hummingbird stuck in a garage.

Only she's not stuck. I am. The kind of stuck that makes me start to instantly envy Scratches, who's back home with Mrs. Williams, our neighbor, getting spoiled with tuna and long naps on the woman's cushy lap.

Some graduation gift this is turning out to be. Me watching everybody else rub it in my face that they still have the thing they love the most. Seems pretty callused, if you ask me. Suddenly in need of someone to scream at (or at least text), I pull my cell from my shorts. I have no reception here, though, as I haven't for almost an hour. (I *hate* my bare-bones cell, but it's not like I had any room to complain about Mom not wanting to spend a wad of money on a phone. After all the money *I* blew this year, I should be grateful to have anything more high-tech than a smoke signal.) But I realize, as I run my thumb across the useless buttons, that I won't even have Gabe on this vacation. I feel like tearing every last strand of my hair out.

"We're almost there," Mom says, finally settling herself back into her seat. "It's been a long drive—"

"Still don't know why we couldn't have flown," Brandon says, glancing into the rearview mirror.

"We have college to pay for," Dad growls. "And medical bills."

I feel myself hardening inside.

The Explorer finally slides into the resort parking lot, spraying white gravel everywhere. Brandon stomps the brake and we skid to a complete halt, directly in front of the main lodge. An enormous sign with a green, open-mouthed fish in the center announces we've officially arrived at Lake of the Woods fishing resort. Brandon slams the gearshift into park and pulls the keys from the ignition, completely killing the annoying strains of "Iron Man."

"Bet nobody around here's seen an entrance like that," I mumble as he launches his skinny body out of the driver's seat, then rushes to the back door of the SUV to check on his bass.

"Brandon, bud, we're gonna need this car for deliveries when we get back," Dad says gently. "It's our business car, remember."

Road-weary and worried about Annie, Brandon refuses to take the criticism well. He instantly starts shouting— "Did you want to get here tonight or *not*?"—and Mom chimes in with all that "We're just tired and need something to eat" business.

I push my door open and step out. The bold block letters of the White Sugar logo shine in the moonlight, then disappear back into the darkness as I slam the door again.

I just stand there, absorbing it all: the midnight blue sky, the fringy black silhouettes of pine trees, the white full moon. The longer I stare, the more the trees look like a black lace formal, the moon like an opal pendant. When the breeze hits the pines, the black lace sways, as though the sky-woman's dancing to the yodel of the distant loons.

Behind the loons—on the opposite side of the darkness, it seems—water crashes. There can't be a tide here, but maybe it's rapids running over rock? *Hush,* that rushing pulse urges. *Hushsshhh ...*

I close my eyes and listen, no longer thinking about the hourglass that basketball has become, all the sand piled into a pyramid on the bottom. For the first time in months, my mind empties completely. I feel—calm. Of all things.

"Chelse!" Brandon shouts. "Come on. Before you grow roots."

He and Mom are standing in the entrance of the lodge staring at me. Light skips across the tips of Brandon's crazy hair and washes across their impatient frowns.

"Sorry," I mumble, hurrying to follow them inside. As I cross the threshold, though, my phone goes off. Shocked, I scramble to fish it from the pocket of my shorts, the unripe-tomato glow of my screen washing out into the black of night.

The text is from Gabe: *miss u already.*

I start to go all caramel-goo inside. *miss u crazy,* I text right back, afraid the phone will quit working again if I take a single step forward or even lean in the wrong direction.

As soon as I send it, Gabe texts back, *carlyle 23 days.* It makes me feel a little scared—the same way I felt just before having to get up in front of my old speech class.

That's a girl thing, I try to tell myself, *Every girl feels self-conscious about losing her virginity.*

"Enough of the drama, Keyes," I scold myself.

When I step inside, my eyes rest on a pay phone attached to the wall of the lobby. *At least there's still one solid link to civilization,* I catch myself thinking. I take a few steps forward to join my family, who have already clustered around the check-in counter.

A man who's definitely playing the part of the stereotypical outdoorsman—khaki fishing vest, hat decorated with lures galore—shouts, "Earl here, owner of Lake of the Woods fishing resort. Welcome!"

Dad starts shaking the guy's hand, saying, "Keyes."

Earl's eyes light. "Keyes!" he repeats. "*Chelsea* Keyes."

My brain starts spinning. The egotistical part of me starts to wonder how it could be possible for Earl to have heard about my basketball legacy so far from my home. *Maybe,* I actually catch myself thinking, *he remembers USA WEEKEND.*

"You're in luck—Clint's still here," Earl announces, darting out from behind the counter and slipping into what looks like a dimly lit dining room, full of rustic bentwood chairs and tables.

Clint? I wonder, squinting into the candlelight. It's not about basketball at all. My legacy's not even so much as a footnote. The reality stings. Again.

"Here he is," Earl announces.

The man he ushers into the lobby? Good God.

Okay—here's the deal. I am not a romance-novel kind of girl. I'm not a giggler. Or a flirt. I've never doodled a boyfriend's name in any of my notebooks, not even Gabe's. I don't twirl my hair around my finger and bat my eyelashes. Sure, Gabe can turn my insides into hot caramel, but that started only after we'd been dating awhile. I'm not the sort of girl who has ever, in her entire life, gone all mushy-mushy at the mere sight of anything male.

But *this* guy? Hair as shiny and black as the feathers of a raven. Skin licked by the sun. And a body sculpted by sheer strength. The width of his chest, the curve of his biceps beneath the short sleeves of his T-shirt, the smooth tapering of his hips … he smiles at me, and I recoil. Not from him, but from the way my entire body is responding to him.

What is wrong with you? I ask myself. In response, I instantly start to make excuses: *Everybody notices the opposite sex, no matter how involved they are with someone else. Human nature.*

My stomach lurches a little when I notice that his T-shirt has *Lake of the Woods* embroidered above the pocket. But I tell myself he's probably just somebody who helps with luggage. And then we'll go on our separate ways. Never to see each other again. Thank God.

"Nice to meet you, Chelsea," he says, the pitch of his voice deliciously low—like the dark filling of a chocolate truffle candy. He smiles at me with this look … like we're only at the beginning. Like the game clock has only just kicked into gear and four full quarters of action lie ahead.

"Clint's going to work with you over vacation," Dad says.

"What do you mean, *work*?" I ask.

"He runs a boot camp here at the resort," Dad says. "I set it up for you yesterday. Your own personal trainer."

I actually start to feel a warmth break out under my

rib cage. And just as I begin to realize that the warmth is actually *hope*—hope that Dad might actually be doing something thoughtful, that he might be giving me something I'd enjoy, like we were still the old friends we used to be before the accident—he says, "We spent a lot of money on this graduation gift of yours. I didn't want you to have to waste it sitting on a cabin porch."

As if I'm the kind of person who *always* wastes the opportunities that come my way. Like I'm someone who has good things land in my lap all the time, and I'm not gentle enough or thoughtful enough or careful enough to protect those things. He says it as if I squandered basketball, even. The warmth of hope instantly turns to the burn of anger.

Dad accepts the keys that Earl jingles. "Cabin number four," he mumbles, staring at the key chain.

It's my fault. I get it—I wasted everything. I screwed up college, even. Destroyed any hope for a full-ride scholarship. And it's obvious that Dad's never going to forgive me. In that moment, my hip is an open wound he's just emptied an entire salt shaker into.

Clint smiles at me, saying, "You'd never know you got hurt."

That just goes to prove, right there, how little this guy really knows.

Clint
body checking

"One of these days, I'm going to come out with you,"
Kenzie promises. At first I think "one of these days"
means "today," but instead of climbing aboard, she stays
on the dock and picks up a fistful of fishing poles.

"Don't know why you haven't yet," I say, in the same
tone I'd use talking to Greg or Todd. Friendly, open. Not
like I *have* to have her out with us. Not like I'm pining. Or
foaming at the mouth, like Todd. *Sure, you can come out
with us. But the world won't end if you don't.*

I lean over the edge of the boat to accept the poles,
then carry them beneath the cover that shades the passengers' seats on the Lake of the Woods launch—one of the
twenty-five-foot motorboats that Greg, Todd, and I use
to take out ten or so vacationers at a time. We could fit

in as many as fifteen, but Earl likes to keep the groups a little smaller than that. And it's such a great gig, none of us would ever think about testing Earl's rules.

"Sure do bring a lot with you," Kenzie observes as I motion for her to hand me my boxes of tackle, too. I learned on day one that it's best to bring the just-in-cases—because there's always at least one weekend fisherman every trip who realizes, halfway out into the lake, that he's accidentally left something behind in his cabin. Or there's always a couple of tourists, usually women, who swear they hadn't intended to fish, but now that they're here, and it's such a beautiful day, and *pretty please, any way we can fish, too?*

Once I've placed all my stuff in the boat, I climb back out onto the dock. I've learned, too, that it seems more welcoming this way—if I'm waiting on the dock, vacationers assume there's still space for them on the boat. And this morning, I want to get as many onboard as I possibly can.

I glance over at Kenzie. She's smiling at me, one of those all-knowing *I'll get you yet* grins. The early morning sun plays off the waves in her hair.

But I've got too many worries right now to get all upset about maybe leading Kenzie on just by being nice to her. I'm remembering the words I bounced around in the lobby two nights ago, when the Keyes family first arrived: *Fishing's about as low-impact as it gets. Easy way to start. And if you all come out, you'll get a chance to see how Chelsea and I are going to work together while you're here.*

Her dad had frowned at the suggestion. Tried to back

out of it, but her mother persisted, nodding, liking the idea.

You guys take tomorrow to get settled in, I'd offered. *The next morning, I'll take you all out on my first run of the day.*

Talk about dumb. Now, instead of impressing one person, I've got to work her entire family. If I can take four or five vacationers in addition to the Keyes family, the others will offer a little bit of a distraction. But probably, I think as I spot the Keyes family in the distance, making the trek from cabin number four, it won't be enough to really soothe my nerves. The mom and the brother don't worry me so much—frankly, that gangly brother of hers is no concern of mine at all, and the mother seems like she'll be pleased with just about anything (the whole lemonade-from-lemons type). The dad, though? And *Chelsea*?

I keep thinking about the way Chelsea backed away from me at the lodge when I introduced myself. And the way she ignored me yesterday, turning her back on me from the large front porch of cabin number four when I waved from the dock. Makes me wonder why her dad signed her up for boot camp at all.

"What is it?" Kenzie asks. She follows my gaze up the dirt path toward the Keyes' cabin. She pinches her face, lets out a long sigh. "Is that your ball player?"

I nod. Kenzie shades her eyes. "Broke her hip, huh?" she says, her voice sour.

"Yep," I say, motioning another cluster of vacationers toward the dock—I count five heads. Five in addition to the Keyes family. *Thank God...*

"Too bad somebody didn't break her *face*," Kenzie mumbles, so quietly she probably doesn't even think I've heard.

But I have—and it makes my eyes shoot back up the path stretching toward cabin number four. Kenzie obviously sees Chelsea as some sort of competition, and this is the perfect opportunity for her to nitpick, to convince me Chelsea really isn't *that* pretty.

She can't, though—because Chelsea's damn near perfect. But without flaunting it. Khaki shorts, white T-shirt. None of that obvious look-at-me crap girls put on in the summer, tiny sundresses and skimpy shirts that don't even hide so much as a belly button. Chelsea's breasts and waist and hips tug at her simple clothes, filling them out in all the right spots, turning a plain old pair of shorts and a T-shirt into one of the sexiest outfits a girl has ever worn.

Ouch.

My eyes trace the outline of her hips, troll down her thighs. I remember her mom telling me, that first night, that Chelsea'd been swimming for exercise. My mind fills with the image of Chelsea in a bikini—a white one that has a tendency to turn see-through when wet. It's the first time in two years that the sight of a woman has given me a fantasy like this. I feel a little dizzy; I even squat and tighten the laces of one of my sneakers as an excuse to put my head between my knees for a minute.

Kenzie raises her eyebrow at me when I finally look her way, like she's reading my mind.

"Get real," I tell her. "She's only eighteen."

"And you're only nineteen," Kenzie says.

"She's my *client*." There. That sounded professional enough. Forget *sounded*, it's true. And besides, I'm not interested. After burning your fingers to black crisps, how smart is it, really, to put your hand against a red-hot burner a second time? A pointless summer fling. Who needs it?

"Client. Sure," Kenzie mumbles. "Here," she growls, pushing her camera into my hands. "Maybe one of these days you'll buy one of your own."

I shake my head, still protesting, but she rolls her eyes and says, "I gotta get to the lodge." Her legs swallow the dock in three strides, and she scurries off. Kenzie and I have never been a couple, not even close, but the way I've just looked at Chelsea has smacked her—and that makes me feel like the crud Earl sometimes gives me the distinct honor of scraping off the bottom of the Lake of the Woods canoes.

As Kenzie grows smaller, Chelsea approaches the dock, her long blond hair rippling and her incredible legs flexing with every step. And I know—nothing about the next three weeks is going to be easy.

Chelsea
nothing but net

elp you in?" Clint asks when I hit the end of the dock. He stretches his arm out, waiting for me to take his hand.

In the sunlight, his eyes are bluer than the sky or the lake, and somehow even purer than either. And the face that surrounds those eyes stands out far more clearly than it did inside the lodge the night we arrived—chiseled features, tan skin, teeth like glazed white pottery, a lock of dark hair tumbling across his forehead. His face sends shockwaves through me. Betraying the order from my brain to stay cool, my eyes are already traveling down the length of his body, taking in his muscular shoulders, his strong arms, tapered waist, sun-darkened calves.

The mere idea of spending an entire morning with

him makes my face grow hotter by the millisecond. And my entire family's going to be watching my every move. The whole outing is made infinitely worse by the fact that I had the entire day yesterday to think about it. To remember the way my body rang out like a cymbal just standing next to him in the lodge. To wonder how I'd feel, spending the morning sitting next to him on a boat…

"Just take my hand," he says. "I won't drop you. Promise." He's smiling, flashing his perfect, straight teeth. My stomach starts doing some weird acrobatic routine. *Gabe,* I start chanting in my mind. *Gabe, Gabe, Gabe…*

I'd like to stick my nose in the air and step onto his stupid boat myself, knocking him onto his butt in the process, but I'm afraid of falling. Sure, the boat's enormous. But after the year I've had, I'm terrified of anything that isn't solid ground. To me, the boat looks about as steady as a rubber ducky, the way it bobs. What if I were to lose my footing, slip, and hit my hip on the way down? Doctors have warned me about the dangers of falling a second time. And I don't particularly think spending what should be my freshman year of college recovering from hip *replacement* surgery would be a blast.

I glance behind me, but the rest of my family and the five other tourists who plodded to the end of the dock are all onboard. There's no one else to push ahead of me, to give me half a second to catch my breath. I'm all that's left.

Reluctantly, I slip my hand into his, the touch of his skin causing my heart to beat double time. I try to hurry into the boat, eager to pull my hand away, to wiggle from the crazy beehive-swarm of emotions he arouses in me. But my foot slips on the ramp, and my heart stops.

My very worst fear of all time is coming true. I'm falling, in terrorizing slow motion. My whole mind replays the footage I've watched hundreds of times—me in the last moments of my last game, body twisted, arm raised above my head as the ball rolls off my hook shot, my hip hurting, sure, aching already, but that pain was nothing compared to what hit me when I slipped and crashed and broke...

I open my mouth—*not again, not again*—and I'm about to scream when I fall into his arms. All I let out is a pitiful "*Ee—*." His chest is strong, and—*oh, God*—he smells so good. Like clean summer shirts just brought in from the clothesline.

"Thanks," I manage to mumble.

"Don't worry," he says. "I'm lifeguard certified. I'll rescue you from the lake if you fall. Actually, I'd be glad to jump in on a hot morning like this."

Actually, I might just jump in on purpose if you're coming after me. The thought explodes into my brain from nowhere, rattling me like an earthquake. How could these thoughts be coming to me when I'm already in love with someone else? I can feel my cheeks turning strawberry pink. I finally squirm out of his grasp and hurry to take a seat next to Brandon, one of the twenty or so seats that surround the railing along the back of the boat (or is that the bow? The helm?). *That's good, Chelse. Distract yourself from the way you feel with a list of vocab words.*

"What's the deal?" Brandon whispers, seeing right

through me. "Why are you acting so weird? You'd think you'd never seen a guy in your entire life." He raises his camera and takes a picture, recording my sheer mortification.

"Knock it off," I snap.

The truth is, I feel exactly like I did when I'd insisted on riding the Tilt-A-Whirl ten times straight on my tenth birthday—dizzy and weak. My mouth is dry. My hands are even trembling a little. While I'm still trying to get myself under control, Clint suddenly appears and wraps his hand around my biceps, hauling me to my feet. Lightning flows through me at his touch. So help me God, *lightning*.

"I need a model," he says, leading me gently toward the center of the boat. We turn to face the passengers.

"We call these things Mae Wests," he says, holding up a life jacket by the shoulders. I turn and slip my arms through the holes.

Clint works me like a top, spinning me around. His face—his *beautiful* face—is right in front of mine. I can feel his breath on my cheek. My mind reels. I need something to say. Something to distract me from the fact that his hands are reaching toward the ribbons on the life jacket—ribbons lying right over my chest.

"So—so why's it called a Mae West?" I manage.

"Oh, I bet I'm the only one here old enough to know who Mae West was," a gray-haired woman shouts as she laces up her own jacket. "That lady's boobs could fill up an entire movie screen! The only way I'll ever get 'em that big is to wear one of these things."

I look at Clint, horrified. He nods. "Yep," he says. "You

ever fall in the water, all you've got to do is pull this cord down here, and *poof!*" He holds his arms out like he's illustrating ample bosoms. "You'll be an instant Mae West."

I'm sure my entire face is now maroon as I scramble back into my seat. Brandon's ready to swallow his tongue he's laughing so hard. "This is too great," he tells me. "I'm so glad we came. I don't think your face will return to its normal color ever again."

I glare as he snaps another picture.

Clint quickly steers the boat toward the middle of the lake, then slows the engine. As we putter along, he calls out, "Get your lines in the water! We're going to troll."

Instantly my mind fills with images of elves—wrinkly and short, in pointy hats and shoes. There's no way that's what the guy's talking about.

"Hey, Chelsea, you want me to help you get that line in the water?" Clint offers. He stands right behind me, his arms around my shoulders. I bite my lip.

"Here, let your line out. Just let it drag beside the boat."

A whoop steals Clint's attention away from me.

"I got one! I got a bite!" the old woman who made that awful Mae West crack shouts. "Get your net, Clint! It's a big one!"

Clint rushes to help her. I breathe a very grateful, yet (do I even admit it to myself?) slightly disappointed sigh of relief.

"It's a beaut, Gladys," Clint shouts as he pulls the fish into the boat. He holds it up for everyone to see. "Nice largemouth bass," he says. "Good eating size. Chef Charlie at the lodge will love to get his hands on this guy. Gladys will have a fine dinner tonight." He places the fish on a stringer in his ice chest while everyone onboard congratulates her.

"Chelsea!" he shouts, turning his attention right back toward me. "You've let out so much line, I think you're actually fishing in Canada! The fish you catch will all need passports."

I grimace, shift my weight, and try to reel my line in. "Jeez. I think—I'm hooked on something," I say.

"Just keep it rolling. Slowly," Clint says, coming over.

I clench my shoulders, but it's been too long since I've done anything that could be classified as *strenuous*. I feel like some klutz in gym class, uncoordinated and praying that no one tries to watch me dribble. As I attempt (ridiculously) to reel the line in, wishing Clint would just *cut me free, already,* an enormous fish breaks the surface. His greenish scales glisten iridescent against the light blue water. He jumps so high that he looks like he's actually standing on top of the lake.

"You've got one!" Clint cheers. "A big one, too, and he's trying to break your line. Hold on tight. He's trying to pull the hook out."

My heart jumps higher than the fish on my hook. I glance to the side, waiting for Clint to come swooping in with his net. But he just stands back, even though that colossal fish probably weighs more than Brandon's bass amp. I was barred from helping Brandon and Dad hoist that unwieldy Marshall into the cabin—so why isn't anyone trying to help me here? Why is Clint watching me struggle? The beads of sweat on my forehead feel so big, I figure I look like I'm wearing some gaudy rhinestone tiara.

"Don't stop—keep reeling—slow and steady," Clint is saying.

I shoot him a glare and grunt, just to emphasize my annoyance.

But by now, no one, not even my parents or Brandon, is watching *me*. Everyone's leaning against the side of the boat, watching the end of my line. Even a particularly rotund middle-aged guy has carved a viewing spot for himself; a dad's holding his little boy up so that his eyes will clear the railing. The lake's so clear, I'm sure they can all see the scales on the fish that fights me beneath the surface.

I clench my entire body as I crank the reel.

"Keep going," Clint shouts. "You've got him. That's beautiful! I've never seen anybody catch a fish that big on their first try."

I slam one foot against the side of the boat and figure I can safely plant my thighs against the railing. I feel like every single muscle is involved in my fight, and I remember it—the burn of work. It all comes back, how physical tests had fueled me, been the source of my happiness. I keep winding, fighting, beginning to enjoy the battle.

Closing my eyes for a moment, I'm not on a boat but running down a court in the final quarter, fighting for control of the ball. I'm back—I'm whole. Unbroken.

I relish the conflict, flexing my biceps to wind the reel until the fish is so close, he could whisper in my ear.

Finally, Clint's arm flies in front of my face as he scoops the fish into his net—a much bigger net, I realize, than the net he used for Gladys's catch.

"What a gorgeous walleyed pike," Clint says.

It's a funny word to describe a fish—but really not that far from the truth. Its scales shine like an antique gold bracelet in the sun.

"This guy's *huge*," Clint says as he hands the fish to me. The walleye stretches all the way from my head to just past my hip, making my arms tremble beneath the weight.

"We've got to take a picture," he goes on, rushing toward his clump of fishing gear and emerging with a camera that he aims at me. "I'll bet this one's a shoo-in for the biggest catch of the summer so far. If it's *still* the biggest catch in August, you'll win a free week's stay here at the resort next summer."

My heart is racing, the sweat is cooling on my arms, and my legs are wobbly. For the first time since finding myself writhing in pain on a gym floor while my fellow Eagles stared down on me, too scared to help, I actually feel…like me.

"What a great way to start your vacation. We ought to celebrate at Pike's tonight," Clint announces.

Without thinking, I let a smile jump onto my face. But not just some polite, picture-taking smile. Not something smeared across my face out of obligation. I give Clint an honest, true smile of utter happiness. The same smile that, back in my junior year, first won Gabe Ross's heart.

Before he snaps the picture, Clint smiles back.

Clint
odd man rush

She answers the door that night in a pair of jeans and a blue tank top. And instantly I start to sarcastically congratulate myself: *Great job, Clint. You and your bright ideas.*

I hadn't even really meant it when I said it—*We'll have to celebrate at Pike's tonight.* I was just *talking*, the same way I told Kenzie she was welcome to come out with me on the fishing launch. Mrs. Keyes, though—she acted like I'd sent Chelsea an engraved invitation in the mail. *What a good idea*, she shouted. *Of course Chelsea'd love to go!*

So here we stand, face-to-face in the doorway, and I can't quit thinking about the way she looks in that tank top.

Good grief, Morgan, what's wrong with you? You're acting like that twelve-year-old girl with the crush.

This was a really bad idea, going out with her tonight…

"Look," I tell her, "You don't have to go, if you don't want—"

"Of *course* she wants to," her mother says, popping into the doorway. "Just what you need," she says to Chelsea, running her fingers through Chelsea's blond hair. "A night to yourself, right?" She glances sideways when she says it, into the living room of the cabin, where Mr. Keyes sits glaring at the back of Chelsea's head.

"What kind of place is Pike's?" Brandon asks, popping into view behind his mother's shoulder. They look almost exactly alike, Brandon and his mom, with their skinny bodies and big glasses and brown hair sticking out in a hundred different directions.

Chelsea looks like her dad, though—light-haired, tan, athletic. But I get the distinct feeling something's wrong there; it's pretty obvious by the way they frown at each other, by the weird force between them. Kind of reminds me of trying to push two magnets together.

"It's my mom and pop's place," I tell Brandon. "In Baudette. Fried food, live music. You know the kind."

"Live music?" Brandon's voice goes up at the end, almost like a girl's.

"Sure. Greg and Todd—the fishing guides? We all grew up playing together. They play music at Pike's, but they—"

"Wait. Wait. A band. A live band?"

"Couple of guys jamming," I correct him. "Real informal."

Brandon claps his hands together once. "Does one of them play bass?"

I shake my head. "N—no—"

"Whataboutasinger?" he asks, smashing his words together in an ecstatic rush.

I bristle reflexively, remembering a hundred different packed-tight hot summer nights at Pike's, Rosie up there on the makeshift stage, singing to Greg and Todd's music. "No singer."

"Do you mind if I play? I sing, too—"

"Well—I wouldn't mind, but it's not my thing—they do the music," I say quickly.

Chelsea frowns. "I thought you said you all grew up playing together."

I flinch. "Not—not music." Without meaning to, I've let hockey drift out into the open. Actually, hockey and Rosie both.

"What did you play, then?" she asks again. "If it wasn't music."

"Mostly they just do instrumental stuff," I tell Brandon, ignoring Chelsea's question. I don't feel like going into hockey, and why I don't play anymore. Not any more than I feel like talking about the mic Rosie left empty. And why Greg and Todd never tried to fill it. "Sometimes, during the dinner rush, customers will take turns belting out a couple of tunes while they're waiting for a booth to open up," I manage.

"You really want to be backup for karaoke night, Brand?" Chelsea says.

Brandon sticks out his tongue. "I sing," he reminds her. "They'd let me sing. They're *hungry* for a singer, I bet. Come on, Clint. What're you driving? Can you fit my amp in?"

"A truck—yeah—I—" Brandon's already dragging me toward the back of the cabin, barking instructions.

We load the amp. When it's time to pile in, I try to tell Brandon to sit in the middle of the bench seat—"You haven't had hip surgery." I try to reason with him ... three times, in fact.

"That wedge in the middle's pretty uncomfortable. Let Brandon straddle the gear shift," I tell Chelsea. "You'd be better off with a seat of your own."

But Chelsea only shrugs, letting her eyes trail across the rust spots on the tailgate of my ancient GMC pickup, then the sun-bleached bench seat, torn and full of broken springs. It feels like she's saying, *I don't really think I'd be comfortable anywhere in that thing.*

And, in all honesty, she probably wouldn't be.

"I'll sit in the middle," she says. "Brandon's got to hold his bass."

"We could put it in the bed," I try.

Brandon lets out a horrified shriek. Chelsea cringes, touching her ear.

I give in, let my arguments die when she climbs in the middle. But when I slide behind the wheel, it smacks me on the side of the head how long it's been since a woman has sat in the cab of my truck. Since long hair rippled in the wind. Since the sweet smell of shampoo and soap danced off long, soft arms and up my nose.

I accidentally brush Chelsea's knee as I shift out of park. *I do not want this,* my brain immediately starts to chant. But other parts of my body like to disagree.

Brandon wants to talk about music—all the way to Baudette. Which is a little surprising, actually. Way the kid looks, I pegged him for Chess Club Champion. Now, though, as he hugs his guitar case, I notice all the silver hoops in his ears and the vintage Metallica T-shirt.

But at least he takes away the pressure of trying to find something to say. All I have to do is offer a nod and an occasional *mm-hmmm* or *that's cool* to his incessant chatter.

Good thing the AC in my old truck is nonexistent, because that means the window's down and can't be hit with spit when Brandon spews out a weird guffaw of surprise. "What is *that?*" he shouts, pointing at the forty-foot walleye that looms beside a *Welcome to Baudette* sign.

"The fish your sister caught today," I quip. Which actually gets the girl to smile—almost.

"A giant concrete fish? Seriously?" Brandon asks.

"Not just *any* concrete fish," I say. "That's Willie Walleye. He's a legend here. A … mascot."

The word *mascot* isn't really that much of a sports term, but it makes Chelsea's almost-smile fade just as quickly as it came.

"How many people do you think will show up tonight?" Brandon asks as I park the truck.

"Oh, as many as Pop can fit in—fifty or sixty."

"Fifty or sixty," Brandon whispers in awe.

"Leave your amp here for a sec," I tell him. "I'll introduce you to Greg and Todd."

Chelsea climbs out of the cab behind her brother. As Brandon excitedly pushes ahead of me, banging his guitar case through the door, I stare at Chelsea. She's standing on the sidewalk, the orange-neon glow from the Pike's Perch sign washing across her face and arms. She points up toward the inscription in the stone façade of the restaurant: *Bank—1906*. "Is that for real?"

"Pop brews beer in the old vault," I say, still holding the door open. The sounds of early evening dinner dishes clanking, voices laughing, and chairs scraping trickle out onto the sidewalk.

"My parents own a place kind of like this," she says. "I mean, not a full restaurant, but a bakery. In this row of shops and businesses that've been a hundred different things over the years. Somebody's taken over the original town bank there, too. It's an office building now. I've always loved that about my town—how it kind of keeps getting reinvented without being torn down. How history sticks around."

It's the most she's said to me since we've met. And the way she's staring at my folks' place, with that insanely cute smile on her face, makes an uncomfortable warmth spread just beneath my skin.

"Did you grow up working here?" she asks, turning her eyes from the building to me.

"I think I learned to walk bussing tables."

Her smile grows. "Huh. We might actually have something in common."

At first I think she's being sarcastic. And then I remind myself that while I might know her story (or fragments of it, at least), she doesn't know a single *sentence* of mine. She has no idea how much we really have in common.

"Hey," a sweet, happy voice calls from the opposite end of the sidewalk. When I turn, Kenzie's making her way toward the entrance of Pike's. She's all smiles, pushing her hair from her eyes. "I was hoping I'd find you here tonight," she says, pausing at my side. Just as she puts a hand on my shoulder, she glances toward Chelsea. "The ball player," she says quietly.

"Chelsea, this is Kenzie," I manage. "We ... grew up together."

"Lot of training going on at Pike's tonight?" Kenzie asks me, tilting her head. She clenches her jaw, obviously hurt. Or angry. Or both. "*Client*," she repeats through gritted teeth.

Chelsea
out of bounds

H ey!" Brandon shouts, banging his hardshell guitar case against an empty table. "Where's the *band*?" His face twists with utter disappointment.

"Not sure it's really that much of a band." The voice bellows out from behind an ancient teller's booth, now equipped with a modern cash register. The man who steps out from behind it is Clint plus thirty years—black hair, dark tan, broad shoulders, rugged features.

"Brought a new musician, Pop," Clint says, pointing at Brandon.

"Greg and Todd'll be ready to play in a minute," Clint's dad tells Brandon. "Why don't you just sit down and enjoy yourself for a minute? Any appetizer you want, on the house."

As if Brandon could be bothered with food. He bee-lines for the small stage area, pointing to the space behind the microphones. "Right here," he shouts. "My amp'll fit right here." He whacks into a Zildjian cymbal, which brings a protective drum-set owner—a pretty beefy guy in a fraying Corona ball cap—out of the shadows, shouting, "Who goes there?"

"This pretty lady his agent?" Clint's dad jokes, while Brandon introduces himself to the drummer.

"Chelsea Keyes. The basketball player I told you about last night."

"Gene Morgan. The father I'm sure he hasn't said a single word about," Clint's dad says with a quick wink.

Morgan, I think, sneaking a glance at Clint. *Clint Morgan.* It even *sounds* like the character in a romance novel. Or a soap opera. Clint Morgan, the rugged hero. Clint Morgan, the love-interest in the great cinematic American love story. Not that I'm interested. *Gabe Gabe Gabe Gabe...*

"You kids better snare a table while you can," Gene says. "Filling up fast tonight."

Just beyond Gene's shoulder, another guy joins Brandon and the drummer. The drummer seems to be inter-ested in whatever Brandon's saying—or maybe he's just mesmerized by his enthusiasm. But this second guy slips his slender body onto a stool that sits in front of a mic and watches me and Clint with a stare so intense, I'm not sure he even knows Brandon's here to infiltrate his band.

"Greg and Todd?" I ask, nodding once at the stage.

"Yep," Clint answers. "Todd's in the hat."

The slender guy—Greg—raises one hand to wave.

Clint pushes me toward the kitchen, where a woman with a long brown braid pinches the receiver of a phone between her ear and shoulder as she jots down a carry-out order. When she hangs up, she slaps Clint's hand, which has dipped into a plate of sizzling onion rings. "Get your dirty fingers out of that. I've just made them for table seven."

"They're clean, Mom," he protests.

"Clean as a fish, maybe," she says good-naturedly. The whole scene just reminds me so much of home. God—the mom in the back, the dad working the cash register. It's *so* familiar, in fact, that an actual giggle starts to trickle out of my mouth.

Clint's mom turns to me for the first time, her eyes running over me, digging so deep for details that it's almost like I've got newspaper glued to my arms and legs and she's searching my skin for the weather report.

"Chelsea Keyes, fisherwoman extraordinaire," Clint says, piling some hush puppies on a plate.

"Chelsea? *The* Chelsea?" A pleased grin tries to tug the corners of her mouth, the way Scratches sometimes paws and tugs on my foot, trying to get me to play. "Cecilia Morgan," she says, pointing to her chest. "Fry cook extraordinaire." She bites her top lip.

When she doesn't think I'm looking, she gives Clint one of those all-knowing mother gazes. Pats his shoulder. "Didn't expect you two to be out in the evening," she says.

"Didn't expect to see the two of you together in the restaurant at all, actually."

Clint frowns, and does such a rough, violent job of shaking his head at her that it practically gives me a rug burn just watching it.

"I'm just *saying*..." Cecilia's voice takes on a defensive tone.

"No, you were *probing*," Clint says. "We wanted to celebrate a good day on the lake for Chelsea. And her brother's a musician. *Period.* Don't get all private eye about it."

I suddenly get an all-over weird feeling, watching the beginning of a family fight unfold. Especially since I don't even know Clint, and especially since it looks like I'm going to be the source of the argument.

"I—I have a boyfriend," I blurt, stupidly. "Gabe. My—boyfriend."

Clint tosses a frown at me, his look of disbelief and annoyance so intense that my blush doesn't just slowly spread across my cheeks—it splashes across my face all at once.

"Looks like Clint's already fixed you a plate," Cecilia says, rolling her eyes as Clint heaps on servings of everything she's just taken from the fryer or has bubbling on a burner. "One of his Clint Specials. Hope you like barbecue with your fried fish. If you want something else, just knock him over the head."

I'm grateful for her casual words—they hit the air like a shrug of the shoulders that says the past few seconds were no big deal at all. But when the phone rings and she mumbles, "Busy tonight," I get all knotted inside, knowing I'm about to be left alone with Clint—and I've just offended him horribly.

But it's not even like I really *thought* he was going to try to make some kind of move on me. It's just that I was trying to *help* him. I mean, he didn't look like he wanted to encourage his mother in thinking we were going to have some sort of summer romance. You'd think he'd be grateful.

"Come on," Clint growls as he scoops up our dinner plates.

I follow him out of the kitchen into the dining room. It's pretty clear that Clint's something of a local celebrity himself, the way eyes don't just brighten but *illuminate* when he passes. *Only makes sense, with his parents owning what's probably the coolest restaurant in Baudette,* I think.

Kenzie's sitting at a table near the small platform that serves as a stage. Brandon's obviously convinced Clint's friends to let him play, and he and Greg wrestle with the amp, which fills the platform almost like a pro football player would fill a kindergartner's chair. Todd's left his drums for the moment and is leaning close to Kenzie as he talks, working overtime to get her attention. Kenzie's head swivels as she watches Clint snake his way between tables; Clint's oblivious, though.

The red brick walls we walk by are photo albums, filled with black-and-white framed images of turn-of-the-century life at the Baudette bank: women in buns, with skirts long enough to trail the floor, tellers with their faces hidden by those old-fashioned visors. But near the emergency exit, the bank portraits give way to hockey pictures. Indoor arenas with stands full of fans. Pond games with pines lining the shore, their top limbs looking like celebratory fists that pump the air.

The frame closest to the back door holds a close-up of a boy's face, a sweaty black fringe of hair dangling toward his eyes, his white-toothed smile shining. Pads on his shoulders, a rink in the background. It's Clint, obviously. As I stare, I remember the hand-painted signs that had hovered over the crowd during my last game. I glance at Clint, thinking maybe *that's* the kind of celebrity he is. *Clint Morgan, Pride of Baudette.*

Even with his hands full, Clint manages to open the metal door and we step onto a cracked slab of concrete. Some sort of old patio, probably where the wait staff takes their smoke breaks. A couple of wrought-iron chairs and some overgrown weeds line the area; early summer fireflies are beginning to dance above the spindly green stalks of weeds like lonesome boys looking for something beautiful and shiny to flash back at them. Lovers looking for someone to love.

Clint puts the two plates down on an old table—the kind of thing that belongs on somebody's back deck—and reaches for one of the rusty chairs. I take a step toward the table, but stop short when I realize I'm being watched by someone extraordinarily tall—

Make that some*thing* extraordinarily tall, looming on the far side of the cracked patio—a wooden pole, an orange metal hoop, a dirty white backboard. The ratty, soiled remnants of a rotten net dangle from the rim. My heart starts to pound inside my ears, making the same sound as a basketball whacking a concrete floor.

"What's *this*?" I ask, putting a hand on my hip, right above the metal plate.

"Been so long you don't recognize it?" Clint asks. While I stand there stuttering, he dips back inside.

I'm left there alone, blinking up at the towering monstrosity that slices through the warm glow of twilight to cast a cold shadow across my face. I shut my eyes, squeezing my lids the same way I might during some extra-gory scene in a blood bath on late-night cable.

Only when I open my eyes, the hoop is still looming, frighteningly. The terrifying scene has yet to end.

Inside, the band kicks into gear. Brandon's bass lines thunder through the brick, into the warmth of early evening. And that hoop is still casting the shadow of everything I've lost across my skin.

I'm ravenous, suddenly—not hungry for dinner, but for escape. For an envelope in the world where I don't have to feel the weight of my own past.

Something cold and damp hits the back of my arm. When I turn, Clint's face blocks out not only the back wall of Pike's, but the entirety of the Minnesota landscape. He's so close I can almost smell the day's sun on his skin. So close his lips are practically an inch from mine. If I were to just lean forward, they'd actually touch. If I were even to *pretend* to stumble, I'd be able to taste his mouth—

"Here," he says, pulling me away from my thoughts as

he nudges me again with one of the two frosted mugs in his hands.

I give my head a little shake. *What is wrong with you, Chelsea? Why would you ever think about another guy's lips with Gabe at home? You've never had thoughts like this about another guy. Not once.*

I should probably just sit down, but something keeps me rooted here, standing close enough to Clint to see the shadows his eyelashes cast on his face.

"Dad's brew?" I ask, searching for *anything* to say as I glance down into the white foam.

Clint puts a finger to his lips, *shhh*-ing me. "He'd have my ass if he knew I took these," he admits. When I accept, he raises his own mug.

"What're we toasting?"

"Your catch, of course. First place is always cause for celebration."

I clink my mug against his, take a sip. A slight raspberry flavor lingers on my tongue like new love—full of sweet excitement, laced with sour doubts.

My eyes drag down Clint's muscle-bound arms, the bulging calves beneath his shorts. "You're an athlete," I say.

Clint's face turns as black as defeat. "No."

"Sure you are. 'First place is always cause for celebration'? And what're all those pictures inside? The hockey stuff."

"*No*," Clint says, the way people get after their dogs. *No* which actually means, *Shut-up. Obey this command.*

I can't say I much like being ordered around. But there's

another note behind Clint's words—a sad, minor tone that does make me back away.

Silence settles around us like a block of ice. But I want to look at Clint straight on, not through the thick chunk of brutal cold between us. So I start to babble, tossing out questions like a blindfolded pitcher tossing spit-balls.

"Did you happen to catch any of his great moves while you were inside? Brandon's?" I ask. My brother doesn't just jiggle a little when he plays; he literally throws himself around, thrashing, splaying his legs to the side wildly like he's possessed by the ghost of every long-gone punk musician ever to wear a studded guitar strap.

"He gets into it, doesn't he?" Clint agrees.

"Of course," I add, "his performance is probably a bit tamer tonight, since he's also singing."

Finally, Clint smiles. "If *that's* tamer…" His voice trails off as he shakes his head. "Seriously, though, he really did surprise me. He can play. And he's got a decent voice."

"For such a geeky-looking kid," I finish before stopping to think, my voice all big-sister protective. Instantly, the block of ice between us turns into a freaking iceberg.

The whole scene's got this weird undercurrent to it. Forget mere ice—there's something festering between us, already. Something… to forgive, almost. And it doesn't really make any sense. We've only just met.

"That's not what I meant—he's not—" Clint tries to apologize.

"I know." I wave him off and sit at the weather-beaten table. "Never mind. Maybe we should just eat."

The Clint Special, his mom called his dinner. I doubt any other person on the planet could have come up with such a wild assortment of food: onion rings, fried shrimp, barbecued ribs, baked beans, slaw, fresh bread. And pickles. Pickles fill every last available wedge of space, turning the plate into a green polka-dotted display. I put a piece of popcorn shrimp in my mouth, but it kind of turns my stomach. It's not that Cecilia's a bad cook—just the opposite. But nerves always steal my appetite. And being here with Clint has practically set my hair on fire. I didn't get this worked up about taking the ACTs.

It doesn't help, either, that Pike's is close to some sort of swamp or marsh. I can't see what, exactly, because the patio butts right up against an overgrown wooded area, the same kind of woods that line the highways back home. But somewhere not far from our rough chairs and the trees, there has to be some sort of river or muddy stream, or one of Minnesota's ten thousand lakes for all I know. Point is, I can *smell* it—that funky summer scent of a sweaty body of water. And every deep breath I suck in, trying to calm my nerves, mixes with the bite in my mouth, making whatever I'm eating as bitter as a forgotten birthday.

Our silence pulls itself tight enough to feel dangerous. The awkward tension between us is a string on Brandon's bass, getting stretched by a tuning peg. One more turn of the peg and everything we're trying to accomplish with our strained celebration will snap in two.

Clint must feel it, too, because he abandons his dinner, saying, "Come on."

I don't know where we're going, but anything would be better than this. So I eagerly follow.

Clint sticks his hands into a bouquet of tall grass. I'm horrified—literally, *horrified*—when he plucks a large orange ball from the overgrown patch.

"What are you *doing?*" I snap as he dribbles the scuffed ball a couple of times. In slow motion, Clint passes me the ball. It hits the concrete once, then bounces up toward me.

Instinct kicks in—I hold my hands out, and I catch. Good God, I catch it; the ball hits my palms, its skin like a hedge-apple. It's the first time I've even touched a basketball since my final hook shot. Without thinking, I raise the ball to my nose and smell it. Earthy. Alive. Like always.

"Show me what you've got," Clint says, casually swinging his arms and clapping his hands once in front of his hips.

Doesn't the moron know that just touching the ball has caused the worst kind of ache to thunder through me? That it's like touching the warm skin of a man I love while he shakes his head, telling me no? *That's* what it's like for me to hold this basketball. It's like looking into the eyes of the man I love, who suddenly refuses to love me back. *You can't have me.*

I pass the ball back to him and plunk myself back into my chair.

"What're you doing?" he asks. "Come on—simple game of Horse."

Fire eats the inside of my stomach. "I have reasons. I can't jump, okay? The doctors told me no high impact—"

"You don't have to jump, you know."

"It's not the same."

"What was it you said to me outside, before?" Clint asks. "That you love how history sticks around?"

I shrug, shake my head, not sure what he's getting at.

"Basketball's your history, right? Why don't you love it anymore?"

I glare at him. "You don't know anything about what I love. And that's not fair, twisting my words against me. I wasn't … basketball's different."

"How?" Clint presses.

I glance up at the moon, which hangs so close to the backboard it actually looks like a ball about to slide through the hoop. It's crazy, but I find myself even resenting the moon.

"Today on the boat?" Clint says. "I timed you. A full minute and ten seconds passed from the moment you realized you'd hooked that walleye to the time you started reeling. A minute and ten seconds. It's a wonder that fish didn't break your line and swim away."

"So what?"

"So what're you going to do now, sit in that chair like one of those old men who hang around outside bait and tackle shops? Just sit and watch the world go by?"

"Who are you to make *any* judgments about me, ten minutes after you meet me?" I screech, and even as I'm trying to bury my anger, to shove it deep down inside of me, to stay cool in front of Clint, rage keeps popping up like that crazy Whac-A-Mole arcade game. No matter how hard I try to smack it down, it just keeps rearing its ridiculous head.

"What do you *do*, Chelsea?"

"I don't even understand what that question is supposed to mean."

"What do you love? What do you do with all that passion inside, now that the thing you loved the most is gone?"

I hate the way he's trying to corner me, and there's no replacing basketball … there just isn't. I want him to feel just as uncomfortable as I do. I want to attack—want to hurt him back—but I don't know how. I don't know anything about his soft spots.

But then again, I think, as the muffled band launches into a slow song, there *is* that face he made when I said I had a boyfriend …

So I pull myself up from the chair and saunter across the patio, slowly. Knock the basketball out of his hand, let it bounce into the weeds. I raise both hands, place them on his sides. Stare him straight in the eye as the warmth of his skin bleeds through his T-shirt.

"I *dance*," I say, like a challenge.

Clint backs up, his face twisting into the kind of heartbreak I felt when he'd tossed me the basketball.

"I don't," he says.

I'm unable to hide my smile of victory. *Squirm on, jerk.* "Then I guess we're at an impasse," I say.

"Yeah," he agrees softly. "I guess so." As he slumps back into his own chair, he looks like I've just launched the ball straight into his stomach. He stares off toward the musky swamp somewhere in the distance while Brandon's bass thumps out into the night. The orange basketball has rolled into the grass; it glows like a roadside construction cone, warning of impending dangers ahead.

Clint
offensive move

Why, of all the basketball players on earth, did I have to get this one? Why couldn't she have been a guy? Or at the very least, a ball player who'd let herself completely go, and who didn't step out of cabin number four wearing short shorts that show off her long legs? And why did I have to get a ball player who makes it clear, by the angry tightness in her face, that she holds grudges?

"Biking," I suggest, trying to act cool and detached as we stand on her front porch. "Earl rents out mountain bikes up at the lodge. That path behind your cabin goes straight to this waterfall—"

"A *waterfall*?" she repeats, her face softening for a moment. "I've been hearing rushing water ever since we got here."

But just when I think she's about to agree, she shakes her head, crosses her arms. I can't help but notice that when she hugs her ribs, her cleavage bulges out of her tank top.

"We could ride straight up there—" I start.

"And then fly back *down* the hill, out of control, and wreck against a tree," she grumbles.

"Kayaking," I say.

She frowns at me, juts her jaw out. "Kayaking's just asking for it."

Okay, so I deserve the attitude she's giving me today. So I was an ass last night. So I took what could have been a nice celebration and turned it into one of the most awkward nights of all time. All because she'd asked about hockey. Because I'd wanted to hurt her as much as she'd hurt me. So I'd taunted her with basketball. I'm no dope—I knew she'd never play Horse with me. I did it to be mean. So I get whatever she wants to dole out today. As much as I hate it, it's fair.

"I . . . I looked up hip surgery," I try to tell her. "I know high-impact stuff's out of the question, but kayaking—"

"Some wooden banana that hugs my jury-rigged hip and keeps overturning doesn't exactly score up there next to penicillin on the list of *Great Ideas of All Time*. It scores closer on the list to—Beta VCR players and eight-track tapes. The Ford Pinto. Sneakers made out of nails. Rat poison that tastes like grape jelly—"

"*Okay*," I snap, just as the screen door behind us flops open.

When her dad steps onto the porch, I take a step away from Chelsea, drop my hands, relax my face. Stupid of me to start feeling angry with her, anyway. And if her dad thinks we're not getting along, he could fire me.

That'd look real good with Earl.

Forget Earl, the voice in the back of my head starts barking. *It's not about Earl, and you know it. You want to spend time with her.*

I shake my head. *I do not,* I want to convince myself. *I don't care what she does.* But I find myself hoping like hell, as I glance at Chelsea, that she won't tell her dad she's had enough of my boot camp.

"You two have a nice celebration last night?" he asks. It's kind of rough, how he talks to her. I don't know if he means it to come across that way.

"Fine," she growls, staring off in the opposite direction. Refusing to look at his face.

Her dad sighs loudly. He rushes down the front steps, heads down the dirt path toward the lodge.

"What's that all about?" I say before I can stop myself.

"You know what we *used* to celebrate?" Chelsea tightens her lips and raises her eyebrows.

I get it. Another jab at me. Another way to tell me what I jerk I was last night. *Can that whole thing really have only happened last night?* I stare at Chelsea. At this rate, it'll take about forty years to get to the end of her vacation.

"Orchid hunt," I suggest. "Nice gentle hike. Never seen anything as pretty as a Minnesota orchid."

As soon as she relaxes her face, washing the angry

scowl off, I know what I've just said is absolute bull. Chelsea's far prettier than any old flower.

But she agrees—at last. Nods an okay. "Just let me grab a camera," she says. The boards of the cabin porch thunk beneath her feet as she hurries inside to get it.

We get in the truck; my old GMC's the only one willing to do any talking. It creaks and groans and shimmies, but Chelsea only stares through the windshield. And when we get to the lake, she throws open her door and starts stomping toward the water's edge.

I lean forward, fish the camera Kenzie keeps loaning me out of the glove compartment. And I dive out of the truck, rushing to catch up.

"Chelse," I try, but she ignores me.

I stare at her back, wondering what it is about a ponytail. Just a simple blond ponytail, fastened up high on the back of a girl's head. And what is it about Chelsea's ponytail, in particular, that lays a thick fog all across my brain?

As soon as I wonder, the answer appears: *It's the way that ponytail exposes the sweet, soft skin on the back of her neck. It's the way the breeze teases strands free, begging a guy to imagine what it would be like to slide that ponytail holder out, to bury his nose in her hair.*

I shake my head. *Knock it off, Clint.*

"Chelsea!" I call, trying to get her to turn around.

But that ponytail is *all* Chelsea's willing to give me. She sloshes through the fringe of the lake in a near-stomp. She doesn't press forward like the athlete I'm told she once was, though; her feet don't have purpose, her arms flop around sloppily. She's rusty. Out of practice.

"Careful," I try to warn her.

But she only slams her feet against the earth more forcefully. Shoves the soles of her sneakers so deep into pockets of mud that she occasionally has to pause to wrench herself free.

I press a little faster, trying to catch up. When I get close enough for my toes to kick water onto the backs of her calves, she starts to pump her arms and rush ahead, increasing the space between us.

Just as I decide to let her have it, the space, she takes her long-sleeved shirt off and ties it around her waist. The tank top underneath shows off the curve of her slender shoulders. I swear, her tanned skin is the same shade as a just-baked piece of pastry. It literally makes my mouth water.

I do not want this, I remind myself. My body, yet again, disagrees.

The sun reaches through the branches of the swamp maples overhead, spills across my shoulders. But Chelsea is what warms my body.

This is stupid, I try to tell myself. But my body feels what it wants to anyway.

"Chelsea," I call. "Chelse!"

"I'm *on* it," she shouts over her shoulder. She's kind of mall-walking, pumping her arms, the silver exterior of her digital camera catching the sun and tossing it around wildly. "Look—I'm hiking, see? Don't have to ask me twice, don't have to wait a whole *minute and ten seconds* to get started. No way. Not quitting, not me."

"Truce!" I finally shout.

For the first time since she stepped from the truck, she stops. Just stops, without turning around, her breath gasping out of her body so harshly that her shoulder blades heave up and down.

"Look, I'm sorry, okay—I was out of line last night," I say to her back. "Let's forget it, just move on from here. Nothing high-impact. Just a nice hike. Photograph a few orchids along the way. Never—never seen anything as pretty as a Minnesota orchid," I say again, even though it sounds ridiculous. "No busybody trainer handing out advice you never asked for. Promise."

She sighs so loud, the sigh has an actual voice to it. "I just *miss* it. Miss it so much, it makes me crazy. Basketball, I mean." She turns only enough to show me her profile. "To be out there, on the patio behind Pike's … To be around basketball, to be on the fringes, when I can't really have it. Not like I used to. It just—it kills me. It's like—like I'm in jail, and I haven't had food in two days, and there's a cheeseburger and a chocolate shake on the other side of my bars, just beyond my fingertips, out of my reach when I stick my arm through. Maybe that sounds over-the-top, but I guess that's how I feel. Over-the-top."

"Okay," I say.

Her blue eyes dart to me. "Okay?" she repeats. "Just okay."

"All anybody can ask for is an honest effort." Good personal trainer talk. No emotion. The way it should be.

"But I—I'm different now, after the accident," she says. "I mean—honest effort—it's not the same now. I'm—not what I used to be."

"Okay," I say softly.

She nods, turning a little more, showing me the pink glow of both her cheeks. But the knots under my skin refuse to loosen, because this feels close, too. Like we're a couple, and we're making up after a fight. No matter what I do, Chelsea keeps burrowing herself deeper—only I don't know when I allowed her in. Wasn't every door inside me already padlocked before she even came to the resort?

Still, I'm staring at her beautiful face and the only thing I can think is, *I wonder what he's like, the boyfriend.* A twinge of jealousy pops up, followed by a rush of anger, just like it did last night when Chelsea announced she had a boyfriend. But why? Why would I even care?

Why *can't* I stay non-emotional?

We slosh farther along the cool edge of the water, into a marshy area that smells a little like sweat-soaked skin. A stream cuts across our path, shallow and gurgling. Chelsea starts to follow it, walking upstream, putting the lake behind her. Above us, cars careen down a highway, the roar of their engines slicing through the still air.

My eyes dart down the stream, past Chelsea's shoulders. A shiver travels down my back as I realize where we've wound up.

"Did you find one?" Chelsea calls to me. "An orchid?"

"No," I say, my voice wobbling. "Look, let's go back the other way."

What's wrong with you, Morgan? I start chastising myself. But I know—I'd been staring too hard at the curve of Chelsea's shoulder to realize just where she was headed. To realize she was heading to *this* ravine.

Never should have driven here in the first place, I try to tell myself. But I'd been too upset, too focused on the silence in the truck, to think about anything else. Anything but Chelsea.

"I did! I found one," Chelsea shouts triumphantly. She hurries even farther ahead of me, toward a white and pink bloom.

But the bloom disappears, and so does Chelsea. I'm not feeling the heat of a summer morning, but brutal cold. It's not the first week of June, but early March, and winter's still got northern Minnesota in her icy clutch. I look down to find that I'm holding the silver lid of a thermos instead of a camera. Pop's pouring black coffee into it. And I'm not standing in the ravine; I'm looking down on it as I steer my GMC along the highway above. Snow has painted the world pure white. My breath comes out in clouds. My arms are covered in the sleeves of a parka. My forehead itches against the rim of a wool stocking cap. Through the windshield, I see the sun slowly rising. Marking the beginning of yet another day of unanswered questions.

"What you *really* need is some sleep," Pop is telling me. "You need to try, at least." He says it loud, because the radio is on. That damned radio.

"...the search for missing teen Rosaline Johnson continues," the local DJ announces. "Last seen leaving to attend the local pond hockey tournament..."

"And I knew it, right away," I say. "She didn't show up, and I *knew* something was wrong. But I kept *playing*?" I grip the steering wheel even tighter.

"Not your fault, Clint," Pop insists, as he has for the past eight solid hours of driving. "If you'd just get some rest—"

"Yeah, well, we still don't know where she is. We still don't know what's happened to her. And something *has* happened. That's *somebody's* fault. I'm not going to stop just to sleep. No way." I hit the brakes and skid onto the shoulder. I slam the gear shift into park.

"So why *are* you stopping?" But even as Pop asks it, I think he already knows.

Up ahead, red and blue lights are splashing across the snow-covered branches. Police cars are parked on the highway, blocking traffic. And suddenly I'm out of the truck. I'm running.

"Clint," Pop calls. But I'm already sliding down the bank, my boots sinking into inches of snow. Pop's feet crunch behind me as he tries to catch up. My lungs are on fire, burning against the cold.

Black uniforms stand ahead of me. One of them sees me, holds his hand up. "Son," he shouts, "you don't want to be here."

"Rosie?" I screech. "Rosie?"

Pop catches the back of my parka, but I break away.

I race forward, feet sinking. Everyone is screaming, and ahead—I can see it now—a windshield, cracked, and that paint, that damned white paint, camouflaged by the snow. A Miata, roof caved and crunched. *It rolled,* I think, my eyes darting back up to the highway. *I drove by this place a hundred times the past couple of days. I just didn't see her. She always drove too fast anyway, like a maniac, even in bad weather. How many times did I warn her?*

The officers all join in, raising their hands, all of them calling, *son, son*... I slowly begin to realize that the scream bouncing against my skull is coming from me. *Rosie, Rosie*...

"Hey—over here." Chelsea's voice makes the landscape turn green and muddy and empty of police officers. Cars fly down the highway above my head, oblivious to what happened two years ago in this very ravine. But I'm still shaking all over.

Rosie's gone.

As I make my way toward her, Chelsea kneels down next to a fleshy-looking bloom. Her camera flashes. She reaches for the orchid as though about to pick it, but I lunge forward and grab her arm, wrench her away.

"Come on," I snap. "We're leaving."

"But, I—"

"Don't argue with me," I bellow, because being here, reliving it, makes the accident seem fresh. Not like a memory at all, but like something that's happening *now*. I can't believe I let my guard down long enough to wind up here.

Chelsea
restrictions

What they say about absence isn't true, Gabe writes. *It doesn't make the heart fonder—it makes the heart want to break, it hurts so much. Just like a compass, my heart keeps pointing me straight to you. If I didn't have this stupid job, I'd be on my way to Minnesota...*

I sigh as I balance the netbook on my knees, wiggling my toes on the front step of cabin number four. My cell phone reception might be iffy all the way out here, but Mom had to get the bright idea of bringing her netbook so she could check the incoming emails and orders at White Sugar. (It's driving her crazy to be away from work this long... in addition to tweaking the annual cookbook, she's already brainstorming ideas for an August wedding cake whose order came in yesterday.) And the stupid Wi-Fi connection in our cabin's pretty rock solid. Which allows me no breather from Gabe.

Not that you need one, I remind myself. *You love him as much as he loves you.*

Right. Exactly.

I miss you, too, I reply, in what has become my daily exchange of emails to the guy who, according to his latest message, writes me at one in the morning when he can't sleep for thinking of me. I wish I could come up with something beautiful to tell him. Something that would make his heart turn as sticky as a half-melted lollipop.

My mind drifts forward, wildly, like a raft on the rapids near the resort, as I imagine how it will feel to finally not just touch Gabe's hand or his mouth, but experience the *entirety* of his naked body against my skin. I imagine the moonlight seeping in through a window of the Carlyle, playing off the golden curls on his chest. Imagine wrapping my entire body around his...

But I can't write this down, can't even begin to bring myself to type such a thing. So all I manage to come up with is, *Carlyle: 15 days and counting...*

After pressing *send,* I absentmindedly pick up a pair of binoculars Dad's left on the front porch and hold them to my eyes.

The lenses fill with a head of black hair as Clint steps out of the lodge. I feel a gasp kick the inside of my throat as I'm forced to admit to myself, yet again, just how much I hate the idea of losing a day with Clint. He's taking a group out kayaking today, and stupid me, I had to go and tell him that snotty stuff about thinking kayaking's as dumb as an eight-track tape. Now I'll lose the entire day. And the last two haven't exactly been so great. Ever since that weird hike, when he yanked me away from an orchid and practically tossed me into his truck, things have been—*uugh*. Professional, of all things.

But kind of detached, too. He's acting like the guy behind the counter in a fast-food joint who doesn't really give a crap if I supersize or not. So when I said no to golf or waterskiing (I mean, really—*waterskiing?*), he just sighed and shrugged. Hadn't pushed back. Hadn't tried to convince me I could do more, like he had when we were at Pike's. We just hiked again; we went bird-watching.

One full week of my vacation is now gone. Another pyramid of sand is building at the bottom of another hourglass.

Maybe Dad's right. Maybe I *am* wasting this vacation. (*Bird-watching?* Not exactly the outdoor adventure he and Mom had probably envisioned. But I have reasons. Stacks and piles of them. Right?)

I get tingly when I realize that Clint's walking toward me. Because I start to think, maybe he *hasn't* decided I'm the world's biggest bore. Maybe he'll ditch the kayakers so we can spend the day together. The idea makes my lungs burn with excitement.

Brandon comes banging out of the cabin behind me with his guitar case. I jump, lose the head of black hair in the distance.

"Don't those guys have jobs?" I ask. Brandon's been

completely monopolizing Greg and Todd's time, practicing with them incessantly. I jerk out of the way as he flops his uncoordinated, skinny body across the porch and down the front steps, banging the case against the railing and nearly knocking me in the head with it, too.

"We jam between their fishing runs," Brandon says, so excited he's actually out of breath. "And besides, Greg's got a gig for us later on today. A real gig!"

"Where?" I ask through a frown. "Are you going back to Pike's?" I shout after him, hoping he won't be around to ruin things if Clint and I decide to grab a bite later.

What is wrong with you, Chelsea? Forget about that email you just sent... to your boyfriend? Hmm?

"Brand!" I shout again. But he's too busy shuffling off, his case flopping against his calves, to answer.

"And what about you?" I call after Mom's skinny back as she scurries along behind him.

"The oven in the cabin's no good for baking," she replies, tossing her words over her shoulder with a careless wave. "Chef Charlie's going to let me use the kitchen in the lodge, in exchange for teaching him how to make a decent pie crust."

"Don't you think a chef already knows—" I start.

"He's a chef, but definitely not a baker. Don't you have something planned with Clint?"

I certainly hope so...

I glance down at the computer screen, realizing I've missed the P.S. in Gabe's last email: *Anytime you feel we've been apart too long,* he's written, *just look for the Chelsea Keyes Star. I'll be looking at it, too.*

I'm not exactly in the mood for a guilt-fest. So I sign out of my email account and raise the binoculars again, easily zeroing back in on the head of black hair and the muscular jaw that clenched throughout our ride back to the cabin after the orchid hunt. Clint's shoulders sway with each step he takes up the brown trail that leads straight to cabin number four. I aim the binoculars just low enough to get an up-close view of his slim sides, remembering how his skin warmed my hands through his T-shirt when I touched him on the patio behind Pike's, challenging him to a dance.

There's just something about him. It's like he's hotter than a steering wheel in August—he burns me every single time I get close enough to touch him. But the thing about a steering wheel in the summer is, even though it stings, you still have to touch it in order to get where you want to go. And besides, sometimes that burn feels kind of good against your hand, anyway.

I shiver. *Where did all that just come from?*

I put the binoculars and the netbook aside, try to act like my heart isn't attacking my ribs.

"Just saw your dad up at the lodge," Clint says, his faded hiking boots pausing at the edge of the bottom step. "I think I convinced him to try out the golf course at Oak Harbor. Seemed pretty excited about it."

As soon as he mentions my dad, I can't help picturing the way it might have been if we'd vacationed here *last* summer. I imagine Dad sitting next to me on the cabin's front step; I picture him jabbering with Clint and me like he's forgotten he isn't actually eighteen anymore, dropping in the occasional *awesome* that must have been every other word out of his mouth in high school, judging by the way he'd lean on it. But I haven't heard him say that word *once* since my accident. He hasn't felt much about our situation has been awesome, I guess.

I feel myself tense up, my entire body turning so stiff I could practically pass for a brick wall.

"It's tougher sometimes on other people," Clint says, slicing into the sudden silence. "It's—got to be hard on your dad—the whole basketball thing."

I frown, not exactly in the mood for this conversation, either.

But Clint holds up a hand, stops me from telling him how wrong he is. "At Pike's, when you said I was an athlete, you were right," he admits. "I *was*—played hockey. When I had to quit, it hurt—my folks—as much as me, even."

"Yeah, but I've seen you and your folks," I mutter. "They—*talk* to you, at least. Not like him."

"We were always pretty close, I guess," he admits. "Only child and all."

"What happened?" I ask, my stomach plummeting, like an elevator with a broken cable. *Do we actually have this in common?* "Did you get hurt?"

"You could say that."

"During a game?"

"No, I didn't ... *have* to give hockey up. Not physically,

like you did. But I couldn't compete at the same level anymore. I tried, but my mind wasn't in it. I wasn't focused. They were beating me up out on the ice. Or avoiding me, which was maybe even worse. Like I wasn't even playing. Like I wasn't really part of the team. They ignored me. So I decided—no more team sports for me. Not just hockey, either. I still exercise plenty, but the only battle I get into anymore is between me and the occasional walleye."

"Better to let them remember you when you were great."

He shrugs and nods. "Yeah. Something like that."

I try to picture what it would have been like if I'd broken my hip, but not as badly; if I'd been allowed to get back on the court, only to discover I was half the athlete I'd been before. I imagine college scouts trickling out of the gym before halftime. Rushing to the mailbox only to find the phone bill, checking my email only to find a message from Gabe. No news of athletic scholarships. No letters of intent. A heart that didn't just break once, but had tiny pieces broken off with disappointment's hammer hundreds of times, every single day.

"It's a lady slipper," Clint says, pointing to the picture of the orchid I loaded onto Mom's netbook. "You got a terrific shot." When he looks back at me, his eyes travel around my face the way fingers dart through the bottom of a drawer, searching for batteries in a blackout. I start to feel my excitement bubble over... this isn't the passive way a guy looks at a girl he's completely uninterested in. But

Clint just shakes his head, clears his throat, points again at the computer screen.

"State flower of Minnesota," he finally says, still just talking about the lady slipper, still not offering even a hint of an explanation for the way he'd flared up with— what *had* it been? Fear? Anger?—during our orchid hike the other day. And here I am just sitting on the step, not sure how to even broach the subject even though I'm dying to. "If you ever find another one, don't pick it," he says. "Protected by law." As though this somehow explains why he was so rough about hauling me from the ravine. And we both know no one could ever care that much about a flower.

"Are we talking, *Do not remove the tag on this mattress under penalty of law* or *Do not drink and drive under penalty of law*?" I ask. I'm trying to tease, but the way Clint's face clenches, I know this has hit him in the way the Chelsea Keyes Star hit me.

"Even if there wasn't a law," he says, "you shouldn't pick them. They're pretty rare. Takes them sixteen years to bloom."

"*Years*? A late bloomer," I moan, glancing at the screen saver. "How ironic."

Instead of an orchid, I see bilious, neon-orange letters pulsing at the top of the picture: *VIRGIN. VIRGIN. VIRGIN.*

I imagine myself stepping onto the screen, throwing an enormous rock at the glowing letters.

"Where'd you go?" Clint asks. He tucks a piece of flya-way hair behind my ear.

I don't stop him, or flinch, or pull away. I just stare up into his eyes, at the irises that are every bit as dark as his pupils, their depths swirling about me like an eddy. I'm afraid to speak, afraid I might scream out the words lying in wait beneath the touch of his fingers: *I want more.*

Gabe Gabe Gabe Gabe...

"Listen," he says finally. "Since I know you don't par-ticularly like the idea of kayaking, I wanted to ask if you'd like to make up for a day off by going to a birthday party tonight."

"*Yes,*" I say. His invitation reduces me to a giggly, romance-novel-reading pile of girly mush.

Clint
sin bin

A birthday party for a *fish*," Chelsea says, shaking her head in disbelief. But she doesn't look like she really thinks it's stupid at all. Her eyes sparkle, and her shoulders are so relaxed that the strap of her sundress keeps falling off and dangling across her upper arm.

Just as I start telling myself to stop looking at her, to stop thinking about how pretty she is today, my eyes hit the bottom of her sundress. The yellow material ripples around her knees, which are as pink as the wads of cotton candy that dot the crowds. *And I bet they're just as sweet...*

"A *fish*," Chelsea repeats.

"Not just any old fish. A two-ton *concrete* fish. Willie's a legend," I remind her.

She smiles, her sandals scraping against the pavement

of Baudette's Main Street, which is overtaken today by a carnival. Booths line the curbs, advertising homemade jams and pickles, wire jewelry, door wreaths twisted out of grape vines. Runners who competed in the morning's 5K still wander through the crowd, easy to peg in their running shorts, numbers still pinned to their backs. Entries in the lumberjack chainsaw-carving competition are still perched on a wooden ledge outside a camping gear store: a bear, an old man's wrinkled face, and three different versions of Willie Walleye himself.

Umbrellas cover wooden tables, shading jugs of frozen root beer, plates of fried food, laughing faces. And there doesn't seem to be a single face here that *isn't* smiling, isn't laughing.

For the first time in my life, Willie Walleye Day sure seems like some sort of magical cure-all.

At least, it's a cure-all for everybody except me. I just can't make my brain shut up. Or get my nerves to calm down. I keep asking myself what we're really doing here. I mean, it's not like we have something to celebrate, not like the day she caught that walleye. And it's not like this can pass as some boot camp exercise. Sure, we're walking. But so what? *Walking?* Not even hiking. She wasn't hurt so bad that walking would be considered a real workout.

What are you doing, Clint?

"This is nothing like the Heritage Festival back home," Chelsea admits as she takes it all in.

I nod, staring down the street, doubting that her heritage festival looks much different. But the fact that she said it, that she's so *happy*, makes me feel insanely good. Kind of adrenaline-high good.

"Frozen lemonade," she says, reaching for the little purse she's got twisted around her wrist.

"No," I say, kind of offended by the way she's reached for her money. But why should I be? I fork over a few dollar bills. It's not like we're on a date here—right?

Only I *did* put on a clean shirt before I left to pick her up. I shaved. And when I swore I could still smell the lake on my skin, I took a shower. I feel like an idiot for picking out a button-down shirt that looks like it should be in a sit-down restaurant instead of an outdoor festival. At least I put on jeans instead of khakis.

I pay for her lemonade and steer her away from the booth with the flashing lemon sign. Point out the sign above a large tented area that proclaims *Beer Garden*.

"Hmm," she says, swirling her straw through her lemonade. "That makes me feel a little silly for wanting this. If I'd known you were going to have a *beer*…"

"Just come on," I say, pushing her toward the garden.

"Don't make me card you two," Pop calls from the side of the tent as he flicks the caps off two amber bottles and hands them to thirsty runners. "I don't want to know anything about fake IDs."

"I don't have a fake ID," I tell him, but Pop rolls his eyes.

"Everybody has a fake ID. I had a fake ID when I was your age. But I guess you don't need one, do you?" Pop's tone lets me know that he found out about the two raspberry brews Chelsea and I drank at Pike's Perch.

What Pop's hawking here at the beer garden is his award-winning Pike's Porter. Dark as the backs of eyelids staring into the sun, with the same warm, red tint running through it.

"Get you two some fresh chips?" Pop asks, pointing at Mom, who's sweating over the fryer. She tosses us a wave until she notices who I'm with. And then a grin grows. She purses her lips in this *uh-huh, I see exactly what's going on here* kind of way.

I start to shake my head. But a drum steals my chance to tell her that she's got it all wrong.

Pop points over his shoulder at the makeshift stage just behind the beer garden. "That brother of yours has whipped Clint's friends into shape," he shouts at Chelsea. We both turn toward the stage, where a hand-painted sign announces, *Appearing Every Night At Pike's Perch!*

"Hope your family doesn't mind me giving him a steady gig," Pop tells her. "If it puts a kink in the rest of your vacation plans..."

Chelsea laughs, shakes her head. "No way. You've made his entire year."

She puts her lemonade down, tugs my arm until we hit the edge of the crowd clustered for the band. This is a real treat—usually there's no music at all until the street dance kicks into gear. I'm about to tell Chelsea this when my eye travels to the far side of the crowd, where Kenzie sips from a bottle of Pike's Porter. She raises the bottle in greeting, but her smile tumbles when she notices who I'm with. She stares down at her hands and chews her lip before disappearing into the crowd.

"Live, from Willie Walleye Day in Baudette," Brandon announces into his mic. "It's ... the Bottom Dwellers!"

Chelsea tosses her head back and laughs. I'd call it a belly laugh, but it seems deeper even than that. Before I can stop myself, I think *Man, that's a great sound.*

"Your brother's becoming quite the celebrity."

She turns, then jerks backward a bit when she finds Kenzie about half an inch from her nose.

Kenzie's got her long hair stuck through the hole in the back of a ball cap; her Lake of the Woods T-shirt hangs out of a pair of scruffy capri pants. She looks like she came straight from the resort. Slowly, she runs her eyes over my stupid shirt and Chelsea's sundress. She flashes me a *come off it—just admit what's going on here* frown.

"He'll have groupies tagging along behind him everywhere he goes," Kenzie says.

"*Brandon?*" Chelsea laughs. "No way."

"Just might have to join them," Kenzie adds. "What do you think about that?" She says this last part to me, and just stands there weighing my reaction. It's some kind of crazy test. "I like his wild hair," she prods. "I told him so."

I feel like climbing up onto the stage, pushing Brandon aside, and tapping his mic. *Attention, Baudette,* I want to say, *see that girl over there in the sundress? I am not here on a date with her. I'm her trainer. She has a boyfriend. I'm not interested.*

But how am I supposed to deny what Kenzie thinks when Chelsea's standing right here? Wait—why *can't* I deny it with Chelsea standing right here?

I can't because, when I glance at her, the devil on my shoulder just keeps telling me how nice it would be to know what she tastes like.

I take the coward's way out, and step to the side a little, separating myself from Chelsea—but not too much.

Kenzie's still staring at me when Chelsea takes my hand and starts moving her feet to a decidedly garage-band version of an old Rolling Stones song, "Waiting on a Friend." And before I can completely take my eyes away from Kenzie, before I can mouth something at her like *not my type* or *you've got it wrong,* Chelsea pulls me deep into the crowd in front of the stage. Before I know what I'm doing, I'm swaying with her.

"Careful," Chelsea teases. "This seems awfully close to dancing."

From the corner of my eye, I watch Kenzie slam her bottle into one of the metal trash cans and stomp away.

Chelsea
ball reversal

We walk up and down Main Street so many times, my arches are throbbing like they do after one of my long hikes with Clint. At some point during those slow and easy treks, he always takes out some old compass and stares at the dial—and then the horizon—and sighs loud enough to make me suspect he finds our pace *too* slow and easy. Make me wonder if I need a note from my orthopedic surgeon to convince him that *push yourself* is a relative term.

But Clint's not sighing this afternoon. He seems to revel in the fact that our stroll is punctuated by funnel cakes and fried Twinkies and kabobs and root beer. Trying on silly ball caps. Watching the kayak races. Picking lumberjacks to cheer for in the log-jumping competition.

The pink watercolor shades of sunset shock me. We've

spent hours here, but it feels like a moment. Clint's beginning to seem a little antsy, as if the encroaching night is a floor we've begun painting without paying any attention to where the doors are. Like we're about to be trapped by—what? A darker shade? Isn't that all night is?

Only it's not. Night has a whole different connotation—I know that. Baudette knows that, too. The families clustered around picnic tables are giving way to hand-holding pairs. Couples that look a little like fireflies, the way they flitter about, flirting in the sweet summer air. And I'm here with *Clint*. Anyone who didn't know better might suspect we're dating, too. My face warms as I wonder what it would be like if I were free to take his hand. If I could wrap an arm around his waist.

Gabe Gabe Gabe Gabe Gabe...

We're coming to the end of the booths again; it's time for us to leave, I know it is. But I elbow Clint, delighted to find a way to stretch out our day just a little longer. "Come on," I say, pointing to a booth where hairdressers are braiding hair, weaving ribbons into the plaits. I take a seat, close my eyes, and allow my brain to play with daydreams the way the local stylist plays with my locks, twisting them tightly around the base of my head. I imagine that I'm a Baudette girl, going to college in Minnesota. That I have all summer to spend with my boyfriend, my Clint, whose skin is the utter fire of thrill—the closest thing I've ever felt to launching my body into the air, shooting the ball out of sheer desperation, and triumphantly snagging the final, game-winning three-pointer.

When the hairdresser's done, she sticks a handheld mirror in front of me. "Whaddaya think?" she says, her voice bouncing with a light accent.

I think it looks just like a little-girl hairdo. I might as well have happy faces and rainbows painted on my cheeks.

"Thank—thank you," I stutter, my entire face growing red as I push myself out of the chair. My hair is pulled so far from my face, I have no hope of hiding my horrendous blush.

"It's silly, isn't it?" I say, reaching to take it down.

But Clint just wraps his warm, strong hand around my wrist, stops me from pulling out the pins. "You look really pretty," he says, without even a dash of sarcasm. *Pretty.* The word gives me goose bumps.

His stare grows intense. I start to wish, as I stare back, that I could see his unspoken fantasies reflected in the shiny pupils of his eyes. More than anything, I wish I could see that the person he's been fantasizing about is me.

His head—good God—his head leans closer to mine. My entire body beats as though I'm being dribbled against a gym floor.

Clint's grip grows painfully strong against my wrist. But instead of pulling me toward him, like I want him to, he pushes me away.

"I—I'm sorry—I—" I try, but Clint just shakes his head.

"Let me go see if Pop's going to need any help at the beer garden. Gets kind of hectic at night," he says, turning away from me.

I'm left standing there alone. Feeling like a complete and total moron.

Kenzie catches my eye from the opposite side of the street and starts stomping straight for me. Okay, now I wish I could *stay* alone. *Please go away*, I think. *Please go away*. But she heads right for me anyway.

"You are *so* barking up the wrong tree," she says, glaring at me from underneath her ball cap.

"Excuse me?"

"You're working awfully hard at *pretending* to be exercising—or—whatever this little thing's supposed to be."

"What do you know about it?"

"I know a lot." She shrugs. "Like the fact that Clint will never fall in love with you, if that's what you're thinking."

My eyelids fly backward, as if the idea completely shocks me. "That's not—I'm not—I have a—" But somehow, this time, I can't even say the word. *Boyfriend.* I can't make it come out of my mouth, any more than an iPod could play some old vinyl record. I'm so busy trying to think of a way to tell her she's wrong, it doesn't even occur to me to tell her to buzz off, mind her own business.

"He's damaged goods," she tells me. "Broken. Incapable of love." She turns away before I can pry my tongue off the roof of my mouth.

Boyfriend. Still, the word refuses to show its face in the sweet summer-night air.

———

The night is black enough to make me feel blindfolded as we drive back to the resort. Clint's truck jiggles and jostles down the paths so forcefully, I have to grab the dash to steady myself.

"Don't worry," he says, his voice chipping away at the awkward silence that's followed us from the festival. "She'll get there. I know this truck looks rough—"

"No—I love your truck," I say. Or more truthfully, I love being inside it. Because sitting next to Clint, I'm light-headed with anticipation. Adrenaline burns my lungs, in a way that it hasn't since I last ran out onto the court.

God, I've missed this feeling. And *I want more.*

Clint snorts a laugh. "Yeah, it's real classy."

"Seriously," I insist, nerves making me babble. "I can practically see all the camping trips you've taken in this truck. The fishing trips. Nights you spent stretched out in the bed, hands behind your head, stargazing..."

My voice trickles off as I glance through the windshield toward the sparkling white stars. I zero in on one of the specs in the sky: *the Chelsea Keyes Star.* Its twinkle turns to a slit-eyed glare as it accuses me of horrible things. True things.

But instead of feeling embarrassed, I imagine putting that stupid star in a slingshot and shooting it straight into another galaxy.

When we get to cabin number four, Clint throws open his squeaky driver side door. "I'll get it," he says when I grip my own door handle. "Wait." He races to the passenger's side, where a matching squeak sings out, almost as if to answer the first.

In slow motion, I steady myself by reaching for the metal handle on the door with one hand and putting my other hand on Clint's shoulder. I start to take a step out of the truck; as I lower myself to the ground, I come far closer to Clint than I'd intended. I actually slide down the front of his body—when my face reaches his, our lips meet.

At first it surprises me, the wet touch of his lips. Shocks me so much I almost start to pull away. But something inside me—some instinct—fights the shock, presses my face closer to his. As I'm balancing there, one foot dangling above the ground, one hand on Clint's shoulder and the other still on the door handle, Clint's mouth opens against mine. He wraps his arms around me. As our mouths close, he parts my lips open again with his tongue.

Our kiss is a Midwest summer storm, swift and frightening. It's dark clouds and the sweet smell of impending rain all at the same time. It's knowing I should run inside, take cover, but not being able to pull myself away from the danger, the thrill.

He's holding me—but he's lowering me, too. By the time our mouths part again, he's already put me down on the ground.

He snatches his arms away. By the time I open my eyes, he's hurrying around to the driver's side.

"Clint—" I try, but he's inside the truck and it's starting to roll away.

"Clint—" I repeat. The door's still open on the passenger's side, and all I can think to do is slam it shut for him before he speeds away.

Clint
protective equipment

I practically kick the gas pedal to the floorboards. Instead of revving and racing forward, the GMC just kind of flinches, as if to ask, *What'd I ever do to you?*

The black sky beyond the windshield doesn't just swirl, it weaves itself back and forth, reminding me of the pigtails Rosie used to wear.

That sky's telling me I *ought* to be full of remorse. Instead, my mind insists on *imagining* ... I'm seeing my hand reach right up a sundress to smooth the indentation of a surgical scar.

A horn blares behind me. But I'm speeding away from the resort so fast, the orange lights of the cabin windows zip straight out of my rearview mirror. Still, though, that horn gets closer, almost like it's challenging me. The horn blares again as a truck flies around me, passing me, nearly clipping the front bumper of my pickup.

I hit the brakes; so does the blue Chevy ahead of me. In the glow of my headlights, two doors open and Greg and Todd step out, talking at me at the same time.

"...been looking for you..."

"...had to drop Brandon off at his cabin..."

"...you at Willie Walleye..."

"...never saw Kenzie so mad..."

"Got *two*," Todd says, laughing as he shakes his head at me. "*Two* women on the line. From zero to sixty in two seconds, flat."

Rage takes control, balls my fist, sends my knuckles racing for Todd's face. His jaw cracks against my hand when my punch lands on the side of his face.

Chelsea
violation

I've barely stepped inside the cabin when a low, "Hey, Chelse," makes me yowl like Scratches does when I sneak up on him.

"Brand?" I croak.

"Yep."

As my eyes adjust to the darkness, I can make out the silhouette of his head above the edge of the small living room sofa. The ratty sides of his Vans glow in the strip of moonlight that filters into the room from a nearby window. Judging from the smell wafting from the plate in his lap, he snagged some sort of barbecued late-night dinner before leaving Willie Walleye Day.

"What'd the two of you do, come home by way of Brazil or something?" he asks.

"You waiting up?" I tease, trying to sound cool and nonchalant. But the truth is, Clint's mouth still burns against my own. I touch my top lip, thinking maybe he's even left some sort of print behind, the way girls stain boys' mouths with their lipstick.

"Yep," Brandon says again, his voice muffled by a mouthful of whatever he's eating.

"What for?"

"Because you are the most transparent person on the planet," he snaps.

It crosses my mind that maybe he even saw us through the front window. *Does he know I just kissed Clint?* My whole body feels as stiff as a petrified tree.

"There a reason you left today without taking your cell?" he asks, leaning into the moonlight to toss his paper plate onto the small wooden trunk that serves as a coffee table. He glares at me, disgusted, as he tosses my cell onto the coffee table, too.

"It gets crappy reception out here—you know that," I insist.

"It'll work in town—you know *that*," he challenges.

I flinch as he frowns at the little purse that's still wrapped around my wrist, a purse that's in no way too small for my cell. My Whac-A-Mole anger pops, even though I'm attacking it with my rubber mallet like a mad woman.

"What are you, my conscience?"

"Do I need to be?" he asks, his upper lip bulging out over the top row of his braces. "Greg and Todd had to stop by the lodge before they dropped me off." He tugs a wad of paper from his back pocket. "Know what these are?"

he asks. He flicks his wrist; small squares of paper scatter across the coffee table, next to the stacks of batter-smeared notebooks Mom's been writing recipes in.

I shake my head at the small pieces of paper.

"Messages. From Gabe. He's been calling the lodge looking for you."

My stomach dips down, and I feel a sick tingle travel the length of my arms.

"How come you got back *after* me, even though I played at the festival all day?" Brandon asks. No, accuses.

"You obviously just got here yourself—haven't had time to completely finish your dinner," I counter. "Besides, it's not late. You couldn't stay too late—you had to get out of there before the *real* band showed up for the street dance." I'm speaking so quickly that my excuses trip and pile all over each other, becoming as indistinguishable from one another as a heap of football players after a tackle.

I touch my mouth again. It's a dead giveaway, I know it is. So is the way my eyes are surely pleading with Brandon not to say anything else. But he's my little brother, and if there's anything little brothers never do, it's bite their tongue.

"What's the deal, Chelse—" he starts.

I actually stomp my foot and shoot out a *shhh* at him.

"Are you—"

"I'm *nothing*, okay, he's my—we just went—because—kayaking—" These words come out pathetically, even though I'm trying so hard. Kind of like when you shake and shake a nearly empty bottle of shampoo, pumping furiously, and all that comes out are a few watery drips of foam.

"It's not like *you're* not seeing people," I say. "Going out. I'm on vacation, dope."

"A vacation from Gabe, you mean?"

"*Brand*," I hiss.

"I don't like this, Chelse. Gabe has been with you through all the shit, you know? He stood by you through everything, after the accident. And now you're—"

"Calling him tomorrow."

"No way," Brandon barks. "You've called him later at night than this. I know how you guys are—used to be—at home."

"There is no 'used to be' about me and Gabe."

"Then prove it," Brandon says.

"There is *no cell reception out here*," I growl.

"You really think you'd have to fight a hundred people to use the pay phone in the lodge? Place is completely empty right now—"

"Why don't you lay off? I'll call him when I want to," I shout.

But Brandon shakes his head, shouts back. "You'd have complete *privacy* right now. Why *wouldn't* you want privacy to talk to your boyfriend on his—"

"There a problem in here?"

I flinch, look up to find Dad standing in the doorway, a solid black silhouette like those outlines of heads and shoulders I always see on TV, at target ranges on prime-time police dramas.

But I'm the one that feels like the world's aiming right at me.

Clint
out of play

Todd reels backward, his shoulder thumping against the bed of the truck.

"Damn it, Morgan," Greg shouts, pushing me away from Todd, sending me stumbling backward. "This is getting old. You think *we* didn't lose somebody, you stupid asshole?" He pushes me again. I'm already off-balance, so my feet tangle and I trip. The seat of my Levi's smacks against the dirt road.

"Not like I did," I shout.

"I'm not *talking* about Rosie, I'm talking about my *friend*," Greg says, towering over me. "You're here, but you're not. You hide away in textbooks, in fifteen stupid summer jobs. And I've had enough." He kicks my foot, then lunges forward and grabs the collar of my shirt. "You want me to beat the bullshit out of you? I'll do it, Morgan. And I'll feel good about it. Gimme a reason."

His face is less than a foot from mine. The hand that isn't gripping my collar is clenched into a fist.

I finally swivel my arm, pull his hand off my shirt.

"Ass," I spit, standing and dusting the dirt from the back of my jeans.

Todd's still wiggling his jaw back and forth, testing it to make sure it works.

"We got a six-pack and we're headed to the lake," Greg says. "You gonna follow us or not?"

Calm hasn't taken hold of me completely, but looking at Todd's face, red from where I hit him, I instantly feel bad. And I'm really not sure what I'm so pissed about anymore. Not sure why *any* of it—Chelsea telling Mom at Pike's she has a boyfriend, or Kenzie flirting with me, or Todd making assumptions—should make me so angry.

"That's gonna leave a mark," Todd says, squatting to get a look at his face in his truck's side mirror.

"Whatever," Greg says. "Anything'll help you look better."

"Don't I even get any sympathy?" Todd asks. "I bet some pretty girl at Pike's would give me sympathy."

"No Pike's. Not tonight," Greg says. "Just drive."

I shake my head, climb into the cab of the GMC. I follow the Chevy, under the moonlight, already tasting the tinny cold of a can of beer.

Chelsea
double dribble

N o," I snap at Dad. "There's no problem."

Brandon reaches for my cell and all the paper messages, but I snatch them away from him so furiously, I accidentally scratch him.

"*Hey*," Brandon yelps.

"Chelsea," Dad chastises. "What's *wrong* with you?"

"I need to make a phone call," I snarl through my teeth, glaring at Brandon.

"Don't be too overjoyed about it or anything, Chelse," Brandon mumbles. "I mean, he's only your boyfriend."

"A phone call," Dad repeats, oblivious to what Brandon's just said. "At this time of night. You can't do it tomorrow?"

"*No*, I can't do it tomorrow." Every last drop of my

pent-up anger comes out in my words. "What do you care, anyway?" Suddenly, out of nowhere, I'm not talking about phones. I'm talking about the last few months. I'm talking about the way I've been watching some crummy recording in my room late at night, because one of the things I ache to remember is what it was like when he cheered for me.

Dad takes a step into the moonlight, his arms crossed over his chest. "I don't understand you, Chelsea. Ever since the accident—I tried to give you time. I tried to make excuses for you. If anyone had a right to feel badly, it was you. But this—this doesn't make any sense anymore, Chelse. The way you lash out—"

"The way *I* lash out—"

"Yes, the way you lash out. Just like you're doing to Brandon right now. And the way you mope—"

"The way I *what?*"

"You don't even try, Chelsea. The old you would have found a way—some way—to keep going."

"What?" I bellow. "I didn't quit! It was *taken* from me."

"You're no one I even know anymore," Dad says, reaching for Brandon's hand. The way he examines it, you'd think I'd done permanent damage.

I can't stand to be in the room. I stomp out of the cabin onto the porch, where I swear the kiss I've just shared with Clint has a lingering smell . . . like a fresh pan of Mom's white-chocolate brownies. The hot sweetness still clings to the air. And I'm a girl on a strict diet who's just downed the whole batch. Guilt overpowers me.

I have to get away from this, too—the thought of kissing Clint. I race through the cool moonlight toward the lodge.

I stop just outside the door, tears cascading. There's no way I can talk to Gabe now, not like this. Maybe though, I think as I stare at the messages in my hand, Brandon's on to something. Maybe Gabe would be more suspicious if I didn't return his call—make that calls. About a hundred of them, from the looks of all these messages.

So I push through the door of the lodge, toss all the messages into the wastebasket in the lobby. I wipe my face, fish some coins from my little purse, drop them into the phone. As soon as Gabe's cell starts to ring, I pray that it'll just go to voicemail.

"Hey, babe," Gabe says, surprise lacing his tone. "Didn't think I'd ever catch you. Where—I mean, what've you been up to?"

Gabe Ross, you are as transparent as a Ziploc bag.

"Birthday party," I blurt.

Gabe chuckles. "Don't I wish."

I instantly feel the burn of shame creep up my entire body, starting with my toes, inching toward my knees, my neck, my face...

"Thanks for the present," Gabe says.

I hold the phone away from my face a moment as I spit a few whispery curses at myself. *You're an ass, Chelsea Keyes. An ass.* The picture of a braying donkey actually fills my mind.

At least I had the foresight to leave Gabe's present with

his mom before I headed out of town. But little more than one week after driving away—just one measly week—I've already done the unthinkable. I've forgotten to call Gabe to wish him a happy birthday. I didn't even wish him a happy birthday in the crummy email I sent earlier.

No, no, no. That's not the worst of it. That isn't even *close* to the worst. And I know it. My hand flies to my mouth again. When I close my eyes, I can feel Clint against me. His lips pulling me closer, but not just my mouth. Pulling my legs, my arms. I'd wrapped myself around him for the brief moment before I'd slid down, before my feet hit the ground. What kind of person *does* that? And Clint knows I have a boyfriend. What must he think of the way I just acted?

What if Clint doesn't want to work with me anymore? How can I explain that to Dad without the word *quitter* glowing in his pupils?

And if Clint doesn't want to work with me, would that just confirm everything that Brandon suspects? Would it be the proof he needs? Would Brandon decide to side with a guy, squeal his suspicions to Gabe? I don't want to lose Gabe—not that comfort of sliding my hand into his. Not the daydreams that pop up as I linger in the grassy green of his eyes.

This night could not possibly get any worse. At all.

"You win," Gabe mumbles. "You one-upped me in the gift department."

Correction, I think, as a new tide of guilt washes through me. *It could always get worse.*

"It's not a star or anything," I say.

"An eternity symbol is definitely more than a star," Gabe protests. My heart twists painfully, feeling tight and tiny and desperate inside my chest.

"I bought it after prom," I say softly, my hand turning into a fist around the receiver as I think of the black titanium ring I'd purchased with the lazy, sideways "8" carved into it. "After you traced the symbol on my shoulders—"

"—while the sun rose," Gabe says. "First thing I thought of when I saw it."

My tongue is melted. I've forgotten how to speak. *Please, Gabe, don't suspect.*

"You all right?" he asks. "You sound funny."

"Fine," I say. "My cell gets crummy reception around here, and I'm on this old pay phone. That's why—why I wasn't carrying my phone. Why I haven't called more."

"Yeah. You told me that in an email. I just really wanted to talk to my girl on my birthday. Haven't taken my present off since I unwrapped it, though," he says, and I'm eternally grateful he's decided to make a u-turn in the conversation, veering away from my lame excuses. "You know, I got pretty nostalgic tonight. Dug up that old picture Brandon took of us the night we went out for the first time. You remember the one, right? I swear it probably sounds all mushy, but the way we're looking at each other, it's like we knew, even that first night, that we'd found something special."

Okay, now I'm not so grateful. I can feel the tracks of Clint's lips shining like glow-in-the-dark paint against my mouth. My eyes tingle, and I know I've got to hang up before I say something completely stupid. "You sound tired—I should—let you go—you're probably working really hard."

"Yeah. I just couldn't let my birthday go by without talking to my girl. Love you, Chelse."

"I'll—I'll call more. I promise. Everybody at the resort has to share the same pay phone, and I just—happy birthday, Gabe." I hang up and gasp all in the same motion. I probably look like a near-drowning victim who's just broken the surface of the water.

I hurry out of the lodge and start to drag myself back up the trail to cabin number four when it suddenly hits me—this is the first time in more than a year that I've ended a phone call to Gabe without actually using the words *I love you.*

Has the thought occurred to Gabe, too?

God, I hope not.

Clint
neutral zone trap

C an't kayak, maybe, but you can canoe," I say, really slathering on the chipper voice. *That's it, Clint. Just pretend nothing happened last night.* "No exercise like rowing."

But the truth is, I just keep replaying the whole scene—cabin number four, the open door of the GMC, Chelsea's body pressed against my own. The way my heart sprung open when I felt her lips on mine. And as I remember, the devil hovering over my shoulder tells me to drive Chelsea down to the edge of the lake, where summer love always blooms along with the water lilies and occasional lady slippers.

"Good for core strength," I tell her, trying to turn my ear away from the devil on my shoulder. He knows that just looking at Chelsea is making my entire body vibrate. "Rowing, I mean."

The Rainy River flows gently, barely moving at all, less than a foot from where we stand. Luckier folks are at Clementson Rapids, whitewater rafting down a more exciting branch of the Rainy. Of course, when I'd suggested it to Chelsea, she'd immediately started shaking her head.

Now, I'm stuck spending the day on a *float trip*—which isn't exactly all that exciting. And it also isn't going to take my attention away from how insanely pretty Chelsea is.

"Or paddling, at least," she teases.

"Paddling?" I repeat.

"Yeah. Core strength? Hello—" she says, pointing at the two short wooden paddles I've placed inside the canoe.

"Right," I say. "Rowing—*paddling*. Core strength."

I help her into the boat, only to find that her skin is more enticing than the Rainy on a hot day. Just touching her makes me want to immerse myself, put my head completely under the surface of her. I want to drift, to let her carry me away, down her current.

Once she's seated, I settle into the canoe, too. As soon as I sit down, I notice the way her shorts have ridden up her thighs.

Concentrate on something else—the feel of the paddle in your hands, I tell myself. *The way the wood's worn smooth from so much use.*

Too bad, I think, that letting the same thought run through your mind over and over doesn't turn your soul as smooth. Too bad it does the exact opposite. For more than a week now, I've been thinking of long yellow hair and the peachy-sweet smell of Chelsea's skin. And all it's done is made me feel rough and splintered inside.

"All about the rhythm, see?" I tell her as I use my paddle to push through the water on one side of the boat while she works the other. "Just think of Brandon and his bass."

"If I try to row like Brandon plays, I'll wind up breaking *both* our hips," Chelsea jokes.

The smile on my face makes me feel a little calmer deep down.

"Look," I say, deciding to tackle the damn elephant already. "Last night, I—"

"Don't worry about it," she says. "Totally my fault. I just—fell onto you. Accident."

"Right," I say.

We both know this is a horrendous lie. A ridiculous lie. But at least the whole subject has been picked up and put aside. So I lay my paddle down in the bottom of the boat and say, "You take over. Paddle once on one side, once on the other. I'm just going to enjoy the scenery." I turn my back on her, looking out across the green fringe of pines, the white ripple of light down the river.

"What is this?" Chelsea asks. "Your own personal gondola ride?"

"You're the one who needs exercise, not me. Hey, what's that?" I ask, holding a hand to my ear. "It's the ghost of your former self," I tease. "Wants you to get your flabby butt in gear."

She lifts the paddle up in the air, tossing a spray of water on me. A giggle burbles out of her chest. I turn, dip my hand into the river, and send a spray right back at her. She squeals, her voice bouncing down the riverbank like the squawk of a bird. Like something wild and free that has never known sadness. Hunger, maybe. Physical pain occasionally. But never sadness.

She raises her hands to protect herself from my splash. The world turns slow motion as her paddle starts slipping deeper into the Rainy. "Chelse," I say. "Chelse, watch—"

But she doesn't listen. She's still holding her hands up, waiting for the next spray of water. I reach for her paddle, but by the time my hand arrives, all I wind up grabbing is my own fist.

The paddle dips down beneath the water and is gone. All that remains is the circle of a ripple—the kind of thing that appears after a fish has eaten the bug on the water's surface.

We both gasp, but when we look at each other, our laughter spills over. Thank God—*laughter.*

"It doesn't have to be all serious, does it?" Chelsea asks.

Chelsea
full-court press

It's really good to see him smile. The kind of good that zings through me. I'm the one who *put* that smile on his face. Clint's shoulders relax; his chest is no longer like the armor knights wore in the Dark Ages. And in that moment, he doesn't seem so far away, so unobtainable.

"Good thing we're not too far from the shore," Clint says. "Water's pretty shallow here." Still, he pulls his compass from his pocket and places it in the bottom of the canoe before easing himself out, rocking the boat slightly. The river barely reaches his waist. Holding his arms out above the water's surface, he wades across the Rainy and grabs the paddle, easy as fishing a pebble from a bowl of tap water.

But before he can reach the boat again, I've already

eased myself out, too. The surface of the river circles my body like lips around a straw.

"What're you doing?" he says, his easy smile now flickering, threatening to go out completely. He tosses the paddle into the canoe, grabs my wrist. "You know how slippery this river rock can be?" he scolds, shaking his head.

My body starts acting on instinct, as though this is a play I've practiced hundreds of times in preparation for game day. Only I've never reached for a man when he shakes his head. I've never pressed forward, searched for a hole in his defense, charged for the goal, sought to win a heart that was held just beyond my reach.

Gabe's heart was given to me. It was a necklace I took from the box and held to the light, staring at for a moment before deciding it really was something I'd like to wear.

I've got my hand on Clint's wrist—I don't even know when it happened, when we switched positions. But *I'm* touching *him*. Lightning is flowing straight up my arm, across my shoulder. My breath grows ragged.

Clint's muscles tighten as he pulls away a little, but I can see in his eyes that he's afraid if he wrenches himself free, he might knock me off balance. He might hurt me. I've got him—and all I can think of is how his lips felt against my own outside the cabin. It's all I *want* to think about.

"Chelsea—" he says, his voice coming out in a whine.

But I'm not teasing. I'm completely serious. Both of my arms circle his waist. My brain is screaming, *Gabe! Gabe! What's wrong with you?*

But I don't care. Not now. Not with Clint standing in front of me. The world behind him blurs, becomes unrecognizable. We aren't in the middle of a river, we aren't in Minnesota. We're nowhere. There is no right, no home, no boyfriend. I draw him closer to me.

"Chelsea." He whispers it this time, but not to complain. Not to tell me to stop. He just whispers my name as if he wants to hear it, to feel it on his tongue.

We're exactly the same height. We match up—our eyes, or noses, our lips. When I lean forward, our mouths meet, gently. But my insides pop, like a string of Black Cats have been lit and are going off one after another. The explosions start going off in my chest, but soon start popping lower and lower.

I open my mouth, and Clint's tongue works its way behind my teeth.

Firecrackers pop behind the fly of my shorts.

But I'm not afraid. I'm not embarrassed. I'm not thinking of a thing except how he feels, his mouth closing, then prying my lips back open again, his tongue touching the tip of my own.

I put both hands on Clint's back, pulling him toward me. But Clint's muscles tighten again. Instead of leaning into me, he grabs my wrists and pries my hands from his body.

"Clint—I just—I want to be with you," I find myself babbling, the words spilling out of my mouth without any command from my brain. "Not because my dad's paying you. Not for boot camp. I just want to—"

"I can't," Clint says, avoiding my eyes, looking into the water that swirls around us.

"He's not *your* boyfriend," I plead. "He's mine, okay? Let me worry about that. He's my problem, not yours."

Clint just stares at me all horrified. I've done something wrong. What, though? I have no idea where I've messed up, so I just keep pressing forward.

"I'm the one with the boyfriend," I say again. "And—I don't know what you think cheating is. Maybe—maybe we're already cheating. Maybe it's already happened. But I just—I can't help myself. So what if this thing's got an expiration date stamped on it? Really. That doesn't mean we couldn't have the absolutely most amazing experience—the kind of thing you always look back on and are grateful for—"

Clint keeps shaking me off, every time I try to touch him. Running a hand through his hair, shaking his head.

"Get in the boat," he says.

"Clint, please, I—"

"Get in the boat," he shouts.

He helps me in, his fingers tight and unyielding. Climbs in, grabs the paddle, and begins to steer us toward shore.

"Clint, don't go back. Let's just have our day," I try. But the muscles in his jaw clench.

"I can't, Chelsea. Okay? I'm not doing this."

When we get to the shore, I try to touch him again, but he flicks me away hard, like I'm a swarm of insects gnawing on his arm. "He's *my* boyfriend," I say, as though he didn't hear me the first hundred times. "And don't *worry* about my dad—"

"Stop it, Chelse. You don't know anything," he says. "I *can't*, okay? Not because of your boyfriend, and not because your dad's paying me. Just please let it go, okay?"

Clint
breakaway

I slam on the brake in front of her cabin, feeling scraped-up inside.

As we sit in the truck, the seconds pulsing like a toothache, I wonder why Chelsea won't just get out of the cab. Why she won't give me some peace.

Why would she expect me to help her out of the truck after what happened last night? I don't want to kiss her again. I don't want to—anything—with her. Didn't I just make that perfectly clear?

"What do you *want*, Brand?" Chelsea moans.

My head shoots up and I realize that her brother's standing just beyond the passenger side door, some enormous black roll under one arm. Kenzie's standing beside him, cradling a stack of paper.

They're both looking into the cab with identical horrified expressions. Like they're afraid to find out what they've just interrupted.

"You can drive Brandon out to Pike's, right, Clint?" Kenzie says. "I told him you wouldn't mind."

"What do you need to go to Pike's for?" Chelsea asks.

Brandon shifts his weight, points to the roll in his arm. "Kenzie helped me print up a giant banner. For the Dwellers. And flyers, too," he says, nodding at the sheets in her hands. "Up in the office at the lodge. And Earl was there— he said Clint didn't have anything booked this afternoon. And you're—done—canoeing, right?"

The word *canoeing* hangs in the air. I can feel my soaked shorts sticking to my legs. Chelsea still smells like the river. My sneakers have lakes in them. Canoeing—I just hope that to Brandon and Kenzie, that's *exactly* what it looks like we've been doing.

"I thought—we could hang the banner in the front window, and put some more flyers up in town," Brandon says.

"Brand, did the thought ever occur to you that his parents might not *want* you to mess up their place with your junk?" Chelsea asks.

"Only way to find out is to ask," Brandon says. "But they have to *see* the banner before they can refuse it." A squeaky groan erupts as he opens the passenger side door. He pushes Chelsea across the bench seat, closer to my side. *Stupid Brandon…*

"I—don't have anything else going on right now—I

could help hang some of these," Kenzie offers, holding up her flyers.

"We'll get them. It's fine," Chelsea says.

They're not going to fight over me, are they? I shake my head. The whole thing's just so stupid. How many times does a guy have to tell these girls *no*?

"Thanks, Kenz," I say. "We got it, right, Brand?"

Kenzie's face falls a little. But what am I supposed to do? There's no room for her in the cab—three's pushing it as it is. And if I kick Chelsea out, it would look bad—wouldn't it? It's not that I want Chelsea to come with us. Right?

Kenzie hands Brandon the stack of flyers. "Come on, already," Brandon says, his voice bouncing against the dash. "Let's *go*."

Chelsea
pivot

Clint," I say, as we all pile out of the cab. Brandon flashes me a look as he rushes toward Pike's. I flash him a nasty one right back. The silence that filled the truck all the way to Baudette was unbearable—he had to notice that. And I'm going to burst if I don't get to the bottom of this, find out why Clint keeps pushing me away.

Brandon shakes his head at me the moment before he disappears through the door. I hurry after him, trying to catch up with Clint.

"Come on. *Clint.* Talk to me," I plead, following him inside.

The lunch rush has left every table in the entire restaurant decorated with wadded-up napkins, and plates empty except for the stray French fry and uneaten tomato slice.

Ice-filled glasses have created random patterns of watery circles on tabletops. The air hangs heavy with the smells of cooking oil and sunscreen, lake water and Noxzema.

My tears are like a whole pack of dogs on leashes; no matter how I try to tug them back, they just keep barreling forward. I tilt my head toward the ground while Brandon attacks Gene, flopping his banner out onto the floor. Cecilia smiles at him as her hair hangs down over her tired face.

But when she looks back our way, at me and Clint, still river-soggy and awkward, her eyes hang on awhile. She stares at Clint's angry, clenched jaw, and at my face, hot with embarrassment, until Brandon finishes his breathless sales pitch to Clint's dad.

"Brandon," she says, tossing a long brown strand of hair away from her eye as she pinches two empty glasses between her fingers, "we'd be happy to hang the banner in the window. In the meantime, why don't you let Clint walk you around town? He can show you all the best places to post your signs. Chelsea can stay with us until you guys get back."

Brandon sprints toward the door, grabbing Clint's arm on the way out. He races onto the sidewalk, dragging Clint, so happy he's half-skipping. He starts joyfully singing Paul Simon's "Cecilia."

I'm still shaking my head at him when Cecilia calls, "Come back here, Chelsea," nodding once toward the kitchen.

I follow her into the kitchen, but I still feel like crying—maybe even more so now. I think if she says one word to me, my eyes will turn into lawn sprinklers, spraying water all over the entirety of Pike's kitchen. The stainless steel appliances will all be dripping, exhaust hoods to grease traps.

"You don't mind helping me out in dish?" Cecilia asks.

I don't—even though it's a little weird. It'll give me something to do with my hands, at least. And I won't have to look Cecilia in the eye. I can tuck my head down, stare at my hands, and she'll never have to know that I'm ready to bawl over her son. That I'm ready to lose it because he's told me no. He doesn't want me the way I want him.

I'm about to start searching for a towel—sponge—pair of gloves—I can't *bear* to open my mouth to ask Cecilia where to begin—when I realize Gene's standing just behind me. Cecilia was talking to *him.* She grabs a Coke bottle from the refrigerator while Gene crosses to a dish sink, then motions for me to follow her down a short, narrow hallway lined with red brick. She swerves into a tiny office, desert-like in its decoration. A laptop marks the center of a wooden desk, the screensaver casting a funky blue glow on a gray metal filing cabinet, rusted at the corners. A desk chair is the only other piece of furniture in the room.

Cecilia puts the Coke next to the laptop and stands in front of the screen, typing as she tells me, "Clint hasn't had a girlfriend for two years. It's probably a strange thing for a mother to be talking about—Clint would kill me if he knew I was—"

"Clint's my trainer," I protest, fidgeting just inside the door.

Cecilia glances up at me through her eyebrows. A grin spreads crookedly into one cheek. "I'm not just someone's mother," she informs me. "Believe it or not, I had a whole life before Clint. Before Gene."

I twitch uncomfortably. What does she want from me? Why is she telling me about Clint's dating history? Why is it any of my business? When will this stupid day ever *end*?

"Clint had one girlfriend growing up," she says, squinting at the print on the computer screen. "A childhood friend who became something more."

She clicks her way into a site and stares at the screen, her jaw locked. "But I suppose a story from somebody's mother doesn't have as much weight as a text message, does it?" she asks. "Or, say, an old article online? I understand you've been hurt, Chelsea," she adds softly. "From what little Clint's told me, I think you have every right to be scared."

I open my mouth to protest, but only get out an "I—" before Cecilia holds up her hand. She eyes me like Scratches does when I interrupt his hunt to call him inside to dinner.

"Clint told me you're scared of everything he wants to do. Scared to bike," Cecilia says. "Scared to go kayaking. Just imagine how terrified Clint must be. I know how he—" Cecilia cuts herself off, tugging on her bottom lip. "Wounds of the heart are the hardest to medicate. The slowest area of the body to heal." She steps away from the computer and points at the office chair. The soles of her sandals click as she leaves the room.

By the time I dislodge my own feet and circle behind the desk, the screensaver's come back on—an old photo of Clint in a hockey jersey, a sweaty fringe of black hair hanging down into his eyes.

I pick up the Coke and take a long pull, my eyes glued to Clint's face. I finally jiggle the mouse and find myself staring at the website for *The Northern Light*, the Baudette newspaper.

Bold print stomps horrifically across the screen: *BODY OF MISSING TEEN FOUND IN RAVINE.*

I frown as I start to read. *After an extensive two-day search for Rosaline Johnson, the car belonging to the missing teen was spotted below Highway 72. Her body was discovered in the wreckage; paramedics indicated Johnson died on impact. Police suspect recent snowfalls impeded the discovery of the white Mazda.*

Still not completely sure what I'm reading, I skim the rest of the story. Stare at the picture of the wreckage, thinking something about it seems awfully familiar.

I scroll down the screen, click to the second page of the story. Here, the details swirl around a hockey tournament that Rosaline never made it to, and about a distraught boy who'd made appeals on local news stations to *anyone who might have seen Johnson*... A second, smaller picture shows someone crumpled into a heap on the back of a squad car. *Johnson's boyfriend, Clint Morgan, at the scene of the accident*, the caption proclaims.

Whoa! *What?* My eyes spring straight back to the beginning of the caption. I reread it six, maybe seven times.

In the picture, Clint's slumped against the police car, his chin against his chest. He looks a little like a forgotten doll, the way he's propped on the trunk. But the area behind him—I've *seen* that place before. I recognize it, even though the snow has long since melted. I can smell the earthy wet scent of a nearby creek, feel Brandon's camera in my hand. As I stare at the black-and-white photo, dots of pink pop—patches of orchids. I *know* this is the ravine Clint dragged me out of. And now I know why.

I'm on my feet, hurrying down the brick hall, not even feeling my legs.

"Bo's Bait and Tackle," Cecilia calls out as I pass the kitchen door. Her words are a lasso around my waist. I backtrack until I'm standing in the doorway of the kitchen. She's bent over the sink, one eye looming just above her shoulder, a trail of brown hair dangling over her cheekbone. "Clint knows the owner's family," she explains, flashing a crooked smile at me. "And I know my son."

———

I'm not running, exactly, but I'm close. My blond hair flies behind me as I pump my feet. And I can feel my arms flopping kind of crazily, like I'm making my way toward the scene of an accident. I can feel urgency scrawled all over me, bright as a smear of red lipstick. The kind of urgency that doesn't exist between "just friends." Or a trainer and trainee.

The old guys clustered outside of Bo's, swapping old-time stories, let their voices trail off to watch me. They have the same kind of shock plastered on their faces that they'd have if one of their bosom buddies showed up at Pike's with a woman other than his wife.

This can't be happening, I think I hear Clint mutter when I reach his side.

"Clint—" I say.

"I'll go get Brandon," he tells me, acting like he's got to go inside to find him, like Brandon's not standing in the front window taping the four corners of his poster, his Pink Floyd T-shirt in full view of the street. Clint's trying to pretend his way out of this conversation.

But it makes sense now. I get it. Why he acts the way he does. Why he shakes me away. I want to tell him—*it's okay, Clint.* I want to convince him. God, we're just alike.

"Clint," I try again, grabbing his elbow to keep him from disappearing inside the bait and tackle.

"Mom told you," he blurts, his tone sharp with annoyance as he turns away from the front of the store (and the men watching with round eyes and drooping mouths) and hurries back toward the street. "The whole tragic poor-Clint story."

"That's what you were talking about before," I say. "Why you gave up hockey."

"She was coming out to watch me. Stupid hockey tournament," Clint mumbles.

"It's impossible to play hurt," I say. "We both—we couldn't play hurt."

He clenches his jaw, like he's clamping his mouth shut on his response.

"I think—" I whisper. "I think you feel what I feel. When you kiss me, it seems that way."

He turns, staring over his shoulder, reminding me we're still being watched.

"I don't want any promises from you," I say, too quietly for the old men outside the tackle shop to hear. Even as the words come out, they sound stupid. But it's not like I'm used to begging a guy for his attention while standing in the middle of a street. *What am I doing?* "And look, I don't want to feel this way about you either," I add. "But I do. I can't stop it, and I can't take it back. I just want a chance."

My whole body is throbbing with desperation.

Clint runs a hand through his hair. "You're just going to leave."

"Yeah, I am. But not today. Not for a while yet."

Clint starts to shake his head, his arms crossed defensively across his chest. I can see his answer floating up there in his head: *No.* But before he can say it, I take a step toward him so we're standing as close as we did in the river when we'd kissed. I slide one finger behind the waistband of his shorts, snaring him, while I slide my other hand down into his pocket. He stares at me, eyes like a cornered raccoon's, while I fish for the compass he always carries, liking the feel of being so close to his skin, not wanting to pull away too soon.

I finally pull my hand out, dragging the compass into

the light. "Look," I say, staring down at the dial, which is pointing right at him. "This thing knows which way I'm supposed to go." I feel as exposed as a sweatshirt worn wrong-side-out, or like pocket linings dangling outside of a pair of jeans. My heart, my hope, hang in the afternoon sun.

"Hey, guys," Brandon shouts, bounding down the steps of the tackle shop. "What's up?" He scratches the back of his neck nervously as he hurries toward us.

"Just give us a chance to see where it goes," I say. My eyes are wide with fear, my tongue so dry my words stick against the roof of my mouth. "It doesn't have to be all serious, right?"

"Guys?" Brandon calls. "Got my flyers hung—did you see, Chelsea?"

No, I didn't. My eyes are pinned to Clint. His face is chiseled with the kind of concentration I've only seen on my own face, flashing across the screen on the TV in my bedroom.

Clint opens his mouth, like he's about to say something, finally, but Brandon is on top of us now. He'll hear everything.

"Tomorrow night," Clint whispers as he takes his compass back, his words coming out so quickly I'm not quite sure he's actually said anything. Maybe, I think, it's just me playing out a fantasy. I follow him to the truck in a kind of daze.

"Come on, time to get you guys back to the resort,"

Clint tells Brandon, swinging open the passenger side door of his GMC.

As I climb inside, he places his warm hand in the small of my back, as if to let me know I haven't just dreamed the whole thing up.

Clint
restart

The Twilight Drive-In has been in business since the
1950s, and everything about it is original. *Everything*—including the concession stand selling popcorn
with real butter, not that oily junk they squirt over the ker-
nels at the city cineplexes.

"When's this thing start?" Chelsea asks, eyeing the glistening tub of popcorn I've just bought.

"When it gets dark," I tell her, pointing at the sunset hues that have only just started to spill across the sky.
"Haven't you ever been to a drive-in before?"

"Too high-tech for me," she teases.

"'Bout as high-tech as I ever want to get," I say, hoping
she can't hear the clicking sound of my tongue against my
dry mouth. I'd buy an extra-large Coke to get me through

the night, except then I'd have to go to the bathroom fifteen times before the stupid movie was over ... and ... am I really worried about how many bathroom breaks I might take? *You've lost it, Morgan,* I scold myself.

We make our way back toward the truck, parked in the back row even though there were plenty of spaces closer to the screen when we arrived. But I have a whole laundry list of reasons why I don't want the two of us to be seen together, reasons that involve word getting back to Earl about me having a fling with one of the girls at his resort, *after* he trusted me enough to tell her dad about my boot camp idea. And reasons that involve the hurt that found me two years ago. Hurt that would split me in two if I had to live through it again.

Am I really doing this?

We settle into the cab. Chelsea crunches away on the popcorn while I stare through the windshield, watch the sun use the distant mountains as a staircase down to the bottom of the nearby lake.

This entire night is balanced on a stack of lies. Her folks, who are taking it easy at the resort, think she's at Pike's. Brandon, who's playing yet another gig for Pop's summer crowd, thinks she's on a moonlight bicycle ride with fifteen other vacationers. My folks think I'm at the resort, helping the kitchen with inventory (of all the lame excuses). Kenzie thinks I'm on a stargazing hike. *If something is right, should it really involve this much sneaking around?*

"I don't even know what's playing tonight," I mumble,

just to have something to say. "Bound to be something as vintage as the theater, though."

"Ah," Chelsea says. "The black-and-white days when men lit the ladies' cigarettes and the women wore high heels to bed." I guess I toss her a stunned look, because she teases me with a shocked expression of her own and shoots a popcorn kernel at my head.

We laugh—in that moment, it's easy. And maybe, I think, it's supposed to be. Still, something in me keeps pressing closer to the door, like any minute I might just jump from the cab and bolt.

Chelsea crosses her legs, making the hem of her sundress fall back an inch. Licks the tips of her butter-greased fingers.

Ouch.

You want me to beat the bullshit out of you? I can still hear Greg yelling at me, telling me it's time to move on, as he kicked me in the middle of that dirt road. And as I listen to those words circle through my head, I think of the compass—and remember that when Chelsea pulled it from my shorts, its arrow pointed straight from her to me.

I'm still nervous, but as I stare at her profile, desire starts to bubble inside me. Starts to eclipse the fears I've been carrying around for two years.

This is what I want.

The blond, beautiful, peach-scented creature sits next to me, waiting for me to touch her.

Chelsea
charging

After a Road Runner cartoon, the opening credits reveal that the night's feature is an Alfred Hitchcock number—*Vertigo*, with Kim Novak and Jimmy Stewart. The movie makes me wonder what it'd be like to love someone so much, you'd stalk their double. Really—what would it be like to be *that* infatuated?

I glance sideways at Clint. In so many ways, this black diamond of a man, his insides obscured by darkness, is nothing like the overtly romantic Gabe, who wears his love for me like a screenprinted message on a T-shirt. Is it completely bizarre to be drawn to two guys who are practically polar opposites? What does it mean about how I feel for Gabe when I'm drawn to someone else who's so completely different?

Clint begins to run his fingertips down my arm, erasing the question marks that have been swirling through my mind, replacing them with bold-print exclamations. His touch is gentle, but I feel like he's just lit my skin on fire.

He's never reached out and touched me this way.

I lean toward him, locking his gaze for a minute before closing my eyes and finding his lips on mine.

God, he tastes as good as the butter-laden popcorn—better. Forget Jimmy and Kim—Clint and I are the night's hottest couple.

Wait—*couple*?

"Chelsea," he murmurs in my ear. "Do you give a crap about this movie?"

I flash what feels like a devilish grin, shake my head no. He throws himself back into his seat, starts the engine, and reaches for my hand as he steers out of the drive-in.

I'm soaring as I feel Clint's hand in mine. I swear—Publishers Clearing House winners couldn't be any happier when they peer through the curtains to see balloons and a five-foot check waiting for them on the porch.

Clint and I ride quietly back toward the edge of the lake. The eerie shriek of loons and the creaky-screen-door call of crickets fill the cab with their music.

He cuts the engine in a secluded area—a rough and rugged section of shore. No dock, no kayak rental, no signs proclaiming when the next fishing boat will leave the dock. Just the moon, the crickets, the loons, and the trees.

Without a word, Clint covers my lips with his own. I savor the feel of him a moment before deciding to test him a bit; I strengthen the kiss. But Clint doesn't pull away. He answers back—his mouth plunges deeper against my own, no reservations. I sink my fingers into his hair.

We make out for who knows how long. Kissing like that—deep, soulful—it just doesn't seem to have any time attached to it at all. We kiss until kissing's not enough. Until Clint's hand starts to stroke one of my thighs.

A need builds deep inside of me, more powerful than anything I've ever felt before. A hunger unfolds—only it isn't coming from my stomach. It's coming, to be honest, from a region decidedly lower. I close my eyes and nearly drown in our seclusion, our solitude. Clint reaches up beneath my sundress as his lips start to rove toward my neck. But I wiggle until our mouths meet again.

Clint draws his hand out from underneath my dress and slowly begins working his way up, resting gently on my breast. In a single swift tug, he pulls the top of my sundress down.

A gasp escapes my throat—it had still been too hot, in the early evening hours when I'd dressed, to mess with a bra. My mind starts swimming. I'm not quite sure how to handle being naked from the waist-up, in full view of any die-hard fisherman who just might happen to wander by. But when Clint's tongue starts tracing my nipple, my mind falls quiet. I'm immersed—only instead of being underwater, I'm under-*desire*. My hands race all over Clint, even though I've never made a conscious decision to touch him. My fingers dive under his shirt, exploring his skin.

Clint tugs at my thighs until I start sliding, my back

coming down to rest against the bench seat. His kisses grow deeper as he stretches out on top of me. He slips his hand between my legs, rubbing me through my underwear.

When Clint lifts his face from my mouth, a moan, unlike anything I've ever heard coming from my own body, peels out from between my lips.

But it isn't just that I have this itch I want scratched. It isn't that I want Clint to do something to me; I want to do as much to Clint. I want to devour every single inch of him. Boyfriends and pasts and right and wrong be damned. I want Clint—wildly.

My hands travel down Clint's side. I massage his thigh, inching my fingers around to the front of his body. Inching closer to the fly on his shorts.

"Wait," Clint barks. He flinches as he knocks my hand away. He pushes himself away from me, sits himself up in the driver's seat, turns his face toward the window.

"Sorry." I hastily adjust my sundress as I hoist myself back up. "I thought—you seemed like—I didn't mean to push—"

I stop, wondering if I'm still the same Chelsea Keyes who'd been nervous about losing her virginity in one of the most romantic locations of all time, a swanky room her boyfriend had rented at the Carlyle. Why would I want to give up that kind of first-time perfection? Had I really been ready for—*that*—to happen *here*? At the muddy fringes of a lake, with torn-up upholstery scratching my back?

"I *do* want to," Clint says. "That's the problem. I want

to so bad that if you touch me, I don't think I'll be able to stop."

"Would that really be such a bad thing?" The words pop out so quickly, I wonder for a moment if they've actually come from my own mouth.

"I don't know," Clint admits, pushing his hair back from his face. "This is so far from where I thought this night would go—so much faster."

"I'm scared, too, you know."

"You don't exactly seem like it."

"I am—have been—" I sigh. "First time is scary."

Clint's frown has crevices deeper than the Grand Canyon. "I thought you had a boyfriend."

"I do. Hip surgery doesn't put you on the fast-track to losing your—" I stop short. There's that word again: *virgin.*

Clint's face grows a cloud. He seems to shrink a little, in that moment.

"Don't freak out on me," I say, reaching for his hand again. "I know it's a lot—the boyfriend. The broken hip. The ... virginity. I'm not the easiest girl in the world to take on. But I'm not about to add to your load, you know? My issues are mine, not yours."

"But if I'm complicating things—"

"Then I'd have to smack you upside the head. Don't forget, *you're* the one who just put the brakes on *me.*"

Clint leans away from me, puts an elbow on the door, rubs his eyes. But there's far more than just space between us. Including, I remind myself, Rosaline Johnson. The seriousness of the moment weighs as much as Clint's truck.

My mind drifts back to our laughter—and I want desperately to find a path back to it.

"You know what we need?" I ask him, grinning playfully. "A small step. To tackle something that scares the both of us. Together."

Clint stops rubbing his face to stare off into the distance. He's wearing a look like a dead-end road sign. My stomach starts to sink in on itself, as I think he's about to tell me it's too much, all this history, heavy as an eighteen-wheeler, that the two of us are dragging around.

But I know I have to be delicate here. As much as I want to hang on to him, stay with him until this mood has passed, I know the worst thing I could do would be to press him, turn clingy. *Strategy, Chelse,* I tell myself. *You're a smart girl. Get yourself a game plan.*

"Tomorrow," I say, nudging his side. "Something that scares both of us. Actually, me more than you."

"What would that be?" he asks, perking up a little.

"Nope. Tomorrow. Not a word until then."

Clint
man on

So where do I turn, anyway?" I ask. "We're definitely not headed to town."

"Not to Baudette, anyway."

"How is it that *you're* telling *me* where to drive? Wouldn't it be easier if you'd just tell me where we're going?" I raise my eyebrow, waiting for Chelsea to answer.

"Nope." She sticks her nose in the air, the wind making her ponytail dance a frenzied salsa routine. "I Googled this place three times over. I know exactly where we're going."

"Not even a *hint*?" I ask, the same way I'd asked when we were on my group fishing expedition earlier that day. Even now, with evening creeping over the tops of the pines, I still have no idea what she's got planned.

"Eyes on the road, bub," is all she says, pushing my cheek so that my face turns back toward the windshield.

"One hint."

"If you don't mind, I thought we could do something a little—physical."

Physical? I remember the way the curve of her breast fit in my mouth the night before, as we draped that thick blanket of steam across the windows of my truck. *Just how physical is this thing she has in mind?*

She scolds, "A little professionalism, please, sir," like she knows what I'm thinking. "A *small* step, remember? Something a little scary for us both to tackle. Turn here."

As I ease the truck across the cracked asphalt of a parking lot, Chelsea points to a large warehouse-looking building.

"You're kidding," I say, my stomach bottoming out.

A huge pink neon sign, complete with flashing white bowling pins, announces that we have just arrived at the Rose Bowl.

"Are you fifty or something?" I tease her as we pile out of the truck. "Bowling."

"Small step—how many times do I have to tell you?" she asks playfully. She hurries ahead of me, grabs the door to the Rose Bowl, and opens it for *me*. Already she's messing with my mind, showing me she's got the upper hand. Showing me *I'm* the weaker one. She's challenging me, even though I told her sports were behind me.

I give her a hard stare to let her know I'm on to this strategy. But she only widens her eyes and shrugs, acting completely innocent. Still, I don't really appreciate having a challenge forced on me. Especially since I've spent the entirety of her vacation playing by her rules. Making sure we don't do anything too strenuous. Watching out for her. Doesn't really feel like she's doing me the same honor. And for a second, it kind of pisses me off.

"Smells like I remember," she sighs as we step inside. "Like sweaty shoes and cigarettes and stale beer."

"Like you remember," I mumble, dragging my feet. "This is my neck of the woods, isn't it?"

"Like *I* remember," she repeats. "All bowling alleys smell the same. And, yes, I've been bowling before. What were you expecting? That you'd get to wrap your arms around me while you showed me how to roll the ball down the lane?"

"That's not—look, Chelse, I wasn't kidding when I said I left competitive sports behind me. You can respect that, right?"

But she puts her hand on her hip and says, "If you think bowling is a serious competitive sport, you really *have* been on the sidelines too long."

"I'm done. I *meant* that," I insist.

"What is this, some sort of martyr complex?" she asks. "Really. Is this the same person who insisted *I* looked like one of the old men wasting their lives away outside of bait and tackle shops? Is this the same person who wanted to know where all *my* passion had gone?"

"Is this the same person who wouldn't even attempt to toss a basketball?"

She juts her chin out. "See that? The way you just volleyed

the conversation back at me? Your competitive spirit is *crying* to see the light of day."

She wants me to smile at her, but I refuse. She slumps a little, then says, "The other day, at Pike's, when you and Brandon went to hang up the flyers, your mom used the word *scared* to describe me. 'I know you're scared,' she said."

"So?"

"So—she used it like it was just some *obvious* word anybody would use to describe me, you know? Like—*blond* or *tall*. And I keep thinking about how I refuse so much of the stuff you suggest."

"That really doesn't matter," I tell her. "You're working—you know what you can handle—"

"I'm not sure I do," she cuts me off. "I'm starting to wonder if it really is my safety that's keeping me sidelined, that's making me say no. Or maybe I'm just—really—afraid."

I stare at her a minute—long enough to know this isn't a tactic. She's serious. There's no way I'm going to be able to back out after that little mini-speech. *Great,* I think as I turn toward the counter.

"Size twelve," I tell the man at the shoe-rental counter. He's wearing one of those fancy league shirts, this one with "Burt" embroidered over the breast pocket. He nods a hello, and I offer a hello that sounds more like a grunt.

Chelsea leans against the counter, staring at the rack of shoes. "Got any baby booties back there?" she asks. "Might need them for the little man here."

"Little man," I repeat. She's doing it again. This is a tactic—no doubt about it.

"It's okay, sweets," she teases, petting my arm. "Don't worry. Your mom'll still love you, even after you get your butt whipped by a girl."

"Where'd you find her?" Burt asks, wagging a thumb at Chelsea in disbelief.

"Yet again, this is definitely not where I imagined this night going," I say.

"Get used to it," she announces, sticking her chin out defiantly. Cute, cute, cute. Damn her.

"You going to just *take* that?" Burt asks.

"Okay," I say. "I'll bite, Keyes." I point at the shoes Burt's put on the counter, asking, "You did give her a pair that's completely covered in athlete's foot, right?"

"Doesn't really sound like this is gearing up to be a friendly game," Burt says.

"Don't worry about it. He's just trying to intimidate me," she explains to Burt. "But little does he know, I'm unshakable."

Burt chuckles. "You guys've got lane three."

She races to the ball rack. I take my time walking there, deciding to show her that I'm *so* good, I have no worries. I can take my time—I could, in fact, beat her at bowling while cleaning a fish with one hand and taking a hundred pictures on Kenzie's digital camera with the other.

"Here," I say, in a sarcastic tone. "Here's a pretty little pink ball. A good one for you. A two-pounder."

"Sorry, did you *see* that enormous fish I reeled in all

by myself? The one that's going to win my family a free week next summer? Need I remind you?" She bats her eyelashes, waiting for my response. Just as I open my mouth to answer, she interrupts by screaming, "Clint! That swirly little blue ball has your name on it. Look! Sparkles!"

"I'm so going to kick your butt," I warn her. Just to intimidate her, I grab a green sixteen-pounder—the heaviest ball on the rack—and head for our lane.

"The taller you talk yourself up, the more it's going to hurt when you fall."

"In for a little wager, Keyes?" I say. I flinch when I realize I used to do the same thing on the ice—use last names.

"What'd you have in mind, *Morgan*?" she says, playing along.

I pull myself together, tell myself to forget hockey. There's just right now, nothing else. "The loser has to kiss a fish."

"Kiss a fish," she repeats. "What kind of bet is *that*? Loser buys drive-in tickets, maybe. But kiss a fish? Besides, it's unfair for me to take a bet. You being such an underdog to my insane bowling abilities."

"We flip for the first frame," I tell her, pulling a quarter from my shorts.

"Heads," she shouts, and grimaces when my *tails* shines under the fluorescent light.

I dip my fingers into the holes on the ball, line my body up with the lane. But it feels like falling off the wagon, being in here. Playing. Competing. *Suck it up, Morgan*, I tell myself. I pull my arm back, knock down a respectable spare, and swagger back toward our bench. "Take that," I say proudly.

"Not bad," she admits, sinking her fingers into her ball. She lines her body up with the arrows on the lane, swings the ball up close to her chest, starts to raise a foot, then stops.

I know what she's doing. She's thinking of all sorts of horrible scenarios: tripping on a loose shoelace, getting the ball stuck on the knuckle of her middle finger just as she tries to launch it down the lane and losing her balance. Falling. Just like she did before.

She glances back over her shoulder. I just raise an eyebrow at her, shrug and hold a hand up, palm out. "It was your idea," I tell her. "Can't chicken out now. You do, it's a forfeit."

She narrows her eyes—that got her. Stiffens her back, tightens her hold on the ball. She takes three long, graceful steps and releases the ball. The pins fall, every last one. Strike.

"And so the competition truly begins," she says, trying desperately to suppress a *gotcha* smile. She fails miserably.

"Better get your game together, buddy." We both turn to find Burt leaning over the railing behind our lane, watching us. "She's good. But surely you can beat her."

"I'm going to, already," I defend myself as I grab my ball. "She just had a lucky frame, is all."

Chelsea bristles. I try to tell myself I'm just pushing her, like any good coach would. But it's more than that. I don't want to lose.

Her next two balls are strikes, too. "Easy as cuttin' butter," she taunts as she points to our score screen, where the image of a turkey flashes.

"Hey," a rotund older guy says, pointing at our lane with his cigarette. "That girl's good."

Having seen the turkey, Burt wanders down from the front counter again. "What's going on?" he calls to me. "You're not losing, are you?"

"No," I shoot back. But on our screen, it's clear that after my spare, I've left two open frames.

"I think you are," another man yells, putting his beer down just long enough to point at the screen.

"It's not over yet," I snap, frustrated.

Maybe I snap it just a little too loudly, because Chelsea sort of droops. Like she's decided, in that moment, not to push it any further—like she's decided I feel bad. That she thinks I might even be a bit of a sore loser. That it's not worth getting me completely peeved.

But when she gathers her ball for the next frame, two women at the concession stand start whistling through their fingers, hollering and clapping like Chelsea's somehow standing up for every downtrodden female throughout the history of all time.

"I can't exactly let them down, now, can I?" she asks me as she lines herself up again.

Another strike for Chelsea. Six pins for me. Without thinking, I growl and slump into my seat, cross my arms over my chest. I start to wonder why I care so much. Why I can't stand to lose. But I know the answer—I had no idea

182

how hungry I was for a clean rivalry. A battle. I had no idea how much I'd been needing this very thing. I feel like *I'm* the one getting mended. By bowling. Of all things.

When I catch Chelsea smiling at me, I figure she knows it, too.

Two strikes later, every woman in the alley—including the woman who's been sweeping the floor and the girls who've been leaning on pool tables while their boyfriends play eight-ball—are all crowding around our lane cheering, while the men start shouting, "Come on," and "Get 'er," and "What's the matter with you?"

Chelsea scores a spare on the seventh frame, which the men take as their shot to rally. But I'm pathetic—rusty. Not that I was ever much of a bowler, but when I was still playing hockey, I must have been better than *this*. I've only snared two spares the entire game.

With the hopes of the entire male population resting on my shoulders, I hit one measly outside pin, then roll a gutter ball.

I've definitely forgotten what it's like to shoulder pressure.

"I'd regret the ass kicking I've just unloaded on you if that pouty look on your face wasn't so adorable," she murmurs in my ear.

For the first time, I *feel* the pout on my face. Laughter starts to pour out of me, surprising me. When a jokester throws me a small white towel, I say, "No way. I'm not quitting. I'll never hear the end of it if I do."

Chelsea's last frame's another strike, landing her two

more chances. "You want them?" she teases. "Might improve your score."

I drape the white towel over my head. "Just go on. Let me know when it's over."

Spare.

Her feet click right up to where I'm sitting on the bench. She peeks under the towel and whispers, "Want a rematch?"

"You're joking, right?" I grab the towel and wave it. "Complete and utter defeat," I announce, while the men slink away and the women give each other high-fives.

"You've played professionally before, huh?" I ask as we untie our rented laces.

She shrugs. "I just used to play a lot."

"A lot," I repeat.

"I played in a league for about three years," she says, patting my knee. "Don't feel bad."

I snort. "Don't feel bad," I mutter, trying to act like I'm peeved. But the lightness in my chest reminds me how long it's been since I've felt ... free.

"Listen," I say, nudging her. "Seriously. Are you okay?"

"Okay?" she asks, tugging her left shoe free and tossing it to the tile.

"Your hip. It doesn't hurt, does it?"

Her hand freezes before she can pick up my sneaker. "I forgot it," she says. "Completely. As soon as we started playing." Her voice begins to scatter down our lane in laughter.

———

The sun is setting as I edge the truck through a field maybe a mile from the back door of Pike's, up toward a creek bed. Excitement burns as hot inside me as it did the first time I tried hang gliding. *Hang gliding.* Dumb comparison. This is nothing like hang gliding.

I cut the engine, climb out of the truck, and extend a hand behind me without looking. Chelsea slips her warm skin against mine. It's a simple gesture, but it's also so familiar, as if we've been holding hands for the past ten years. The ease is shocking, and—the word pops into my mind before I can second-guess it away—*wonderful*.

"Thanks for bowling," I say, still on a high even though our game ended almost an hour ago. "It's crazy, but I haven't felt that—I haven't—" I can actually feel a happy light start to swirl through my own eyes.

"Yeah, I thought so," she says, squeezing my hand back.

Does this really happen? Does life actually start to feel beautiful and whole again? Are second chances real?

When we reach the end of the stream, I tighten my clamp on Chelsea's hand and make a mad dash for the lake, dragging her into the water with me. The afternoon heat is still clinging to the air, so the water is soothingly cool as it swallows our legs, our waists. Two more steps, and the depths stretch all the way up to our chins. Chelsea dunks her head underwater, soaking her hair.

"Don't go any farther," I warn when she comes up for air. "There's a drop-off pretty close to here. You don't want to get in too deep."

"Maybe I don't want to stay where it's safe," she says, looking me straight in the eye.

"Come here, anyway," I say. "I have to make good on that bet I lost—I know exactly which water-drenched fish I want to kiss."

It's corny, but Chelsea giggles anyway as she floats toward me. She wraps her legs around my waist and her arms around my neck. As our mouths meet, water streams from her hair, running down both our faces. My hands fly up inside her wet shirt, her chilled skin cooling my palms. Our kisses turn deeper than the lowest point of Lake of the Woods. Without any real command from my brain, my hands are peeling back the soaked hem of her T-shirt. Shivers race down her body as I raise the shirt over her head. She pulls her arms out, the cool water leaving a trail of goose bumps across her chest—a trail I want to travel with my mouth.

She peels her bra away; my eyes trace the curves of her naked breasts while her shirt floats on the water beside me. As we come together for another kiss, I trace the lines of her breasts with my hands, squeezing her nipples gently, tugging a moan from her mouth. Her voice vibrates against my lips.

I don't really know how much of this is new to Chelsea—how far she's been before—but it's been so long for me, it all feels new.

I push her away, but only slightly. Reach below the surface of the water, tugging at the waistband of her shorts. The water's turned the material of her shorts stiff, but I manage to unfasten the top button and wiggle the zipper down. I want to touch her, touch everything.

"Clint!" a voice calls out through the encroaching darkness. "Saw your truck back there. *Clint!*"

Chelsea splashes about frantically, searching for her tangled-up T-shirt and bra. When she finds them, she maneuvers behind me, hiding as she struggles to put everything back on.

"Well, hi, uh, George," I say, recognizing the voice and the burly silhouette at the water's edge. "Gonna do a little night fishing?"

"You bet," Pop's old friend answers. "Figured you were, too."

"Just cooling off. Had a couple of long hot days on the fishing boat."

"Man, that sun will get you every time."

"Sure will. Sorry to be trespassing on your land—just wanted to get away from all the tourists. See enough of 'em during the day," I lie. *Can't seem to ever see enough of one,* is all I can think.

"You don't have to apologize, Clint. You're welcome out here anytime, you know that…"

As George rattles on, I turn my head and hiss, "You decent?"

"Yeah," Chelsea whispers back.

"Think I'll head for home. I'm really bushed—you enjoy yourself, George," I say, dragging myself—and Chelsea—out of the water.

Chelsea crosses her arms over her chest as we hurry toward the truck, the two of us drenched and dripping.

"See you, George," I call, waving over my shoulder.

"Well, now, you—ah, well, you and your, ah, friend, well, there, you two don't have to run off on my account..." He's shocked. Foot-on-a-downed-power-line shocked. He's got to recognize that the silhouette of my friend is decidedly female. Clint Morgan ... *he's not as dead as we'd all started to think he was.*

"You catch one for me, all right?" I call as we hurry back along the creek.

"All—all right. Well. Okay," he says.

We jump in the cab. Chelsea's muttering, "Shit, shit, shit" as the engine coughs to life.

But laughter's rolling out of me, and there's no way to turn it off.

"*Clint!*" she shouts. "What if he says something—to my folks or something?"

"He'd never recognize you," I tell her. "Trust me. It's getting too dark out. You know what *his* face looks like?"

I can tell, by the way she stops to consider this, that she agrees. "But it's not funny," she insists. "*Stop,*" she yells, making me realize that I'm still laughing.

But my laughter just rolls on. "It doesn't have to be all serious," I remind her, picking up her hand and kissing her knuckles.

As the truck ambles back toward the resort, I don't think I've ever felt quite so light in all my life.

Not even with a girl with two black braids.

Chelsea

turnover

Minnesota is a poem. Minnesota has black hair. Minnesota is a summer kiss under the stars, scald of a sunburn, ache of a heavy sweet lodged in the crevice of a tooth. Minnesota is a morning on a lake, an afternoon under trees, stolen kisses, the smell of a man's neck, the rough callus of his hand under my lips. Minnesota is a sky full of stars and the edge of a lake and wading farther and farther away from shore.

At least, that's what it feels like over the next few days. Weird, but around Clint, I don't think about metal plates and screws. I don't think about falling. I don't wish for a pause button that could keep me from ever moving forward, past basketball. I think about tomorrows. I'm excited—God—about cycling. About hiking. For the first time since my accident, I'm starting to wonder how much farther I can ride today than I did the day before. I'm telling Clint to let *me* row. My pillowy gut is firming, reminding me just how quickly I'd always been able to build muscle. I'm no longer the same squishy pile of dough Scratches kneaded, sitting on my lap just before we left home.

And ever since bowling, Clint seems—freer. He's not pushing me away. He's not telling me he can't. He's not leaning away from me, against the door of his truck. He doesn't apologize for brushing my knee when he shifts gears.

But Minnesota is also Brandon, glaring at me as he stands in the doorjamb of the cabin bathroom. Shaking his head while I hum, tying my hair into a ponytail.

"Don't think I'm stupid, Chelse," he says. "I know what's going on."

"What's going on?" Dad asks as he trudges down the sunlit hallway and glances into the bathroom, eyes hidden beneath a Lake of the Woods cap.

"Hiking," I sing.

"Hiking," Brandon mutters. "Yeah, right."

Dad's mouth curls into a frown. "Aren't you and Clint working out?" he asks.

"Aren't they," Brandon moans. "That's not the problem."

"What's that supposed to mean?" Dad asks, giving his words an angry growl. Suddenly, every cruel and unfair thing he said to me after the Willie Walleye festival—the night I first kissed Clint—comes roaring back.

"Forget it," I snap at him. I'm about to scream some-thing at him like, *Why do you act like I mucked up* your *life?* But Mom starts hollering about Clint being at the door, so Dad just disappears, like he always does, every morning.

We *all* disappear, each of us hurrying out of the cabin and heading off in our own direction. Brandon's guitar case whacks against the porch railing as he passes Clint. "*Hiking,*" he mutters one more time before heading off to the lodge to practice.

But who can care about Brandon or Dad—why let their judgmental crap ruin such a beautiful day? I can't, not when the Minnesota morning has bloomed like a gor-geous lady slipper. Not when I'm dipping into the shade of a cluster of trees, Clint's black hair brushing my cheeks and his mouth working its way around my neck. "Let's go to the waterfall," he murmurs in my ear. "The one behind your cabin. We'll be completely alone there. Promise."

But we're halfway to the trail when my phone, which I'd pocketed that morning just to prove to Brandon that *everything really is fine,* goes off. How is it that it suddenly works? And why *now*?

The text is from Gabe: *turn phone 2 read,* he's typed, *8.* When I follow his instructions, the "8" becomes "∞." Eternity.

The message instantly gives me an off-kilter swing in my stomach. And I don't want to ruin my first view of the waterfall by climbing this hill filled with anything but sheer excitement.

So I grab Clint's arm and drag him even deeper into

the shade. Push him teasingly, tug him down into the tall grass.

We tangle our bodies in the summer wildflowers. When Clint rolls me onto my back, all I can see is the way the sunlight puts a hot, metallic sheen in his black hair. But when I glance past his hair, my eyes land on some familiar small purple blooms dangling just behind him, their yellow tongues hanging out: a vine of bittersweets. The kind that grow by the mill back home.

It's almost like Gabe's planted them there on purpose—to remind me that Minnesota is not the last word. That I will still have to go home.

Stupid Gabe. Stupid bittersweets. I close my eyes; all I feel is Clint.

Clint

tactics

"Greg!" I shout, banging into the dining room of the lodge. "You don't need the Minnow tonight, do you?" The Minnow, the small skiff that Greg, Todd, and I bought together a couple of summers ago.

Putting down his burger, Greg wipes his mouth with the back of his hand. "What for?"

"Night fishing," I say.

"Why aren't you using one of Earl's launches for that?" Kenzie's voice calls out. I turn to find her standing in the doorway of the lodge gift shop, eyeing me skeptically.

Greg stops chewing for a while to eyeball me, too.

"Because I have—such a small—*group*—signed up, checking out a launch is ridiculous," I explain. But my voice is too high, and I'm too fidgety. I'm a crappy liar.

Greg shrugs, like he doesn't care that I've served him up a bunch of bull. "Sure," he says. "She's tied to the dock closest to the lodge." He crams the rest of his burger in his mouth.

"Haven't seen you at Pike's lately," Kenzie tells me as she comes into the dining room. The gift shop door sighs as it falls shut behind her.

Greg stops chewing again, looks up at me from the corner of his eye.

"What?" I say. "It's not like that *means* something. Greg's sitting here eating some crummy old cheeseburger instead of letting my mom feed him."

"Brandon hauls me up to the stage as soon as I walk in the door," Greg says around a full mouth of food. "If I don't eat now, I don't get *any* dinner."

"Everybody asks about you when you're not there," Kenzie presses. "At Pike's, I mean."

"Well, you know—keeping the paying customers happy's a full-time-and-a-half job," I say stupidly.

To prove my intentions, I disappear through one of the staff exits into a supply closet. Burst back into the dining room carrying a couple of poles. I try to make a big show of the poles, jiggling them around before rushing outside. I race right past the Minnow, the early evening sun staining the lake orange, and head straight for cabin number four. I *do* plan to take Chelsea out on it—but fishing's not the goal. I'm thinking more along the lines of a beautiful woman under the moonlight, and long kisses with no one around to catch us.

Chelsea throws the door open before I have a chance to even knock. Her smile turns kind of plastic and forced as Brandon's voice bounces against the cabin walls.

"*Night fishing?*" he screams.

"Just a minute," she tells me as I step inside the cabin. She pushes Brandon into a hallway, out of sight.

Their voices hiss back and forth angrily. I fidget in the front room, wishing the TV were blaring so I wouldn't have to hear their fight.

Sweat droplets form under my arms and trickle down my sides as I wonder if her parents are somewhere in the cabin, listening as Brandon challenges Chelsea's excuse to be alone with me. *Night fishing.* It sounds dumb now, even to me.

"Hope you guys all have fun tonight," she finally calls out, her voice ringing against the air in a hollow way. She's a terrible liar. Maybe even worse than I am. When she steps into view, I realize she's got on a pair of jean shorts that show off her strong legs—all curvy and sexy. I can smell her skin, even from here, and I remember the way her soft body always feels beneath my rough hands.

"Forgot your *tackle box*, didn't you, sis?" Brandon taunts her, carrying his guitar case into the front room.

"Got her covered, Brand, thanks," I say, my crappy-liar voice ringing pathetically. "Drop you off at Pike's?" I offer, trying like hell to save face even though the suggestion is stupid. If Chelsea and I really were going fishing, the last thing I'd want to do is drive all the way to Baudette and back.

"Forget it," Brandon mumbles. "I already got a ride."

"Greg's in the lodge—" I offer stupidly.

"I *know*," Brandon tells me. "Who do you think my ride is?"

"Tell—tell Todd I said hi," I try. But Brandon shakes his head.

"You guys don't fool me," he says. "You don't."

"*Enough*," Chelsea tells him, as footsteps start a stampede toward the living room.

"Sure you two don't want to come?" her mother calls.

"Everyone's leaving—going to Pike's to hear Brand play," Chelsea informs me as her dad steps into view. She shrinks a little when he shows up.

It's uncomfortable, being around the friction between the two of them. The kind of uncomfortable that makes me want to fix it, somehow. So I blurt, "Chelsea's been at me to take her night fishing for a while now." I hold up the poles to prove it's true.

"Night fishing," her dad repeats, his stare turning into an *I wonder what's really going on with you two* glare.

Good idea, Clint, I congratulate myself. *Way to amp the tension right up.*

Chelsea
contact sport

It's a charade—and maybe Dad knows as much. Maybe he's as sure of what's happening between Clint and me as Brandon is. Maybe he thinks even less of me now than he did before we went on vacation. *Is that humanly possible?*

I shift from one foot to the other, my nerves crackling inside of me. I wish they'd all just leave, already. Or maybe they're waiting for me to leave. Wait—how far, exactly, do Clint and I have to take this charade of night fishing? Do we actually have to take a boat out into the middle of the lake? Isn't the goal just to be *alone*? My mind starts turning over the possibilities of what Clint and I could actually *do*, wrapped in the seclusion the water...

Clint grins at me, his smile tearing at the tension in the room the same way two forks pull apart a dense angel food cake. "Hey, Chelse. Think I can trouble you for something to drink before we head out? I had two fishing runs this afternoon, and that sun blazed two-hundred degrees on that boat today."

"Sure," I say, jumping into action. "Sweet tea okay?"

"Long as it has plenty of ice," Clint answers.

As we both head into the kitchen, Mom calls out a final "Good night" and three pairs of feet clomp out the door.

I pour him a glass of Mom's sun tea, the ice cubes growing fuzzy corners as I think about the rough glare that Dad just tossed at me.

"He wants to talk to you, Chelse," Clint says. "He doesn't know how."

"It's not my fault," I growl as I put the pitcher on the counter. "What happened on the court happened to *me*. It was my accident, not his. I'm the one who had something to get over, not him. And besides—he doesn't *know* how to talk to me? I'm the same person I always was—"

"No, you're not," Clint says, coming up behind me. Talk about blazing—he practically feels like a space heater.

"Thanks," I grumble. "Comforting."

"You're not any less special, Chelse. But you're not the same person he knew. You *can't* be. You had a life-changing experience, didn't you? Maybe you just need to reintroduce yourself."

"Maybe if he cared about someone who couldn't be an athlete, I wouldn't have to."

"I don't think he cares about Brandon less because he doesn't play ball."

"He plays *something*," I say.

"This isn't a contest, Chelse. It's a conversation. Remember those?" When he puts his hands on my arms I don't feel skin at all, but the sun's rays. "You don't necessarily have to win conversations. Even though I do kind of like this combative you," he teases.

I turn, put my palm against his chest. His skin radiates so much of the day's heat that touching him feels like wading into the lake, opening my hand, and catching one of the white shimmers of blistering afternoon sunlight bouncing across the water.

"It *was* hot out there today," I say. When I look up at him, our faces are so close that our eyelashes almost tangle.

He kisses me—gently. The kind of kiss that asks for nothing in return. And because it's not demanding a thing from me, it feels like freedom. I swear, over these past few days with Clint, fear has become a shackle with a rusted hinge, weakened and brittle. Ready to crumble apart. And as our kiss lengthens, the shackle of fear gives way, falls off completely. I want to give everything I am to that kiss. To Clint.

"You're *frying*," I insist when our mouths finally part.

"I'm okay," he tells me. He runs a hand down my back, sending a streak of heat through my T-shirt.

"How 'bout we get you cooled off?" I ask.

"Like a swim?"

"Like a shower."

Clint nods. "Okay. I could use a hose-off. Just show me—"

I lead him down the hallway, toward the bathroom we've all been sharing, hoping the place doesn't look like an absolute swamp.

When I flick the light on, I find Brandon's hair gel and zit creams strewn across the counter, but at least Mom's hung the towels up.

I shut the door, showing Clint that I'm not going anywhere.

"Chelse," he says, shaking his head.

I kiss him again—kiss him the way he'd kissed me a moment ago, asking for nothing more than this moment. Telling him with my mouth that I only want this, that I am sure of nothing else *but* this. That the only thing right now that is pure and unsoiled and perfect is the way he feels against me.

Clint takes his red cap off and tosses it to the floor. I reach for his T-shirt, pull it over his head. I pull my own T-shirt off, and Clint reaches around to my back, unfastening my bra. He searches my eyes for a sign to keep going.

Somewhere in the back of my mind, the Chelsea I became after the accident crosses her arms over her chest and taps her foot. Frowning, she juts her head forward and starts to repeat the same word over and over again. I can tell, from the shape her lips take, that's she's shouting *Gabe, Gabe, Gabe.*

But she's a TV show on mute. Her mouth moves but no sound comes. So it's easy to turn my back on her. Easy to ignore her, to turn toward Clint, and toward the fiery-hot feelings that ignite inside me.

Our fingers start peeling back the rest of each other's clothes in big chunks—the way I sometimes peel back the husks from fresh corncobs in the summer. Clint slides my bra off and I unbutton his shorts. After we peel back the thickest layers, we start to take away the tiny corn silks that remain: my panties, his underwear, my ponytail holder, his watch.

We stand naked in front of each other, studying the many inches of exposed skin.

Clint finally takes my face in his hands and kisses me.

As we kiss, I push him toward the shower. Our mouths are still locked as I twist the cold knob full-force, then grope for the hot, adding just enough to take the edge off. We're still kissing as we step into the cool stream. But these kisses are more ... tender, pleading. *Please?* our kisses beg, while answering, at the same time, *yes.*

The water pelts us, soaking my hair and Clint's, making rivers down our bodies, running between our lips.

Clint's body is glorious. The reality of him far outshines any mere fantasy. The cool shower refuses to squelch the passion that radiates far hotter than the summer sun ever thought about. His hands are everywhere—my breasts, my backside, my thighs.

I suddenly realize what he's touching, and I grab his hand. Stare down at my scar. After being pummeled by the shower stream, it looks brutally pink. Raw. Ugly.

But Clint untangles his fingers from my own, traces

the outline of my surgical scar. Against the thick tip of his finger, the scar looks tiny by comparison. Actually disappears beneath his hand.

"Show me where your room is," he mumbles.

I'm already twisting the knob to kill the shower, and we're hurrying our naked, dripping bodies down the hall.

We fall into a twisted, jumbled mass on the bed as Clint kicks the heavy cover back. We're like ocean waves that just keep rising and crashing against each other, our wet bodies and hair soaking everything we touch. My arm flies to the purse at my bedside, tugs the zipper down. *Thank God for Fair Grove commencement night at Hill Toppers'*, I think as I pull out the box of condoms.

Clint grabs the box, tears it open. I close my eyes as our mouths come together, gently. He rustles against me; I'm sure he's rolling the condom on.

He's gazing right into my eyes when I finally open them. I can feel him, hard against my inner thigh, breathing hot on my neck. I run my hands down his back, turning my touch as soft as a summer breeze.

An engine roars up to the cabin.

Clint frowns, turns his head toward my window. When the engine outside dies, he growls, "You gotta be kidding." He jumps off the bed like the mattress has teeth and is threatening to bite him.

"What? What?" I ask, panicking.

"Your parents are here," he says, his feet stomping the floor as he races out of my room.

"*What?*" I repeat, because I'm absolutely sure that I've heard him all wrong. *This can't be happening...*

"Hurry," Clint yells, even though I'm moving faster than I have since my last game.

Clint's already fastening the button on his shorts when I burst into the bathroom. He throws his shirt over his head and tries to hand me the jean shorts I'd been wearing a moment ago. But they're so tight, and my legs are still so wet, I know they'll only get stuck mid-thigh. And I have no idea where my T-shirt landed. Desperate, I grab one of Brandon's concert tees from the bag Mom's using for our dirty clothes, along with the baggy shorts I slept in the night before.

"Come on," Clint urges, dragging me back down the hall while I'm still hiking up my shorts. He grabs his iced tea off the counter, and we plop into a couple of kitchen chairs just as Mom opens the door.

"What—Chelse?" Mom says, her eyes flying wide behind her glasses at the moment she steps into the kitchen.

"You're back awfully early," I say, trying on an innocent tone. It doesn't fit me any better than a pair of size two jeans would, no matter how hard I try to tug on it.

"Brandon—ah—he forgot his strap," Mom stutters. "He's trying to play sitting on a stool, but he's so miserable not being able to dance—jump—whatever he does—that I decided to come back for it. Your dad's still at Pike's."

"Hey, Mrs. Keyes," Clint says, waving coolly before raising the glass of tea to his lips.

"Why are you two so wet?" Mom finally asks, through a frown.

"Turned the boat over," Clint said. "Can you believe it? Not two minutes into our trip."

"You didn't get hurt again," Mom says.

"No, no—Chelsea Keyes, made of steel. Literally," I try to quip.

"Your clothes dried awfully fast," Mom says, running her eyes over both of us. She crosses her arms over her chest and tightens her lips at me.

"I changed," I say with a shrug.

"Me, too," Clint adds. "I had some extra stuff in the truck. Chelse was nice enough to let me use your bathroom." *Is he explaining too much?* He gulps down his tea so fast I'm sure he gets brain freeze. But he doesn't show it—tonight, he's rattled by nothing.

"You don't have to run off—" Mom begins.

"No, no, that's all right," Clint tells her. "I have to get to the lodge. Guy up there does maintenance on the Lake of the Woods boats. I'll get him to look over that motor on the skiff. Greg'll kill me if I did any real damage."

"Which means I can go to Pike's after all," I tell Mom with a plastered-on grin.

"Are you sure you're okay?" she asks.

"Fine," I insist. "It really wasn't a big deal." This could quite possibly be the biggest lie I've ever told. *Not a big deal!* I replay what just happened in my room.

Clint pats my shoulder like we were old pals. "See you,

Chelse. Thanks for the tea—and better luck next time. Rain check, okay?" He winks.

I nod, watch him grab the fishing poles before he walks out of the kitchen.

"I'll comb my hair, grab something a little better to wear," I tell Mom as Clint stomps out of the cabin.

I dash down the hall. But when I think again of what just happened, I can hardly walk—my toes nearly curl under in sheer pleasure. And when I think about how close I've just come to losing my virginity, I mostly just feel like I need another shower. Arctic cold, this time.

Clint
deflection

I'm on the path just behind the cabin, still hoping I'll get one more glimpse of Chelsea, when the cabin door flaps open.

She's wearing a sundress that makes me remember Willie Walleye Day ... and kissing her that night for the very first time. From this distance, her voice sounds like the bells on wind chimes. Chattering on about Brandon, I think, as I pick up a few stray words here and there.

She stands beside the SUV, waiting for her mom to unlock the doors. I'm pretty sure she could never look any more beautiful than she does right now, standing in the soft evening light ... because I can tell, by the way her head keeps turning toward the nearby docks and walking trails, that she's searching for me.

Her mom's on the driver's side of the SUV when Chelsea finally swivels enough to catch a glimpse of me on the trail. A sly smile spreads as she raises her hand, as if to push hair out of her face. But her hand twists, her fingers flap toward me, and I realize she's trying to wave at me without her mom noticing.

Tomorrow, I mouth, and even though I've got to be too far away for Chelsea to read my lips, I swear she nods her head once—as if to agree—before slipping into the SUV and pulling away for the night.

I'm whistling as I wander down the dirt path toward the lodge. Whistling, of all the crazy things. But I can't quit. As I'm walking, I realize I'm jiggling the decoy poles a little so that the bobbers will knock together, jingle. Add a little percussion to my song.

I quit when I see her.

She's swinging her legs from the edge of the dock, a fishing pole at her side. Leaning back on her palms. Wavy chestnut hair going all crazy down her chest. "I finally decided to come out with you," she says.

"Kenzie," I say, "I was—" But I don't have any idea how to finish my sentence. I just sigh, close my mouth.

"Never mind," she says, shaking her head. "Dumb idea, anyway."

"No," I insist, because I feel like a jackass for embarrassing her. "Let's go—come on. I'm free for the night, now, my—my group decided not to—ah—" *Everything* I say is stupid.

She stands, grabbing up her pole. "Forget it." She walks

to the edge of the dock, her sneakers thunking against the boards. She pats my arm, stares at my soaked hair, smiles. "You're awfully wet for never having gotten into your boat," she observes, nodding her head once toward the Minnow.

I just stare at her, not sure what to do next.

"Don't worry," she says with a laugh. "I'm not going to tell Earl about you and your—*client*." She wiggles her fingers as she says the last word, framing it in air quotes.

"There's nothing to tell ... Kenzie!" I shout.

But she walks toward the lodge, deaf to my lies.

Chelsea
brick

I'm *still* dizzy from my near-miss with Clint when I meet up with him in the lodge around noon the next day. All we're doing is splitting a club sandwich, but as our knees touch under the table, I swear the whole world starts to sparkle like sapphire light on the lake.

Kenzie, the girl who'd popped up out of nowhere during Willie Walleye Day to warn me that Clint would *never fall in love with me*, steps out from behind a door branded *Office*. She glares at me and Clint like we're a couple of high school freshmen engaging in some heavy PDA.

I glance back at Clint, worried we're being horrendously obvious.

But my worries evaporate soon enough. Because once we finish up lunch, my thoughts are only of the gorgeous, edible man who pushes me through a door marked *Staff Only*, then presses my back against the wall, sinking a kiss deep against my mouth.

Ha, ha, double ha, I imagine spitting at Kenzie. Clint starts to pull away from me, then comes back for yet another kiss.

"See you tonight?" he asks, while the clank and bustle of the lodge—no, of the entire external *world*—comes to me muffled, distant.

I'm having to get really creative with my excuses for seeing Clint at night, but I don't care. I could write a book on lying at this point. I nod, still spinning from his kiss.

"Coming with me when I take a group out orchid hunting this afternoon, too, aren't you?" he murmurs into my neck.

Yes, yes, yes—anywhere. I'll go anywhere with you.

We ease ourselves out of the narrow hallway that leads to the break room, drop each other's hands, and walk oh-so-innocently into the lobby.

"Chelsea," Earl shouts, waving me over to the pay phone. "Just in time. You have a phone call."

"That's weird," I say with a light shrug.

Clint nods once toward the bulletin board on the opposite end of the lobby, an *I'll wait here* motion. Stands below the picture of me and my walleye—still the #1 biggest catch of the summer.

"Chelsea?" the familiar voice barks as soon as I pick up the receiver.

"*Gabe*," I say, before I can stop myself.

Clint turns on his heel, staring at me with eyes like open wounds.

I chastise myself. *Why'd you have to blurt his name? You can be so dumb...*

"Listen, I'm still at work," Gabe says, "and I don't have much time, but something's been on my mind and I just—I'm sorry. This probably sounds really possessive and paranoid, but is everything okay?"

My head turns into a giant scoreboard, like the one in the Fair Grove High gym. And over my name, the score is a great big glowing zero. Chelsea Keyes is losing, losing.

And don't I deserve to?

"I—what—you—what?" I babble. I don't know if I should scream or beg or start crying. How does Gabe know this—Wait. What, exactly, does he know? Has Brandon called him? What is going on?

"I guess—I mean, I'm just used to us talking on the phone for hours. And even when we weren't talking, it sounds hokey, but you used to drop all those notes in my locker. Love notes. You used to say it all the time, the way you felt about me. *We* said it all the time. Love, we said. We used that word so much, it shouldn't have meant anything at all—it should have been watered down and worn out, the way we used it. But I haven't heard it *once* since you left. I didn't even get a 'love you' on my birthday."

Oh, my God, Gabe, no!

"Chelse? You still there?"

"Yeah," I mumble, staring at Clint while my heart clatters

around inside me like a dropped plastic plate flopping and twirling on a kitchen floor. "I'm here."

"I know you said that you get bad cell reception and all, but it just seems like—like you just don't *want* to talk to me. I can't help it—I just wonder if something's up. I think about you all the time."

A giant tear escapes and rolls down my cheek, even though I'm trying to tug it back. "I do, too," I whimper, my voice all shuddery.

I can't stand to look at Clint. I wipe my cheek and turn my back to him, lower my face down toward the gleaming front of the pay phone, my heart drumming away like an entire marching band. *How can this be happening?*

"Are you okay?" Gabe asks, while Clint's eyes bore hot holes into the back of my shoulders. "I didn't mean to make you cry. I'm a jerk, Chelsea. Okay?"

"I just miss you is all," I murmur, using the tears to my advantage and hating myself for it at the same time. Because I'm also hoping to God that Clint can't hear me. "I do love you," I whisper. "It's been so hard to be away from you."

"Love you, too, Chelsea. It's so good to hear your voice."

"Yours, too."

"Look, just forget I brought it up," Gabe says. "You enjoy the rest of your vacation—I'll see you when you get back, okay?"

"Okay," I mumble, digging a fingernail nervously into the phone cord. "Love you," I whisper again.

Gabe sighs loudly into the phone. "I love you so much, Chelse."

I bite my lip until I can taste blood, until the pain radiating from the clamp of my teeth takes my tears away.

When I turn, Clint's face is maybe an inch away from my own. Earl is gone; the front counter is empty.

"Did you—you heard—he's just—I can't—"

"You love him," Clint says.

"But I—you knew I had—"

"But you love him," Clint repeats. "That's what you just said, anyway."

I'm in the last moments of my last game, all over again. I'm in my Eagles jersey, and I'm jumping, twisting my pain-racked body, bringing my arm behind my head. I'm falling.

"But you *knew*," I insist.

"What are you *doing* with me?" Clint snaps. "You act like—like there's this undeniable *thing* between us—and then you turn around and talk the same way with *him.* I don't understand. I thought—you know about *me,* too, about—what *I'd* been through—and here you are screwing with me."

"I'm not—I've been completely—"

"*Do* you love him?" Clint asks.

My jaw swings open, shuts again. I'm actually disappointed for a second that no words have magically poured out all on their own to explain the entire situation.

"*Damn,*" Clint says, running his hand through his

hair. "Thank God it didn't happen last night. Thank *God* I didn't let you run right over me—"

"That's not—I wanted—"

"From here on out," Clint hisses at me, "I'm your trainer. Got it? You only have a few more days left of your vacation left, anyway. Your trainer. Period. Your trainer, who takes you on the most boring walks through the countryside."

"You *haven't*," I insist. "I've been trying!"

"Your trainer," he continues, "who is helping you throw your vacation away, because you're the most frightened little girl I've ever met."

"*I'm*—?"

"The most frightened. You don't even have the strength to choose between guy number one and guy number two. So I'll help you out. I'll choose *for* you. Trainer, Chelse. That's *it*."

My tears come as soon as he's stomped out through the lobby door. I try to rein them in, but it's harder than pushing a thunderstorm back up into the sky.

When I finally get some sort of control over my blubbering self, I wipe my face and hurry to the gift shop around the corner from the dining room. I make a beeline for a rack of postcards, spinning the metal display as I pick out different shots of the resort.

I pay for the postcards and a pen, then wander toward the bench next to the front door.

XXXXXXXXX, Chelse, I write on one.

One more day closer to you, I scribble on the next.

Don't forget—I love you more than Scratches.

"There you are," Brandon says, bursting out of the dining room. "Look, tell Mom when you see her that I'm going straight to Pike's after band practice, all right? What's the matter? You look like you've been crying."

"Go away. I'm busy," I mutter.

"What're you doing?"

"Writing postcards to Gabe. One for each day we have left of vacation. I'm going to drop one in the mail every morning. To show him I'm thinking about him every day."

"Uh-huh," he says in a knowing tone. "Only by writing them all now, you *don't* have to think about him every day. Which is the point, right?"

"*No.* I just want to get them all done."

"You don't look too happy there, Chelse. Kind of looks like you're doing a homework assignment you forgot about until two minutes before it was due."

"I'd think you, of all people, would be proud of me," I snap.

"Proud of you for finding a way to snow your boyfriend?"

"That's not a very nice thing to say," I grumble. I scribble Gabe's address on another postcard.

"I've *seen* you and Clint together," Brandon says coolly. "And believe me, I could say a lot worse right now."

I'd kill him for that remark . . . if it wasn't so true.

Clint
time-out

I'm too pissed after that phone call to realize just how quickly I stomp through my afternoon orchid hunt. But when we circle back around the trail, winding up back at the lodge, I turn to find my entire group huffing and puffing like I'm their track coach. Like I've just sent them through the most grueling practice session of all time. Some of them have actual sweat stains on their T-shirts.

"Ah—there's ice—iced tea in the dining room," I mumble. Even embarrassment doesn't make me any less angry. But I'm not mad at Chelsea—I'm furious with me. *Of all the people to have a thing for,* I chastise myself. *Chelsea. Due to leave Minnesota in less than a week. What'd you expect?*

I go jogging after the hike. Show up at Pike's before Brandon or Greg or Todd. Throw myself into pitching in for a sick member of the wait staff. Work. I've known it all along—work is what will make everything better. If I'm working, I'm too busy to overthink everything.

After the dinner rush, it hits me that I need to figure out what I'm going to do with Chelsea for the rest of the time we've got together. I don't want to let on how much she's rattled me. I don't want her to know how much I really do care. And I don't want to ruin my chances for another boot camp client, either.

I'm pacing outside the restaurant when I see them at the side of the building. A pair of handlebars—two ATVs parked side by side. And I know exactly what I'm going to do with Chelsea. Tomorrow, at least.

———

"You showed," she says the next day, as she hurries across the porch of her cabin.

"Why wouldn't I?" I ask her, stepping out of the truck. "Your parents paid me to work with you the entire time you're here, right?"

"But I don't—I don't want that," she tells me. "Not—*just* that."

Looking at her, I hear, all over again, the *I love you* she'd whispered to her boyfriend. "Come on," I say. "A mushroom hunt."

I can tell, from the shock on her face, that my refusal to talk about what happened yesterday stings. But I don't care. It feels good to hurt her back. The same way it felt good to throw her off-guard with the basketball out there behind Pike's that first night. Realizing this, I instantly feel like a creep.

We pile into the truck and take off. I snap the radio on so she doesn't feel compelled to talk. All the way to Pike's.

The first shift is preparing for the lunch rush, pulling chairs off tables and filling salt shakers as we step inside. Chelsea follows me through the restaurant and out onto the patio. The weather is as uncomfortable as everything else this morning; the heat swells, feeling heavy and muggy. A couple of waiters are leaning against the brick wall, smoke curling from the ends of their cigarettes.

"Not exactly strenuous," Chelsea says shyly, pointing at the two ATVs I've moved to the edge of the patio.

I give the two waiters the same look Pop flashes when he wants them to get their butts in gear. They drop their cigarettes and disappear back inside.

"Haven't chalked me up as a lost cause, have you?" Chelsea continues.

I instantly start imagining her on the back of my *own* ATV, her arms wrapped around my waist, the sweet smell of her skin in my nose. And parking beneath the thickest patch of tree limbs, where our bodies would be hidden beneath the shade...

Stop it, Clint, I tell myself. This is exactly why I put *both* ATVs out here—because if we're on our own vehicles, I won't have to smell her, won't want her as badly as I do right now just standing next to her. Everything inside me spins when I think of the two of us in the shower in her cabin . . . or the two of us tumbling onto her bed.

I just need some time, I think, even though the devil on my shoulder reminds me there *isn't* much time, that the days have dwindled down to practically nothing, and here we are, nearly at the end of Chelsea's vacation. *Every second you spend trying to sort things out is one less second you have to touch her*, the devil reminds me.

I clear my throat, take a step toward the four-wheelers. *You already sorted things out, remember? She doesn't love you. Not like she loves the other guy. You're setting yourself up for the hurt you want to avoid.*

"Well, have you?" Chelsea presses. "Chalked me up? Because what you said yesterday—about me being frightened—you don't think I'm getting *worse*, do you? You don't think I wouldn't even hike?"

"Oh, there will be plenty of hiking," I promise, keeping my distance, making my tone go cool with professionalism. "Once we get out to where the mushrooms grow, anyway. There's a spot north of Pike's that's always been pretty lucky. It's just that it would take us about a week and a half to walk there, is all." There. Good. I'm treating her exactly like what I've told her she is: a client. No mixed messages. No changing my mind.

When she takes another step closer to me, though, my entire body kicks into high gear. I feel my heart beat faster, my lungs burn, my legs get loose and wobble. Sure. Client. Feels *exactly* like a client to me.

"They really that good?" she asks. "The mushrooms?"

Kenzie flashes through my mind—I remember the way she smiled at me over a plate of morels. Chelsea's got the same look on her face.

But Chelsea's far harder to refuse. I want to grab her, kiss her, bury my face in her hair.

You're just being a guy, I try to tell myself.

But it's not just about skin. If skin was all that was important, I could have gone after anyone without a second thought. I'd have taken up with Kenzie that first night in the lodge.

Chelsea's offering far more than skin. *But what?* I ask myself. *What is she offering that's so incredibly special? You were doing fine without her. You'd better be, anyway. She's going to be gone. You can't rely on her. You can't give in to her. She's just going to disappear.*

I clear my throat, finally get around to answering her question. "Mom sure sells morel appetizers like crazy," I say with a strained smile.

I show her how to start her ATV—turn the key, hold the brake, press the start button. Show her how to use the hand-twist throttle, and warn, "Careful how you accelerate. These are hunting quads, not racers, but if you accelerate too fast, you can still flip up, turn over on your back."

I glance her way, half-expecting her to tell me to forget it if it's so incredibly dangerous.

But Chelsea only nods as she clinches the strap of her helmet under her chin.

"What're you waiting for?" she says, starting the ATV like I showed her.

I figure this is all a bunch of bravado to cover up what happened at the lodge yesterday. So instead of paying much attention to her, I just tug a helmet on and hit my own start button.

I take off, slowly at first—I inch forward so that I can keep track of the engine that putters behind me. She's following along fine, having no problem getting the hang of it—of the ATVs Pop and I used to use for hunting mushrooms in the summer, that Todd and Greg and I took turns riding long before we ever had learner's permits.

Once I know Chelsea's doing okay, I increase my speed, letting my ATV bounce over the terrain. My nose fills with the musty, mossy smell of the nearby swamp; our tires fly across the soft ground, toss the occasional wet splash of mud through the air.

I lead her between trees, weaving, while Pike's grows to a fleck behind us, then disappears completely.

The rumble of the ATV behind me grows louder, starts zinging toward my left shoulder like an arrow. I glance behind me to find Chelsea's head down, her shoulders spread wide, as she crouches over the handlebars. She twists her wrist, egging the throttle like I showed her, forcing the vehicle on faster.

At first I refuse to answer, to take her on. But she knows exactly how to get to me—she closes in on me; automatically, my own wrist twists, my body clenches.

Chelsea gains. Her engine grows louder, closer.

When the front tire of her ATV inches ahead of me, I hunch my own body over my handlebars. Faster.

But Chelsea refuses to just surrender the lead. She urges her ATV forward again, and we dance——I press, she presses. Before I can even think about what's actually happening, we're racing. My tires bounce over roots and old fallen limbs. Our engines roar back and forth at each other, tossing angry threats.

I push, I press. And Chelsea answers. She gets close enough that from the corner of my eye, I can see her hair flying out behind her helmet.

I press again, edging ahead of her. She falls behind. I'm *ahead* of her. I'm winning—I actually start to celebrate inside. *I'm winning*, I think. But then the grumble of her engine disappears completely, and I know I'm *too* far ahead.

I glance over my shoulder, but I don't see her. Just lots of green—branches, grass.

Where is she?

Panic spills through my chest. Chelsea's gone. Instantly, a clock starts ticking in my mind. All I can think is, *I can't do another two days. Forty-eight hours of searching, of wondering.* Chelsea's gone, out of sight, and instantly, I think she's as gone as Rosie.

That's dumb, Clint. I know it is—but I'm terrified.

"Chelsea?" I shout. Why doesn't she just *answer*?

I face forward, just in time to see a fallen tree stretched out in front of me. I stomp the brake, turn my wheels sharply.

It's not enough.

The ATV strikes the tree. I lose my grip and my body flies over the handlebars.

Chelsea
air ball

As soon as I see the tires of his ATV collide with the dead tree, I try to scream his name, but all that comes out is a wheezy squeak.

He soars through the air, his body loose, his arms and legs flopping.

"Clint!" I try again, his body continuing to climb like the sky's a ladder. But my voice is weak—far softer, even, than the muffled sounds of distant cars on the opposite side of the woods.

Needles of fear attack the skin on my arms. I reach for him—a ridiculous gesture. Like I could ever catch him from where I am, the length of a basketball court behind him, stuck deep in a thick, gooey patch of mud I could easily have avoided if I hadn't been so set on getting ahead of him. My voice is caught in my throat, my arms useless. I'm powerless. And Clint, poor Clint, has just been launched like ammunition in a catapult.

His body crumples when he hits the gnarly roots of a nearby tree.

I finally find my scream as I climb from my ATV and race through the soft, muddy space between my four-wheeler and his.

"Clint," I say, afraid to touch him. Afraid not to. His eyes stare at me, wild and frightened as I crouch beside him. "Clint," I say again, panic filling my mouth with a bitter, metallic taste.

I put my hand under his arm, attempting to help him up. But he screams when I touch him.

"Is it your shoulder?" I ask when he struggles to sit up by himself. The left side of his body looks kind of deformed—twisted. Panting, I place my fingertips against his T-shirt, feel an out-of-place bump and muscles that spasm.

"Can you move it?"

He shakes his head and groans.

"I think you dislocated it," I say.

I look up, finding only blue spaces of sky between leaves. The way the tree trunks surround us reminds me of my team, of the way they all stared down at me when I'd fallen. The woods take on the quiet echo of the gym during those last moments.

But I don't have time for this—for remembering, for reliving that one awful thing that happened to me once.

"Come on," I say, standing up. "You have to help me. We've got to get you out of here." I put my hands on his waist, trying to hold him steady as he puts his feet beneath him.

"My ATV's stuck in the mud," I tell him, "so we'll have to use yours." I say it like I'm sure that it'll start, that doubt's a stranger here.

The two of us attempt to squeeze into the seat of his ATV, which is butted up against the fallen tree. I straddle him, bringing my legs around his body. But it's hard for me to reach the handlebars, to see the front of the four-wheeler.

"You've got to start this thing for me," I say, as my foot finds the brake.

Clint turns the key. I pray with more intensity than the most devout woman on the planet, biting my lower lip and squeezing my eyes shut as he presses the start button.

I could cry when the engine coughs.

Clint barks at me about how to put the ATV in reverse. When I finally get clear of the tree, I ask, "Which way back to Pike's? Clint? It all looks the same to me."

"Tracks," he growls, but I know there's no way I can drive, grip Clint's unsteady body, and follow the Hansel and Gretel breadcrumbs that would lead us straight back to Pike's. I try desperately to think of an alternative.

At this point, Clint's making more noise than the engine. He tries to grip the jiggling handlebars, but grimaces when he wraps his hands around it. As I squirm to settle my backside against the seat, I feel the cold metal circle press into my thigh—*oh my God, thank you, thank, you, thank you.* Clint's compass.

My fingers buzz as I wiggle them into the pocket of his shorts. He leans to the side, letting me pull the compass out to check the direction. I remember him telling me the mushrooms were north of Pike's.

South, my brain screams up at me. *We need to head south.*

I keep my legs around Clint's body as I veer back toward the restaurant. Not knowing for sure where I'm heading, exactly, as I steer between the trees. I just trust the compass. As we head south, the compass is actually pointing toward *me,* the only person who can get us out of this mess.

We're moving as fast as Clint can bear; as I suspected they would, the tracks fly past, disappear. I've lost them somewhere along the way. But the compass still points at me, so I try to tell myself we'll be okay. But my throbbing, worried heart lets me know that I'm really not so sure.

Shops appear ahead, but I don't see the old backboard looming over the patio behind Pike's. Because it's not Pike's—*damn it.* I've screwed up. I'm in the wrong place.

Still, though, I force the ATV on, gunning the engine to climb a small incline, then to weave between two businesses and careen onto a street.

The place we've ended up is dusty and sparse, the kind of place where dogs nose the edges of buildings and men in overalls linger in doorways, and afternoons take on the quiet pace of an antique store.

My hair hangs over my face—I pant, sending strands

scattering across my cheekbones. I toss my head, clearing the hair from my eyes, but there's really nothing to see here. I glance both ways down the dusty street. Just pine trees and a red building ahead—a café of some kind, with a few wooden picnic tables set up outside.

"Where are we?" I try to ask Clint. "Which way is Pike's?"

All that comes out of him is a guttural yawp.

I rev the engine and speed down the street toward the café. Because surely *someone* around here has a phone that actually works. Or a car. At this point, I'd go for two sticks we could rub together to start a fire to send out smoke signals. A few diners glance up at the sound of the approaching ATV. Their eyes turn into enormous zeros. Benches scrape. Feet scamper.

I hear my name.

"Shut up, Clint," I bark, because I think he's the one screaming at me.

"Stop, stop! Chelsea! Stop."

My ATV lurches on toward the outdoor seating area, while screams of frightened diners dance in the air and their arms flap like birds' wings as they flee to safety.

"Chelsea!" the cry comes again. "Chelsea. *Stop*."

When I turn, I see a familiar head of pepper-gray hair on top of a pair of broad, ex-jock shoulders.

"What're you doing?" Dad asks, frowning at me.

"I'm—getting him help. He really hurt his shoulder," I say.

Dad's face whitens as he looks at Clint writhing in the seat.

In that moment, there's no last game. There's no year of strained silences or glares over a dinner table. There's no resentment or guilt. Right then, there's really no me and Dad. There's just Clint and his twisted shoulder, which is making a gruesome bulge against the back of his shirt. There's a growl and the way Clint keeps writhing in pain. There's only a person we need to help. Dad nods once, understanding.

"Turn that thing off," Dad says. "Wait there." He jogs away.

When I kill the engine, I notice the horrified faces of everybody who was eating just a minute before. They keep staring, paralyzed, as the White Sugar SUV screeches to a stop in front of the café. Dad jumps out to help me guide Clint into the back seat.

And it should be déjà vu. It *should*—because the GPS leads us straight to the hospital. And we're in an emergency room again, and we're running down hallways filled with gurneys and scrubs and faces that try so hard to appear calm that they look completely fake.

Last time, when I was the one on that gurney, when it was my hip in the X-ray, white lines on black paper glowing through the brutal hospital light, I thought I'd crumble beneath the weight of my fear.

This time, though, when they point, saying *dislocated*, as if this is some big revelation and not a diagnosis in slow motion, I'm solid. I'm sure.

And it's *me* that's holding Clint's good hand while his parents wait in the hall. It's me that's telling him *just a little longer* when he washes a painkiller down with lukewarm hospital water.

And it's me that says *don't watch* when the ER doctor starts to tug on his bad arm, twisting and pulling, trying to figure out how to feed it back into place. I'm the one that says *focus here*, pointing at my eyes while the twisting goes on. I'm the one who supports Clint while he screams like they're doing surgery on him without anesthetic. I'm the one who holds him up. And something in me kicks in— I'm not afraid. At all. No hesitation. No wondering what I'm truly capable of. I know I can handle it—for him.

Funny thing about fear, I guess, is that if you just look *away* from it, toward something else—like dark eyes in a beautiful face, a lock of black hair hanging over a sweaty forehead—you realize you've turned a full hundred-and-eighty degrees away from fear.

You're staring straight into your own strength.

I am, anyway. As I help Clint, I'm staring into my own strength.

Clint
game-ending injury

The pain in my shoulder is so bad, I actually wish for a chainsaw. I wouldn't think twice about cutting the whole rotten thing off, pruning myself as if I were an old oak tree.

I'm woozy and lightheaded. My thoughts come in crazy explosions instead of straight lines. *Everything's* popping up at me—that ravine and the turned-over Mazda, and how wrong the ice felt afterward when I tried to play. And working all the time, like I could somehow get too busy to feel bad, to be as devastated as I really was.

And the funeral, and how I thought that burying my feelings would be just as easy as shoveling some dirt over a gap in the earth. Didn't work, though—it hurt anyway. Hurt just as bad as my out-of-place arm.

And here I am, all over again, in the middle of another accident, but this time, a woman's arms surround me. She's not the source of the pain, she's the one who's holding me up while the pain racks me.

When the bones finally click, the worst of the searing ache subsides. I still hurt, but the relief is enough that I collapse into Chelsea. Even then, when I act like a complete mess, she lets me fall apart for a while.

Chelsea
horse

I'm alone on the patio at Pike's, watching the lightning bugs dance in the grass. Gene is in the distance somewhere, hunting down the ATV I've left stuck in the mud. Clint's at home with Cecilia, getting an extra helping of mothering. Dad's inside, manning the cash register for Gene until someone on the waitstaff can shake away the peaceful dust of a day off and drive to the restaurant. Above, the sunset is so deep red, it's almost purple—but that's how the sky always acts after forcing you to live through a frightening storm. Offers something extra beautiful to look at.

The beer I've stolen is cool, pleasantly bitter on the back of my tongue. Every once in a while I put the bottle against my hot face.

Then the drums start kicking inside the building, life beating on as it always does no matter how much you'd just like the clocks to stop long enough for you to catch your breath.

I drain the bottle, straighten my back, and aim at a metal trash container on the edge of the patio. "Shoots and—" I say, doing a horrible imitation of Fred Richards. Launch the bottle. It soars straight into the container, thuds and crashes against the bottom.

"Scores," I whisper, just as the back door opens behind me. Dad steps outside, staring down at me.

I glance into the tall grass, where the lightning bugs now look like miniature orange basketballs bouncing up from the green stalks.

Before I even realize exactly what I'm doing, I'm on my feet. I'm hurrying across the patio. I'm fishing that old basketball from the weeds. Dad's eyes widen when he sees the ball in my hands.

"I'm lucky you decided to eat at that café today," I say, dribbling.

"You would've figured it out," Dad says. "You don't need me. Never did."

I flinch, bristling automatically against his words. He sounds like he's feeling sorry for himself. I don't really know what else to do, so I start to dribble angrily against the cracked patio.

"Sure didn't need somebody pushing you so hard from the sidelines," Dad adds.

A cold ripple travels the length of my entire body; my anger cools. "You didn't. You—*cheered*. That was all."

"I pushed," he says, guilt washing over his face.

I squeeze the basketball, shaking my head, shocked. Was Brandon right about me being too hard on Dad? Have I been misinterpreting everything? Is Dad angry at himself?

"I was the one who worked too hard," I say. "I was the one who pushed. It was my fault. It was always my fault. Right? I'm the one who blew it."

Dad shakes his head. "I should have known. Brandon said he did—even that night at the hospital, the night of the accident, he said he knew you were hurt. That he should have said something. That he shouldn't have let you play. All I could ever think was, if Brandon knew, why didn't I?"

"It was *my* hip. Mine. I was the one who should have known."

"I still feel bad about it."

"Yeah. Well. Me too."

We stare at each other. Just stare. The sun keeps sinking; bugs keep swarming in the grass; the drums keep beating on through the walls of Pike's. In the distance, I think I can hear the ATV revving to life. Gene will be showing up before too much longer.

"Come on," I tell Dad, bouncing the ball his way. "Horse. Rusty as I am, I'll bet my first semester's tuition I can still kick your butt."

Dad dribbles, takes a shot. The ball bounces off the rim; he catches it and passes it to me.

Feet firmly planted, heart stomping, ears ringing with the echo of the cheering crowd in the Fair Grove High gym, I raise my arms and take the first set shot since my last game. The ball bounces off the backboard and dances on the rim a few seconds before deciding to fall through.

"Still got it, Keyes," Dad says.

"I'm still better than you, anyway," I tease.

He's smiling as he goes for a lay-up.

Clint

hooking

I swear, the couple of days I agree to take off from work after the accident torture me far worse than the actual dislocation. Because I spend the whole time thinking about Chelsea—and how wrong I've been. I *never* should have pushed her away, never should have ignored the way every single fiber in my entire body told me she was what I wanted. I have to talk to her, but not on the phone. I know I have to look in her face to tell her what's swirling through my head.

The day I finally do go back to work, I'm armed with Ibuprofen, the promises I made to Mom about taking it easy, and the promises I made to Pop about doing the gentle range-of-motion exercises the ER doc gave me so my arm won't freeze. I'd promise anything at this point; I *have* to get out of the house.

I can't wait to find her.

I'm sore and tender, but I still rush to cabin number four. When I realize it's empty, I start breaking my promise to Mom by racing around the resort searching for Chelsea. Because yes, maybe there's another guy waiting at home for her. Maybe she does have feelings for him. But isn't there still love inside *me*, too, for Rosie? Won't there always be?

Screw Gabe. Screw all this stupid fear. And screw the clock that counts down the time Chelsea and I have left. I'm already in deep enough that it'll hurt when she leaves. I'll miss her. But right *now?* All I know is that I want her. That I'm giving this a shot.

By the time I rush into the lodge, I'm covered in a thick, sticky sweat. I feel a little beat up, but it's worth it when I *finally* find her in the lobby, staring at the bulletin board that still has her photo tacked to it—the one I took of her and her walleye.

When she turns and sees me, her face smooths out, like maybe my showing up means she's just found what she's been looking for, too.

"You could go out on the boat again," I say, pointing at the photo of her walleye. Not at all what I'd wanted to say, but I don't really know where to start.

"It wouldn't be the same without you." She smiles at me. "And you're out of commission for the next few weeks. At least you don't have to wear a sling. Does it still hurt?"

"The thing is," I say, charging ahead, not able to hold

it back any longer, "you get hurt regardless, you know? No matter how safe you try to stay. Things … you … " *You had two days to think of what you'd say to her, Morgan, and here you are acting like an idiot.*

Chelsea grins slyly. "You decide to change your mind about the trainer thing?" she whispers.

God, did I.

"Listen," she says. "I have an idea. About what we could do tomorrow. If you think you can get away, that is."

"I can get away," I tell her. I glance up to make sure the front desk is still empty, that no one from the dining room is heading into the lobby. When I'm sure we're good and alone, I search her eyes. They curl into a smile as I lean forward to let my lips graze her cheek.

"How about," she says, playing back, her lip running along my jaw, "bowling?"

"*Bowling?*"

"Yeah, a rematch."

"I don't think so," I tell her, running my fingers along the V-neck of her blouse.

"Drive-in got another classic movie playing?"

"Chelse—"

"Okay—how 'bout that rain check?"

I squint at her, shake my head. "Rain check," I repeat, not quite understanding.

"Remember? When Mom showed up at the cabin? And you told me 'rain check'?"

"You want to go *night fishing*," I mumble, but I can't laugh, not with my entire body threatening to explode.

"Meet me at my cabin. Seven o'clock," she says. "Brandon'll be at Pike's by then. So will Mom and Dad." Her voice trails off and her eyes spark as she flashes me a crooked grin.

"Just make sure," I tell her, "to duct tape Brandon's strap to his Marshall this time."

Chelsea
score

Sure you don't want to come?" Dad asks for what must be the eighty billionth time.

I shake my head.

"You and I could go out to the patio at Pike's. Horse rematch. Come on," he pleads. "That band of Brandon's gets a little—"

"—bit better every single time we go," Mom interrupts. "And it's our last chance to hear the Dwellers play. You sure you want to miss out on that?"

You really have no idea how much I want to miss out on that, I think as I try to play it cool, nonchalantly waving them all goodbye.

And then I'm alone, in a quiet cabin, waiting for Clint. And *waiting*. Fidgeting.

I sit on the couch, stare for a moment at the spiral notebooks Mom's stacked on the coffee table—I open one and start thumbing through, flipping past all the recipes she's been tweaking. When I get to the blank pages at the end, I drum my fingers awhile. Hate the empty sound they make against the paper. Just for something to do, I pick up the red marker Mom's been using to edit her recipes and draw a giant heart on the page.

As I run the marker over the heart, quickly coloring it in, I can hear the now familiar sound of the waterfall in the distance. It pulses like the blood in my ears.

My mind races as I begin to cook up a plan, a way to make sure Clint and I won't be interrupted this time. A plan to make sure the wild, excited rhythm of my body— the rhythm that drums every time I see Clint—will get a chance to beat within the world's most perfect setting.

I flip through the rest of the notebook, drawing a giant red heart on each page and quickly coloring it until I hit the last blank sheet. On this page, I write a quick note.

Mind churning, I rip all my pages from the notebook. I grab the comforter off the twin bed in my room, fold it up, and tuck it under one arm.

I hurry out the door, shutting the screen on the note I've just written, and hurry down the front steps. My entire body is throbbing as I tuck myself into a thick patch of leaf-covered branches and wait for Clint to make his appearance.

When he shows, he's rushing. Probably faster than he's supposed to. He hurries up the porch steps, knocks on the door. Takes off his cap and smooths his hair. Raises a fist to knock again when he sees my note. He snags it and reads the message I scrawled for him:

Follow the hearts...

He darts for the porch railing as if to jump it, then pauses, obviously thinking better of it (probably remembering the doctor's warnings about reinjuring his shoulder—don't I know what *that's* like). He hurries down the steps.

I spear my first heart page through the lowest branch of a tree just beside the path stretching toward the waterfall. And I start to make my way up the trail, spearing pages of red hearts onto the lower limbs of trees. I look over my shoulder to see what kind of progress Clint's making. But I keep moving forward, even while glancing back, keeping myself in the cover of low-hanging limbs. I'm not quite ready for him to see me.

He keeps making motions with his hands as if to tell himself, *Just calm down and think.* He finally zeroes in on the first heart I've pinned. When he snags it off the tree, he's not too far away for me to see the smile break across his face.

He glances about, grabbing the heart off the next limb, the next...

I'm absolutely brimming with excitement. Not fear. Just pure elation, anticipation. Adrenaline breaks inside me, scattering warmth through my chest. I return to spearing hearts onto low limbs. I work my way slowly, almost feeling like I'm play-acting what slo-mo looks like. But this isn't a challenge, not like the day out there in the marsh on our ATVs. I'm not racing him. I *want* him to catch me.

Butterflies dance joyfully inside me when his feet snap a few twigs just behind my shoulder. He slips my last heart out of my hand before I can hang it on the tree in front of me.

"Finally ready to see that waterfall?" I hear him ask.

When I turn, he's folding my hearts, putting them in his back pocket.

"I wanted to see it for the first time with you," I tell him. I hold out my hand, which Clint fills with his warm, rough skin.

A fine spray pelts me as we hurry to the top of the hill. My breath bursts in harder, faster spurts as we near the peak. Good God—the sight that greets me as we round the top curve is absolutely majestic. Frothy white foam cascades over the top of a rocky cliff and pummels a small pond below. A stream of clear blue water flows back down the hill. Birds trill and flowers bloom everywhere—mist dots my skin and tangles itself up in my eyelashes.

Clint points out a flat rock where we can stand safely—high above the rest of the world, it seems—and watch bees flit from blossom to blossom in search of the sweetest nectar. We watch squirrels and a raccoon bravely come inches from our toes before racing off again. I gaze down into the glassy stream that flows into the Rainy River. The sound of the water is no mere rhythm—it's a melody. A love song. As I watch a small gray-winged bird (a dove, maybe?) swoop down for a drink, suddenly *I* have to get a taste of that water myself, have to feel it against my skin.

I scurry down the rocks as carefully as I can, Clint following behind me. At the edge of the wide pool at the base of the waterfall, I put the comforter down and start to kick my sneakers off, ready to ease my body into the water, eager to feel gurgles and bubbles dancing up around me. This is the perfect place to pick up where we left off... this is no mere shower, but a *waterfall*. I want him to follow suit, to slip out of his shorts, kick off his shoes. But he just shakes his head.

"No," he tells me, picking the comforter up and motioning for me to follow. "I want to show you something."

He guides me along the edges of the rocks, closer to the waterfall itself. When we're close enough to reach out and touch the brutal stream, he shows me a pocket behind the falls where smooth rocks have formed a tiny little room—a sanctuary of cool peace behind the violent, pounding water.

I'm still drinking in the utter sweetness of our seclusion as Clint spreads the comforter across the stone ground. "Perfect," he says, sitting down on it.

I finally get my feet to move, and I sit on the blanket beside him.

The waterfall's mist dances across our arms. I reach out to draw a small heart on his forearm, the way little kids draw on rain-soaked windows.

Clint picks up my hand, puts it against his chest. I can

feel his heart beating so hard it must hurt. "That's for *you*," he whispers.

We start kissing as though we'd never once been interrupted—not by George on the night we fooled around in the lake, not by my mom, not by nagging guilt. And certainly not by the ancient (or not-so-ancient) histories of our own loves. It's as though all the should-we-or-shouldn't-we's never bloomed and spread like weeds. As though neither one of us has ever worried about breaking someone else's heart or dishonoring the past. As though neither one of us has ever been hurt. Or afraid.

The outside world evaporates. Desire—*that's* the only thing that fills the space between us. Only there *isn't* any space, not when we wrap our arms around each other, pull our bodies together. Somehow, though, even with our chests pressed tightly against each other, we aren't close enough. Clint pulls off my cami and peels his damp T-shirt from his glistening chest. Skin on skin, and still, it isn't what either of us need.

He tugs at my shorts, pulling them down to my ankles. I kick them away and slip my fingertips into the sides of my panties. I'm completely, gloriously naked. Clint's breath draws goose bumps as he kisses the back of my neck…my arms.

We tangle around each other like lady slippers twisting to move beyond the shade. Searching out the heat of our passion the way a flower seeks the heat of the sun.

His mouth is everywhere—my breasts, my nipples. My hands follow the hard muscles in his abdomen. We lie intertwined on our bed as the mist continues to paint our bodies with a heavy coating of dew. Our hair shimmers in the fragrant spray.

We rock together like two boats bobbing on a current. He chases running droplets of mist down my skin with his tongue. I race my fingers down his legs, vowing not to let a centimeter of his skin go untouched.

Mist and sweat and desire tumble down my back and breasts and arms.

This is right. The words keep swirling through my mind like a whirlpool.

Clint quickly rolls on a condom he's pulled from his own cast-aside shorts, his breath heavy with emotion.

Don't stop, I tell myself as I straddle his gorgeous body. I can feel him against the inside of my leg, every bit as feverish as the heat that pulses inside me.

"Chelsea," he moans. "Please—"

He doesn't have to ask again.

Clint
final play

I've got this buzz—my arms feel loose, my legs like mush. Drunk on Chelsea. Even after we leave the waterfall, after I drop her off, drive back home. After I spend hours in my own bed, staring up at the ceiling of my room, the buzz doesn't die. I relive it, what happened at the waterfall. But every time I *do* relive it, my buzz only gets stronger.

Wow. Stupid, but that's what I just keep thinking—*wow.*

The next morning, Mom announces she's scheduled an appointment with our family doctor to have my shoulder looked at. Make sure I'm not overdoing it.

For God's sake. On Chelsea's last day of vacation.

"What's wrong with you?" she asks in the waiting room as I jiggle my leg and snort and rub my face.

I shake my head. Not like I'm going to admit I've got a thing going with a vacationer. One whose dad trusted me to be professional.

By the time the appointment's finally over, *and* Mom drives back home, *and* I grab the keys to the truck *and* I get back to the resort, it's practically dinner time.

I check the dining room of the lodge first, grateful to find the entire Keyes family crowded around a table, an emptied plate in front of each of them.

"We could totally move here," Brandon is saying. "There's got to be a high school for me to go to, and you guys could bring White Sugar up here—I bet you could supply the lodge with all their desserts. Mom said herself that Chef Charlie's not a baker. You'd rack it *up*. And Chelsea's going to be gone anyway."

It's silly, but I start to get excited by the idea. Chelsea coming home to Minnesota during her semester breaks, the two of us having Christmas together...

But her dad laughs. "Think you're just trying to hold on to your good thing at Pike's," he says.

Brandon shrugs, coolly.

"'Course, you realize you wouldn't have much of an audience in the winter," Earl says, passing by their table. "Snows so much here it reaches the eaves of this very lodge. Nobody'd be able to get outta their houses to come hear you."

I catch Chelsea's eye, raise my hand in greeting.

She gives me this smile—the kind of soft grin that can

only come from a woman who's seen you from the inside out.

Brandon and her parents follow her gaze, stare right at me.

"You're leaving?" Brandon asks, as Chelsea's chair squeals across the tile. "She's leaving, but I can't play one more gig," he says loudly.

"We have to get up at the crack of dawn to get back home, bud," his dad tells him. "The way the Dwellers play, you guys would still be onstage when we need to pull out of town. Okay? It's best this way, trust me."

Brandon glares at Chelsea. "I don't get to play one more gig, but *she* gets to do God-knows-what with—"

"Can it," Chelsea interrupts. "I think you'll live."

Brandon's face hardens, and her parents eye me. And here I am without a fishing pole, or a digital camera, or a Mae West. But right now, Chelsea and I only have a few more hours left. And I can't waste time caring how it looks when we race out of the lodge, jump in the cab of my truck, and take off without a single alibi.

———

"It's like some cruel joke, the way time flies," Chelsea says as we walk down a creek toward the edge of the lake. Her hand's warm in mine, but her words are cold in my chest.

"Come on," I say, using a couple of rocks as stepping stones to cross the creek and leading her into a field covered with wildflowers. They're gorgeous—almost as pretty as Chelsea is tonight, her yellow hair streaming across her tan shoulders.

"You know," I add, pointing at the closest orchid, "the moment these flowers finally reach full bloom is the same moment they start to die."

"Cheery," Chelsea says. "Thanks."

"You started it," I tease. "With all that talk about time flying."

I reach out and snap a stem.

"*Hey*," Chelsea moans. "That's not a lady slipper, is it? What happened to all that do-not-pick-under-penalty-of-law stuff?"

I show her the head of the dried-up daisy I've pulled off.

"Just when you meet someone special and start to get close, *wham*. Vacation's over. The moment you find something beautiful," she goes on, staring at my dead flower, "time's up. Got to move on."

"But the thing is," I say, twirling the black bud, "just because a flower isn't going to be around very long doesn't make it any less special when it does bloom—I mean, you *plant* flowers knowing they're not going to be around forever, right?"

She squeezes my hand. "Are we going to talk in flower analogies all night?"

"I think I'm being very poetic and touching. Only took me two years to figure this out. And you," I add. "Two years, and you."

"And a waterfall," she whispers.

She wraps her arms around my waist, stoops a little to tuck her chin into my neck. "You make me feel strong," she murmurs.

"Well, you know, that's how I planned the whole thing. I *meant* to launch myself off that ATV. I had that dislocated shoulder in here all along." I tap the side of my head.

"Mmm-hmm," she says. "Sure. Seriously, though. Strength doesn't just have to do with the physical stuff, with how many miles you can run. How much weight you can bench press. I get that, too. Took me a year, almost. A year—and you."

She lifts her head and juts her chin out, her lip wiggling a little. "So, I told you," she says, clearing her throat. "I told you I didn't need any promises. But I think I've changed my mind."

"Good," I say, pushing a flyaway strand of hair behind her ear. "It'll feel good to make a promise to you."

"Promise me," she says, looking me square in the eye, "that from now on, there won't be any more living timidly. Not like you did these last two years. No more hiding away from *anything* that scares you. From here on out, you'll—get out there and devour life."

"Only if you will, too," I tell her.

"Of course."

"To never living timidly," I say.

"Sounds like you're making a toast," she giggles.

But instead of the two of us clinking glasses, I bring my mouth to hers—sweet and strong.

Our kiss lingers, neither one of us wanting to let go.

When we do finally come up for air, Chelsea's eyes wander past my shoulder, across the landscape. Almost like she's trying to memorize what it looks like.

"They're looking for mates, you know," she says with a grin, pointing into the grass. "The lightning bugs? They blink to kind of hit on each other."

With my arms around her waist, I lower my face toward hers again. Just before I close my eyes, I notice that the fireflies are settling deep into the grass, turning their lights out for the night.

Love found.

Chelsea
handling skills

The ring of a cell phone wakes me from the nap I'm taking in the back seat of the Explorer. I rub my eyes, still trying to hang on to the dream I was having of walking down Main Street, weaving between the booths at Willie Walleye Day, staring down at our hands—mine and Clint's—and delighting in the way our fingers look like saplings that have grown entwined around one another. Trees you couldn't pull apart if you tried.

I don't want to leave Minnesota, I dreamed of breathing into Clint's neck.

Then don't, I dreamed he answered, just before leaning in to kiss me. *Don't.*

I'm still imagining what paradise that would be when

Brandon reaches down to grab my phone from the front pocket of my green handbag.

"Hey!" he says. "Yeah, it was *so* cool. Met a couple of guy who played, too—yeah—no, I took Annie with us. So we formed our own band—the Bottom Dwellers. And we had a steady gig at this kind of bar and grill, Pike's Perch— No, I'm serious. Yeah—"

"Wait," I mumble as I unfold my legs. My entire body feels stiff and cramped after an entire day on the road. "Who called *you* on my cell?" I ask.

"Nobody," Brandon answers with a shrug. "It's Gabe for you."

Noises of disgust rattle in my throat as I hit Brandon on the back of the head. "Give me my phone," I snap.

Offended, Brandon holds the cell just out of my reach. "No."

"Brandon! It's *my* phone!" Our struggle actually rocks the SUV on its axles.

Mom turns around in the front passenger seat, a tired scowl etched into her face. "Listen, you two. What do you think you are, three years old? I know we've been in the car a long time, but we'll be home in an hour and a half. If you don't start behaving like grown-ups, you can walk the rest of the way."

"Fine," Brandon says. "Ask me nice."

"Give me my phone, you nasty, smelly bottom dweller."

"That's more like it."

I snatch the cell and take a deep breath. I haven't actually spoken to Gabe since the day I bought all those postcards—the day he asked if something was up. I'm not exactly sure how this conversation will go, and to add insult to injury, it's going to play itself out with Brandon and my parents listening in. "Hey," I say quietly.

"Hey, Chelse. Sorry—couldn't wait for you to call me. I knew today was the big day. Your homecoming."

Before vacation, this probably would've melted my heart. Today, it hurts for a hundred different reasons. Mostly, talking to Gabe makes Clint already seem like a whole world, an entire lifetime away. And only this morning I'd watched him waving sadly from the dock as we shut the door of cabin number four for the last time. Tears start to bubble. What am I going to *say*?

"Good to hear your voice again," I offer weakly.

"Thanks for the postcards," Gabe says. "I loved seeing your handwriting waiting for me when I got home from work. Mostly, though, I was just happy you were thinking of me every day."

I force myself to swallow a bitter sob as I remember automatically dropping a new, pre-written postcard in the lodge mail slot every morning. "Mom said we'll be home in about an hour and a half," I blab, for lack of anything else to say.

"Really? Tell you what—I'll be getting off work soon, so why don't I just meet you?"

"Well, I … don't know for sure … I mean, it could take longer."

"That's okay," Gabe says. He suddenly seems so needy to me—clutchy, almost. But then again, why would it bother me that he wants to see me? This is the longest we've ever been apart. If Gabe had left for vacation, wouldn't I be anxious to see him?

"See you soon," he says, just before clicking his cell off.

My heart fills with lead.

———————

Two hours later, as the evening haze glistens on Fair Grove's horizon, we pull into our driveway. Gabe's sitting on the front porch—though I'd hoped the extra thirty minutes it took us to get here would have discouraged him, would have sent him back to his own house. He waves and hurries across the lawn to the car door.

What are you going to do, Chelsea? I ask myself. *He'll know. He's got to know…*

But Gabe just throws his arms around me like I've never gone away on vacation at all. Like we're just picking up where we'd left off on graduation night, the two of us standing in a field staring at my star while the rest of the senior class *woo-hoos* at us from the street.

"Man, you got strong," he says. "I forgot what it was like when we met and you were so full of muscle."

"I guess I did beef up a little," I babble. "Probably look different than the last time you saw me."

He shrugs. "No—I mean, yeah, a little. And you're really tan. But it's still you. You could shave your head and wear a burlap sack and I'd still think you're beautiful."

Okay, daggers are flying straight into my heart and tearing out enormous chunks.

"Hey, Gabe," Brandon says, jumping from the car. For the first time in my entire life, I feel grateful the little nitwit's around. "I've got some pictures of my band. I'll show you when I unearth my camera."

"He's really serious," Gabe says, wagging his thumb at Brandon. "I mean, I always heard him and his friends playing when I came over, and they seemed pretty good and all, but—a real band? You guys were gone only three weeks."

I nod. "He's on fire now. He'll probably get another band together around here before summer's over. Good thing I'll be in a dorm room in a matter of weeks," I add with a roll of my eyes.

"Gabe, hon, we haven't eaten yet," Mom calls. "You want to stay for a late dinner? I could go to the store—"

What I wouldn't give right now for a Mother Vaporizer...

"No way, Mrs. Keyes," Gabe says. I've just started to breathe a sigh of relief when he adds, "You guys've been on the road all day. I thought Chelsea and I could drive to Hill Toppers', bring back a couple of deep dishes. How's that sound?"

By this point my heart is so torn apart, I'm not quite sure how it could still be beating. "That's really sweet," I say truthfully. How could I forget how sweet Gabe Ross really is? What the hell have I *done*?

"Come on, Chelse," Gabe urges.

"I'll throw your bags in your room for you," Dad offers.

Gabe smiles as we head toward his 'Stang. "Get a bomb diffused over your vacation, too?" he asks, nodding back toward Dad.

"Yeah," I say, watching Dad carry my bag inside. "Maybe so."

I reach for the handle on the passenger side door of Gabe's car. But I stop, my eyes trailing across the immaculate automobile. I remember Clint's old GMC, all scuffed and banged. Rust spots. Torn seats. Roll-down windows instead of AC. The two vehicles suddenly seem as different as a wildflower in a field and a rose in a vase.

I climb in, aching for the sweet smell of something wild.

Gabe drives around the corner, veers the car straight toward the curb and shifts into park. "Come here and say hello to me like you couldn't with your parents watching," he whispers.

I lean in to kiss Gabe, shocked by the taste of his lips. I've grown so used to Clint, who tasted like sweat and heat and passion and sun and sex, that the taste of Gabe surprises me. He tastes like sweetness and comfort and safety and even, somehow—innocence.

I give in to Gabe's kiss, letting it linger as long as possible. I refuse to pull away—until the thought crosses my mind that maybe I kiss differently now, after Clint.

"I missed you so much, Chelse," Gabe says, running his fingers down my cheek.

He doesn't suspect a thing—which relieves me and also makes me feel absolutely sick.

Clint
substitution

S houldn't be cooped up in here," I say, sticking my head into the office of the Lake of the Woods main lodge. Kenzie looks up, the glow from her computer screen washing her face harshly. Or maybe it's the *frown* that washes harshly across her face.

"Must have bumped your head in that fall, Morgan," she grumbles, then turns back toward the screen.

"Girl like you," I stutter. "Shouldn't—ah—shouldn't—" I can feel my cheeks flaming.

"What's the matter with you?" she asks.

I rub my face. This is harder than I thought it'd be.

"I'm—I'm finally taking you up on your offer," I say. "Or—I'm—you've always seemed like you were open—I mean—"

"Where's this coming from?" she asks, leaning back in her chair. "I'm not stupid. And I'm not deaf, either. I've heard all the gossip around here. You and that basketball player. Talk *exploded* after that little accident of yours. Just confirmed every single thing I already knew was going on after I saw you two at Willie Walleye Day—and when I was out there sitting on the dock, watching you coming back from her *cabin*." She grimaces, like she's kicking herself internally.

My instinct is to just nod and tuck my tail between my legs as I slip back out of the office. But my promise to Chelsea keeps bouncing around inside my head—*no more living timidly*—so I force myself to keep forging ahead, like a moron.

"It's—taken me a long time," I stammer. "To even think about dating. And now I'm finally asking if you—you want to have dinner?"

"As in—dinner," she repeats.

"I'm really bad at this," I say. "Can I just take you someplace nice? This Friday? To make up for all the time it took me to get here?"

She sighs, her shoulders falling. But her scowl is gone, and a smile slowly starts to spread.

Chelsea
switch

"Found my camera!" Brandon calls as Gabe and I step inside with two enormous, piled-high pizzas.

"Nothing formal," Mom adds from the living room. "We're eating in the comfortable chairs tonight."

Gabe opens the two pizza boxes on the coffee table and we all help ourselves, each of us insisting that Hank at Hill Toppers' is in fine form tonight. Everyone but Brandon, who's thrusting his digital camera in Gabe's face.

As he starts to yammer on about the Dwellers, I stare at the browned cheese on my slice and remember graduation night all over again. I think about the me who stood on the sidewalk outside of the pizzeria, bidding her former teammates an awkward goodbye. About how she had no idea what she would discover in Minnesota. My ears fill, for a moment, with the pulse of a waterfall.

"Here's Pike's," Brandon says, pointing at the back of the camera. He tosses his hair away from the rim of his glasses. I notice he's stopped trying to gel the hair into place, letting it go all wavy around his ears; apparently Kenzie really did tell him she liked his crazy hair. I can't stop myself from rolling my eyes at him.

"So we were kind of a cross between Kings of Leon and Fall Out Boy, but we had our feet firmly planted in the *roots*, you know?" Brandon brags as Gabe keeps pushing the button on the back of the camera to view the photos. Brandon's talking like he's being interviewed by *Rolling Stone*. "Sex Pistols and the Stones, and I can see myself really branching out. I've been writing a few songs—"

"Who's this?" Gabe asks. "He's in an awful lot of these photos."

My face falls when he pushes the camera under my nose. In the picture, Clint and I are standing on the dock—open-mouthed, obviously laughing. When Gabe flips backward through the stream of photos, there we are again, on a hiking trail. Or climbing into his GMC. Here Clint is, helping me out of his boat during our first fishing trip. My stomach starts doing somersaults. *Brandon, you moron,* I want to shout. *Why on earth would you take so many pictures of the two of us?*

I watch Gabe in horror, wishing I could read his mind. What is he thinking? Good God, are Clint and I looking at each other in a telltale way in any of those photos? Can Gabe see in our faces what we'd done?

Worse yet—what if Brandon snapped a shot of me and Clint holding hands? Or *kissing*?

"Just my personal trainer," I say, yanking Brandon's camera out of his hands.

"*Chelsea*," Gabe says, frowning.

"Sorry—sorry. Just wanted to show you my—my— enormous catch—my walleye," I lie. "It's got to be here somewhere. I'm not such a bad fisher," I add, trying like hell to seem nonchalant.

"Chelsea found out she's good at lots of things over vacation," Dad says from behind a mouthful of mush-rooms and pepperoni. "She rescued that trainer when he wrecked his ATV."

"Chelsea?" Gabe says, impressed. "No kidding?"

"I shouldn't have been racing him," I say, and instantly regret it. *Why would you race your trainer? Someone you work with? Isn't that something you do when you're goofing off? You don't goof off with a trainer. You goof off with the guy you're fooling around with behind your sweet boyfriend's back…*

"Well, I tend to think Chelsea's pretty good at any-thing she tries." Gabe smiles at me as he adds, "I'd believe she spent the summer catching great white sharks, or res-cuing shipwrecked tourists from deserted islands." But his smile quickly gives way to a concerned frown. "Are you hot? Your face is all red."

"Hot," I agree, stupidly, fanning my face with my

hand. "I think I got overheated this afternoon in the Explorer."

"Get real. We had the air on full-blast," Brandon argues, rolling his eyes at me like I've lost my mind.

"Scratches!" I shout, scooping him into my arms. "Scratches, I missed you so much." I squeeze him to my chest, bury my nose in his neck, let his whiskers tickle my cheek, hoping that everyone will take this little distraction as an opportunity to find something else to talk about.

"Before I forget," Gabe says, wiping orange smears of grease from his mouth. "I bought two tickets to an exhibition game at MSU."

"*Awesome*," Dad says, leaning, as he hasn't in ages, on his high school lingo, his eyes lighting up at the idea of me being back in a gym. Any gym. Even the bleachers of a gym. "Basketball game?"

Gabe nods. "Lady Bears. Figured we could spend the night with my brother at his place so we won't have to drive back exhausted."

"Good plan," Dad nods. "Worst thing you can ever do is drive tired."

Yet again, the Gabe Ross charm has its advantages. Dad (thank God the high school gossip about journalism camp never made its way to the parents) would never even suspect that Gabe and I would do anything other than go to the game and bed down on separate couches.

I begin to relax a little. A basketball game sounds amazing, actually. I can already taste the popcorn. Maybe, by now, I won't even mind so much being in the concession stands during halftime, instead of a locker room. Every athlete has to make that transition at some point. Mine just came a little earlier than I'd anticipated. Right?

"Only hitch is, the game's the day after tomorrow," Gabe says. "It's short notice—"

"Oh, don't be silly," Mom says, waving him off. "We've had Chelsea for three weeks. Now it's your turn. I'm sure you guys want some quality time before your fall semesters start and you both take nose-dives into textbooks."

Ever since the Explorer hit the city limits, I've been so wrapped up in guilt I've forgotten how *easy* it is to be with gorgeous, sweet Gabe Ross. Now, though, I begin to unwind, begin to imagine being with Gabe on campus as soon-to-be freshmen, hand-in-hand, walking across the quad toward the sports arena...

After dinner, Mom gathers our plates and I walk Gabe to the door.

"Thanks for the pizza," I tell him as I shut the door behind us and head out toward his 'Stang. "That really was incredibly thoughtful." *Would Clint ever be that thoughtful?* I wonder. Hard to know for sure, since we were never allowed to admit to being a couple in front of my family.

"And the MSU game sounds—"

"I don't have tickets," Gabe says, his eyes sparkling playfully.

"But you said—"

"Come on, Chelse. You didn't *forget*, did you? Didn't you count down the days of your vacation like I did? The game was the only cover-up I could come up with. The only excuse I could think of to explain why you would be away with me all night."

"There's no game?"

"Oh, there's a game. At MSU, just like I said. And that's why I made reservations for the Carlyle that same night."

The Carlyle. My stomach starts to churn like ocean waves during a typhoon.

"The Carlyle," I repeat. "Night after tomorrow."

He nods, squeezing my hand. "Don't be nervous," he whispers into my ear. "It's just us—there's nothing to be nervous about *us*, right?"

I nod as he leans in for a good-night kiss.

He'll know, I think as Gabe wraps his arms around me. *He'll know I'm not a virgin anymore.*

Clint
long shot

Seems pretty quiet around here," Todd says, cracking open his third can of Bud.

"You drink all the beer, you have to bring it next time," Greg warns, like he always does, though he never follows through on his threats.

Todd's right—out here night fishing (*really* night fishing, not lying to be alone with Chelsea), the whole world seems empty except for the three of us. Our lines drift lazily along the surface of the lake. The water sloshes against the side of the Minnow. Whenever I hear water anymore—a rush, a gurgle, even the trickle from the faucet in my bathroom—I think of Chelsea. For a second, I swear I can taste her.

"That Brandon, man, he kept us busy," Todd goes on,

slurping off the top of his can. "Maybe we could advertise on Craigslist or something for another bass player."

"Maybe," Greg says. "Hard to find somebody that good."

"Or somebody who shows up to practice," Todd agrees in a half-sigh.

"You're quiet tonight, Morgan," Greg says, attempting to stretch his legs in the cramped skiff. "You going to come listen to me and Todd limp along without a bass at Pike's tomorrow?"

"No," I say quietly. "I have a—date—actually."

You'd think my words started some sort of tidal wave out in the middle of the lake, the way Todd grips the side of the boat.

"With *who*?" he asks.

"Kenzie," I breathe.

Todd starts muttering something about *lucky bastard,* while Greg just stares at me, squinting as he leans against the side of the boat. "Huh," he mutters. "And here I was thinking this resort probably felt quieter to you than it did to either of us."

It does, I think, but I just shake my head, tighten my line. Chelsea's a past tense. Summer will be over soon. I can't go brooding over her like I did for Rosie.

I reel in my line to bait my hook again. *Don't live timidly,* I tell myself as I cast out into the lake.

Chelsea
indecisive move

My computer screen glows blue against my skin. I've just finished packing my bag for the Carlyle, filling it with a flattering, nearly sheer azure dress and the raciest panties in my drawer. Which strikes me as a little weird, actually, since I didn't worry in the least about having to dress up for Clint. Just threw on a red cami and shorts and raced up the trail behind cabin number four.

It's late, and my eyes keep trying to close. My entire body begs me to get to bed. But instead of turning my computer off and slipping into the cool envelope of my sheets, I reach into my top desk drawer and pull out a torn-off scrap of paper napkin—the email address Clint gave me before dropping me off at the cabin our last night at Lake of the Woods.

"Whaddaya know?" I'd teased him. "Guess even fishing guides can be a *little* high-tech."

I stare at the address awhile, touching my lips with my fingertip, hoping like hell that being with Gabe won't make me forget exactly how Clint's mouth felt, traveling over every inch of my body.

What's wrong with me? Last month, I'd bemoaned the fact that I was the oldest virgin on the planet. Tonight, I'm planning on sleeping with guy number two—in the same *week*? Have I gone from being a virgin to complete slutsville in a matter of days?

I place the napkin near the top of the keyboard, click on "New Message," and type in Clint's address. I stare at the screen, wishing I could tell him everything that swarms through my heart—how much I miss him. How much I wish we were still bowling and fooling around in the lake and making out in his truck. How much I miss the carefree breeze that blew into my heart whenever I was around him.

My cell phone starts to vibrate, buzzing against the desktop. I pick it up hesitantly.

"Hey, Chelse, it's me," Gabe says softly. "Got a clock handy?"

I glance at the bottom right hand corner of my computer screen. "Midnight."

"You know what that means, right?" Gabe asks.

"It's the day you and I have been waiting for all summer."

"The day I've been waiting for ever since I met you," Gabe corrects. "Love you," he whispers.

"Mmm," I say. "Me, too."

I click the phone off, my eyes falling on the cursor that blinks like an elbow nudging me in the ribs. Saying, *Come on already, write your message.*

Instead, I click *cancel draft* and sign out of my email account.

Scratches pushes open the bedroom door and mews his way across the floor. When he jumps onto the bed, he knocks my purse on its side—and Clint's compass tumbles onto the comforter. I let Clint think I'd dropped it from the ATV somewhere ... selfish of me, since he seemed to love the old thing. But it saved us, in a way. I just never had the heart to give it back.

I pick up the compass and curl up with Scratches, both our heads propped on my bed pillow. As I stare into his sweet sleeping face, I start to get jealous of his simple life. He's never found himself in the kind of tangled mess I'm in right now. He's never felt like his heart was in a tug-of-war.

I place Clint's old compass on the pillow beside me. But the only place it points tonight is toward sleep.

Clint
game time

It's not a completely foreign place, her parents' house. When I was a kid, I'd ride bikes with Greg and Todd past Kenzie's yard, and there she'd be on her porch, giant glasses on the end of her nose and a book in her lap. She was nothing compared to Rosie back then. *But maybe*, I try to convince myself, *it'll be nice to be with a girl who's known me such a long time. Maybe this'll be just what I need...*

I park the truck at the curb and rush to Kenzie's porch, getting so sweaty you'd think I was going to a job interview.

As soon as I knock, I close my eyes to try to steady my nerves. My mind drifts, though, and I see a fleshy lady slipper and the green, tall grass that surrounds the resort. I see flashes of sun-kissed skin. My nose fills with the clean, peachy-sweet smell of soap; laughter rings in my ears.

When the door opens, a simple white dress fills the space. But I start to knot up inside when I see wavy brown locks trickling down the front of her chest. Not blond.

When my eyes trail up and I see Kenzie's face, disappointment rattles me. I try to shove down my wish that it was Chelsea standing in the doorway instead.

"You okay?" Kenzie asks, tilting her head.

"Shoulder still aches a little," I lie.

"Oh," she frowns, using it as an excuse to touch my arm.

"I'll be okay," I tell her. I rush to open the passenger side door of the truck. I hope a little chivalry scores me enough points that she'll forget about how weird I acted when she opened the door.

Chelsea
indoor sport

As Gabe checks us into the Carlyle, the man at the counter eyes us with the most suspicious look I've ever seen in my life. Gabe stares that check-in guy down like he's just daring him to say something. But I don't really have time to care *what* the guy thinks, not with all my seesawing...

Me and Clint steaming up the windows of his truck.

Gabe giving me a star in my own name.

Me and Clint at the bowling alley.

Gabe and the nearly two years we've spent holding hands.

Clint and the roaring excitement I got just *touching* his hand.

Gabe and the sticky goo he could reduce my heart to with any one of his romantic gifts.

Sweet, sweet Gabe, I think, just as every single moment of our history together starts to float through my mind: long talks on our cells at night, kisses on my doorstep, late nights at dances, shared lunches in the Fair Grove High cafeteria. Most of all, I think about my hospital bed, about his face being the first I saw when I opened my groggy, post-surgery eyes. I think about our plan to stay devoted to each other when we go to college.

Okay. So I've taken a slight detour from the plan. But it was only a detour. So I had a summer fling. Big deal. Everyone has summer flings. *Everybody.*

What am I doing, standing here trying to sort things out? Isn't it all perfectly clear? Why would I ever throw someone as wonderful as Gabe Ross out the window over some guy I had a three-week fling with?

Gabe has been mine throughout the toughest year of my life. He loved me even as my whole world broke apart. And I loved him, too—*love.* I *love* him, too. Sure, it was different with Clint. But different isn't necessarily better, is it?

Gabe is the future, I tell myself. Clint's some blip in the past. Clint is over. Gabe is right now—and he's waiting for me.

"Room 403," Gabe says, as he slips my overnight bag from my hand.

Clint
between plays

The restaurant is so uptight and stuffy, I can barely breathe. Yeah, it's nice and all—linen napkins and a guy whose only job, apparently, is to attack crumbs on the tablecloth. But the walls are closing in. And as the silence at my table beats in my ears, I start to wish one of those rescue buttons was close by, the ones on elevator walls— red *in-case-of-emergency* buttons. I wish I could press it, so that somebody could save me from the too-small dining room with no air at all.

Not just *someone.* My mind keeps drifting back to Chelsea.

"Dessert?" one of the stuffy waiters asks.

"No," Kenzie answers. "Just the check." And when he disappears, she says, "Not your style, Morgan. I thought it was weird that you wanted to take me here in the first place."

"Trying a little too hard to impress, I guess," I agree.

"It's okay," she says, running a finger over the top of her water glass. "I like that you're trying to impress me." The skin around her eyes crinkles as she smiles at me.

But this feels tight, too, this conversation. Uncomfortable as hell. "Guess—guess I'm more like a beer and a burger at the edge of the lake," I mutter.

"To the lake, then," Kenzie tells me, leaning over the top of the table, angling so that my eyes hit the drooping-open top of her dress.

Chelsea
fake out

G abe," I breathe as I step inside. "You must've spent every last dime you've made on our room."

"Not every dime. Close, though," he teases as he puts down our overnight bags.

"This is like a suite that some movie-star couple would rent for their honeymoon," I say, staring at the enormous crystal chandelier, the luxurious draperies, the lush coverings on the king-sized bed.

"Why don't you freshen up?" Gabe says, nodding toward the bathroom. "I'll order dinner."

I nod. "Freshen up" means getting out of the darkwashed jeans and plain T-shirt I'd worn to make it look like I really was going to a game in Springfield. I drag my bag into the bathroom, where I slip into my gauzy blue dress with spaghetti straps, racy thong, and a pair of strappy sandals. I try to work magic with my makeup brushes, hoping that an extra layer of concealer is all I need to hide every second thought that keeps bubbling to the surface.

When I finally emerge from the bathroom, Gabe jumps to his feet from the edge of the bed. "Perfect timing," he says, smiling at me nervously. "Dinner just arrived."

He points toward a small table draped with Irish linen and dotted with covered sterling dishes. A bottle of bubbly on ice serves as the centerpiece. I realize that in the time I've been gone, Gabe's changed into a suit coat and tie and has turned down the bed, exposing ivory-colored satin sheets. He's also taken it upon himself to spread rose petals all over those sheets, to light candles, and to place a nosegay of red roses beside my dinner plate.

"You look beautiful, Chelsea," he says softly. He fidgets like he isn't sure what to do next. I have to admit, the pressure of it all is hitting me, too—sure, I've done this before, but not in such a structured way. Which is exactly the way it feels. Not romantic. *Structured.*

Back at White Sugar, on grad night, when Gabe had talked about sex at prom being a cliché, I'd felt lucky that he wanted to take the time to do things on our own terms. Now, it seems like we've spent way too much time *waiting* for the right moment to happen instead of just making it happen, the way I had with Clint. Injury aside, what does it say about us, that we've never made the moment happen in almost two solid years of dating? What does it mean that sex has never been a have-to thing with us? Being at the Carlyle with Gabe, now, makes me feel like we've missed our opportunity and we're here to compensate—like taking a makeup exam or something.

Stop thinking so much, I scold myself. I throw my arms around Gabe's neck and kiss him. I kick off the strappy heels I've just put on and grab his tie.

From the look in his eyes—a mix of thrill and wonder and, yes, maybe even a little fear—*fear?*—I can tell he thinks we're skipping dinner entirely. Or, at least, that I'm skipping the appetizer and heading straight for the main course.

"Wait. First," he says, pulling our bubbly from the ice, uncorking it, and pouring two full glasses. "To tonight," he says, holding his glass as he proposes a toast.

And that's all it takes to bring Clint into the room. Gabe's toast brings me back to that last night—I hear, again, Clint saying, *To never living timidly.* Suddenly Clint's everywhere, showing me everything that's wrong with this night. Everything that's missing. I blink back the tears that well up in my eyes, hoping Gabe hasn't noticed.

Gabe clinks his glass against mine and we both tilt our heads back.

"Sparkling cider," I say.

"Stupid, I know, but I couldn't order champagne—no ID."

"It's wonderful," I say, because even though it's kind of a silly imitation, it really does soften the dry, nervous burn in the back of my throat.

I wrap my arms around Gabe's waist and kiss him,

powerfully. I can feel the beating of his heart against my own. His kisses wander to my neck as we edge our way toward the bed. Together, we tumble onto the slick sheets and rose petals.

It's the first time we've kissed this way since I've been back. *Really* kissed, our tongues tangling, hands running up and down each other's bodies.

But tonight, as Gabe kisses me, I can hear the sound of rushing water. Can feel drops of mist falling across my skin.

Clint
bodies in motion

I park the truck at the edge of the water that sparkles black beneath the moon. I don't even have the engine turned off yet when I feel her hand on my wrist. She swallows the distance between us in a single gulp—her hip against mine, her breast pressing against my biceps. Her mouth an arrow aiming for my own.

She's pulling my shirt from my slacks, tugging me forward. Without thinking, I'm suddenly pressing myself against her, stretching myself out flat—pushing her back against the seat of my truck. Pressing my hips against hers. Her touch is soft, her fingers warm on my skin.

Her lips? They're strong and wet and full of want.

But no *want* in me bubbles up out of my chest to answer hers.

I open my eyes to find her staring up at me.

Chelsea
forfeit

Gabe works his mouth down my chest, kissing me along the neckline of my dress. He tugs at my spaghetti straps and continues to kiss me, making his way toward my breasts. But all I can think of is Clint and how his body had felt against my own. How desperately I wanted him. And I know, as Gabe's mouth travels my chest, that I don't want him. Not the way I wanted Clint.

I can hear the promise Clint and I made to each other: *Never live timidly.* And I know going through with this night is the coward's way out. The tears I've been holding back burst forth, running down both cheeks.

Clint
dirty player

She wrenches away from me, pushes against my chest. She keeps pushing until we're both sitting up again. Bats me away angrily when I try to take her hand.

"This isn't your style, either," she says, pushing her hair from her face. "Lying like this."

"*Lying?*"

"Pretending's as good as lying."

"I want to be here, Kenzie," I insist.

When she finally does look at me, her dark brown eyes are glistening. "I'm such an *idiot*," she says. She raises her hands and lets them fall into her lap. "Just take me home."

"Kenz—let's not end the night like this—"

"I'm not mad, Clint, okay? I'm embarrassed, though. So don't make it any worse than it is—"

"I wasn't lying," I insist. "I really do want to be here."

"I know you do," she squeaks. "Just with somebody else." She rubs her face, shakes her head. "I've known you a long time, and you're a good guy, and you deserve to be happy, and in a way, I'm getting what I wanted."

"What're you talking about?" I ask. This night is completely wearing me out.

"I hoped you'd fall in love again," she admits. "And you did. Just not with me."

Chelsea
man-to-man defense

Gabe lifts his head, staring down at me with a puzzled expression. "Are you all right?"

I shake my head, wiping at my tears.

"Where are you tonight, Chelsea?" he asks. "Because you're definitely not with me."

I put a hand to my forehead. "Gabe—I'm just—"

"It's not nerves," Gabe says as he rolls away. "It's something else."

"You went to so much trouble, and I'm messing everything up."

"It wasn't *trouble*—it was what I wanted. I thought it was what you wanted, too."

"It was."

"Was, not is?"

I can't answer that—the words stick in my throat like splintered chicken bones.

"What's going *on,* Chelse?"

I sigh and sit up next to him; I pull my spaghetti straps onto my shoulders. I can tell, from the tightness in his lips, that anger is really bubbling up inside him.

"The night before you go on vacation, we spend hours making out under the stars," he says shortly. "Now, two days after you get back, you don't want to be here with me. The thought of making love to me makes you *cry?*"

"Gabe," I moan. "That's not it."

"Then *what?* Something's happened. Something's different. You can't deny that. I've felt it ever since you got back. God—even when we were walking into the hotel, I wasn't even sure this night was actually going to happen."

My tears roll one after another, each forging their own shiny path through my powdery makeup.

"Can I ask you something that might piss you off?"

I shrug and nod.

"Was there somebody else while we were apart?"

I turn my head away, and my shoulders heave with sobs.

"I knew it," Gabe mumbles. "I *knew* it," he repeats, louder this time.

"Gabe, please," I manage. I reach for his hand but he jerks away.

"It was the guy in the pictures, wasn't it? Your trainer? *Wasn't* it?" he yells, his voice racked with the kind of rage I've never seen in him before. "Was he even *really* your trainer, or was that a lie, too?"

"No—Gabe—he really was. Gabe—I'm—I'm just so sorry."

"Sorry about what? Me figuring it out? *Huh?*"

"No—about—this. All of this. Me hurting you."

"Mmm-hmm," he growls. "I'm sure you were real sorry when you were out with—whatever his name was."

"Don't be like that. I feel bad enough."

"No, Chelsea," Gabe barks, jumping off the bed. "I don't think you do. There's no *way* you feel as bad as I do. I'll tell you how you feel. You feel caught. But me? I feel like the whole *world's* changed. Don't you think I deserve more than this?" He starts pacing and running his hands through his hair so fiercely he looks like he's tearing his curls out. "Almost two solid *years* together, and you don't respect me enough to tell me to my face that you want to see other people? You just let me go on believing you want to be with me, and you run around on me behind my back? After everything I've done for you—after being there for you when everything else fell apart... I'll tell you something. You thought far more of your stupid fling this summer than you thought of me. And that's *not* okay."

Defensively, I lift my face, my eyes narrowed into slits. All I can think about, suddenly, is the fact that up until a few moments ago, I was ready to go through with this night to keep from hurting him. That I was about to have sex with him even though my heart wasn't in it. Wasn't *that* thinking of him? Wasn't that putting *him* first? Didn't he see how much I'd just been willing to give him?

Fury burns in my lungs. "And *you're* perfect?" I scream.

"Oh, yeah—I guess you are. Gabe Ross, Mr. Perfect. Beautiful Gabe Ross. Smart Gabe Ross. Disgustingly romantic Gabe Ross, who *revels* in reminding his girlfriend she's not a *star* anymore. I *get* it, Gabe. *You're* the perfect one, not me."

"Excuse me?" he bellows.

"Oh—and I almost forgot the best part. Gabe Ross sticks by his broken girlfriend *after* she stops shining. *After* she stops being such a catch. And he *loves* the fact that it also makes him a good guy—look at me, I'm with her even now, even after she's not everything I'd wanted in the beginning."

"I can't believe you're saying this to me," Gabe mutters. "After I *stayed with you.* I even decided to go to MSU because that's where you could afford to go after you lost any hope at a basketball scholarship."

"*There!*" I screech. "You admit it. I'm holding you back."

"That's not what I said—"

"It's *absolutely* what you said. I'm probably holding you back from all that *ass* you could have been scoring, too. With me, you've become some freaking born-again virgin," I taunt.

"You were *hurt,* Chelsea."

"It was more than that," I yell at him. "Everybody knows about you and that journalism geek at summer camp. But with me...?"

"Sex isn't love," Gabe says. "I never once thought we weren't a real couple because we hadn't had sex yet."

"It's part of love," I insist. "Romantic love."

"Romantic love," Gabe spits. "Like you're the expert.

Getting you to tell me you loved me while you were gone was like pulling teeth. Now I know why—he probably was listening in."

"Is that all that's important to you?" I bite back. "Me professing my undying love all the time? There's a difference between being romantic and being completely *stifling*, you know. God—forget Clint. You would have been upset with me anyway, even if he hadn't been in the picture! Was I supposed to be a good little girl and call you at five o'clock on the dot every single night? You were *jealous*, Gabe, and not because of some guy. You were actually getting upset because I wasn't fawning all over you all the time." I stop to get my breath, but the words keep coming. "Did the thought ever cross your mind that maybe I never needed you to rescue me, Gabe? Maybe I'm *still* pretty strong, even after the accident. Maybe I'm not some fragile little thing. Maybe *you* were holding *me* back."

"Don't you dare put this off on me," Gabe yells. "*You* did this, Chelsea. You destroyed us!" He grabs the cider bottle and throws it, letting it shatter against the far wall. I yelp and race into the bathroom, shutting the door behind me.

Never live timidly, my mind screams out. *Face this, Chelse.* But I can't; not yet; I don't know how. Did I really mean all those awful things I'd just said?

I put one hand on the marble counter and cover my mouth with the other. When a knock comes to the suite door, I hear Gabe answer, saying, "I dropped a bottle. I'll clean it up. Sorry to have disturbed the other guests."

I listen as he picks up all the broken pieces. And maybe, I tell myself a little desperately, there are a few other broken pieces we can start to gather—together. I'm not a hundred percent sure, in that moment, exactly what I want from Gabe—I only know that I don't want to completely trash the last two years. And that I don't want him to hate me.

After splashing cool water on my tear-soaked face, I open the bathroom door.

But when I step into the room, Gabe's already changed back into his jeans. He's shoving his tie into his overnight case. A cold electric shock travels through my body. "Gabe—where are you going?"

He doesn't answer, so I put my hand on his arm. He shakes it away. "You can't have it both ways, Chelse."

"But, Gabe, I—"

"Get the hell away from me, you selfish bitch," he says. He zips his case and storms out of the room, slamming the door behind him.

Clint
back in the game

I step inside Baudette Sporting Goods—and for the first time in two years, I let myself glance past the fishing gear that's just inside the entrance. I let myself look toward the shoes in the back. Cleats and basketball shoes and...

"Hey, man," Todd says. "How'd it go the other night? With Kenzie?"

Pulling my eyes from the shoe display is a little like trying to wrench myself out of a dream. I mumble "Hmm?" as Greg pops up out of nowhere, a new fly rod in his hand.

"Sorry. Got the last one," he tells me.

"Last one," I repeat, feeling completely disoriented.

"Rod. On sale. That's why you came, isn't it? When I saw you walk in, I assumed—"

I shake my head. "No—not today."

"So?" Todd presses, adjusting his ball cap by tugging on the bill. "How'd it go? With Kenzie?"

I shake my head. "I think—I've just—known her too long. Takes a little of the mystery out of it, right?"

Greg squints at me. "Known her too long," he repeats, because he knows it's bull. But I don't exactly want to spill everything in the middle of a sporting goods store, of all places. Or even really spill it to the guys, period.

How am I supposed to talk about it without looking like a complete moron? Now that I think about it, the night with Kenzie proved what I'd suspected all along—that the void Rosie left in my life wasn't ever going to get filled by just anybody. I needed Chelsea. Just wish I didn't have to embarrass Kenzie in the process.

If I say anything like that, they'll both swear I've lost it.

I push past the guys toward the shoe display.

"So, you're not interested? In Kenzie? Right?" Todd asks as he follows me.

I'm only half-listening as I scour the shelves for a size twelve. It doesn't seem possible, but the box is already standing out a little from all the rest, like the ghost of the old me's already tugged it out, left it waiting for me.

My heart's practically on fire as I open the box and take out the hockey skate. Just touching it, I can already hear the slice of the blades on a rink.

When I look up, Greg and Todd are staring at me with wide-eyed, shocked faces.

"Are you serious?" Greg asks, nodding once at the skates

"I kind of promised somebody," I say, and turn toward the checkout counter.

Chelsea
advance step

O ne down!" Brandon announces as he bounds through White Sugar holding the keys to the Explorer.

"We haven't made the delivery yet," Mom reminds him. "The deal is, you show me you can *deliver* twenty multi-tiered cakes in one piece—no skidding, no speeding, no careening—and we'll *start* to talk about buying you a car."

"Piece of cake, Ma," Brandon insists. "Pun intended." He grins at me and rolls his eyes.

I smile back at him, just like I've been smiling ever since he lied through his overbite (something about Gabe's 'Stang getting stalled on the highway to Springfield) in order to get his hands on the keys to the Explorer and come rescue me in my hour of need, the night Gabe left me deserted at the Carlyle.

My thumbs fly over the keypad on my phone, finishing up the three-thousandth text I've sent to Gabe these past few weeks: *u hate me u have evry rite im so sorry.*

"You going to be all right here by yourself, Chelse?" Mom asks, knocking on the front counter to get my attention.

"She's not alone," Dad corrects her. "I'm here."

"You'll disappear back into the office," Mom pouts.

"Not necessarily," Dad says, winking at me.

Mom tilts her head at us, a smile of relief washing over her face.

"Aw, don't shove me into the middle of your schmaltzfest," Brandon moans.

"Hey, mister," Mom snaps at him. "You're responsible for getting *two* of these layers into the Explorer. You drop one, no car."

"The way you keep adding on to our agreement makes me think I should have gotten you to put it in *writing*," he mutters.

I think she's nuts for trusting Brandon with one of her precious cakes. But I guess she figures he wants a car so badly that he'd rather lose a foot than dent a single icing rose.

"You'd do just fine without a car," Mom reminds him. "After all, our house is walking distance from school."

"I'm on the up-and-up, Mom. I gotta have wheels, period."

"Then stick to my rules, buster," Mom says. "Or else you'll be toting your Marshall amp around on your old Schwinn."

"Man," Brandon moans. After kicking at the tiles a few

times, he takes a deep breath and eases one of the boxed layers off the counter. "Comin' through!" he screams. "Watch out! Coconut cake walkin'!"

I shove the phone in the pocket of my White Sugar apron, lean my elbows on the counter. Let my eyes go bleary as my mind drifts into a daydream like the Explorer drifts into a stream of summer traffic—or, at least, what qualifies as traffic in Fair Grove.

"Chelsea, I'll take over the front counter," Dad tells me.

"I'm fine," I try to insist, but Dad nods toward the front window, telling me to look.

Gabe.

I clench my jaw, gritting my teeth as I watch him approach the post office with a handful of letters. I'm frozen as he disappears through the post office door. But when he reappears, heading straight for his 'Stang, I finally dislodge myself and rush out into the early August heat.

"Gabe," I shout. "Gabe, talk to me."

He shakes his head. "Just mailing Mom's bills."

"I tried to text you," I tell him.

"I wish you'd quit that," he says, through a mouth drawn tight.

"Please," I say, lurching in front of him, blocking him from opening the driver side door. "I've been thinking a lot about this, and I just—I wanted to tell you that I believe what you said that night we graduated. Remember? About the heart being like a compass. And it leads you either closer to a person, or it shows you another way. And if we were meant to be, our hearts would have led each other straight back here, to us. Not in different directions."

"*That's* what you've been thinking?" Gabe says. "That's the most selfish thing I've ever heard. I didn't go anywhere, Chelsea. *You* did. You don't get to feel good about it. You're not forgiven. Move."

He pushes me aside, leaves me standing stupidly in his old parking space. Watching him drive away.

As I turn toward the front walk, my prickling eyes hit a vine of purple flowers curling up an old trellis in the corner of the White Sugar building. The same flowers that grow in the field around the Fair Grove mill. The same flowers that filled the field behind cabin number four back in Minnesota. As tears threaten to roll, I close my eyes; I can still feel the itch of grass beneath my legs, Clint's breath on my cheek. Even now, I'm thinking of Clint.

My eyes are tingling as I step back inside. I hope Dad really will disappear into the office. At least then I won't have to be a blubbering idiot in front of an audience.

"Haven't seen Gabe around in a long time," Dad says.

Great. This is *exactly* the heart-to-heart I want to have right now.

"Not since the night of the MSU game," he goes on.

I nod.

"From the looks of what just went on out there," he says, nodding once toward the window, "it doesn't seem like he's coming back."

I clench my jaw and shake my head.

Dad pours an iced latte and puts an éclair on a plate,

slides it toward me. Like he thinks a little Bavarian cream might cut the bitter taste of losing my first real boyfriend. "I've seen you when you're passionate about something," he says. "I know what it does to you. Basketball, for instance. It was all-encompassing. But Gabe..." He frowns, shakes his head. "I never thought you and Gabe—you just didn't have that same look on your face. That look you got when you were still playing ball. That—passion. You had it over vacation, though."

My eyes widen.

"Oh, don't look so shocked. I know love...it has different shades. Sometimes, it's passion. Sometimes, though, it's just—"

"More like friendship," I finish.

Dad starts mopping the front counter.

"The heart is a compass," I say. "Steers us back to the thing we love the most."

I reach into my back pocket, pulling out the confirmation letter from MSU that I've been carrying around for a week. I've figured it out, just like Dad said the Chelsea of old would. I've figured out how to keep basketball in my life. But after the year we've had, it's been hard to find the right time to show it to him. *To not living timidly*, I think, as I toss the letter in front of his towel.

"You're already declaring a major?" he asks as he reads the letter. "Psychology?"

"*Sports* psychology," I say, and when Dad's eyes start to get all glittery on me, I cut the éclair in half, take my portion, and push the plate across the counter toward him.

Clint
second half

I sign the postcard and slip it into the mail drop at the lodge. I stare at the darkened slot a minute, a goofy grin plastered on my face.

"Another summer coming to an end," Earl sighs from the check-in counter.

I nod as I turn to attack my boot camp poster, ripping it from the wall. Little white pieces of paper stay speared under thumbtacks at each of the four corners.

"I hear you stopped in at a certain sporting goods store a while back," he says as he leans against the counter. A smile ekes out from under the blanket of his steel wool beard.

I shrug and nod, wadding the poster. "Never do know when a good pond game might break out."

"Just a pond game?"

"Oh, I think the dream of me playing college hockey's over, especially after all the time I've been away from it. But love is love—and you should never turn away from it completely. And I love hockey. Always have, really."

"Huh. Got hope for you yet," Earl says.

I chuckle as I toss the wadded-up poster toward the wastebasket. *Three points*, I think, the way people do when they pretend to play basketball. My nose fills with the peachy scent of soap and skin that I miss so much.

"You know, now that I've had time to think about it, that boot camp a' yours doesn't seem like such a bad idea after all. Sure was good for *you*, anyway," Earl says, giving me an all-knowing look.

I start to deny it, but Earl just shakes his head and says, "Too bad your shoulder put you out of commission, after that ball player. But there's always hope for next summer."

My eyes rove straight back to the mail drop that's swallowed my postcard. "Yeah," I say, my grin now as big as a moon on my face. "Maybe next year."

Chelsea
rebound

It takes a day and a half to cram all the stuff I bought for my dorm into my Camaro. When I'm finally through, I slam the trunk and dust off my palms.

"You sure you don't want us to drive you?" Mom says, worry flooding her face.

"Mom. Cell phone, GPS, not to mention the twelve hundred maps you shoved in the glove compartment. And it's not like I've never been to Springfield. I can practically see Springfield from here."

I kiss them all goodbye for the seventieth time, even Brandon. At least I try to kiss him, but he punches me in the shoulder instead. Once a little brother, always a little brother, I guess...

I slide behind the wheel, fasten my seat belt, and shout,

"Remind Scratches I'll be back to visit in a couple weeks." I can't take prolonging our goodbye any longer, so I put the car in gear and start to edge away from the house.

Brandon, in his true apathetic little sib form, steps off the curb and retrieves the mail from our box while Mom and Dad stay on the sidewalk, waving.

I inch the Camaro down the block. With no other cars around, I can use the stop sign as an opportunity to take a deep breath, shake off the goodbye sadness. I'm still adjusting my rearview when Brandon's image pops into the mirror. He races straight toward me, waving our mail over his head. "Chelsea!" he screams. "Wait! Wait!"

I put the car in park and wait for him to catch up to me. I stick my head out the window. "What is it?"

"Look! Look what came for you!"

I slip the postcard from Brandon's hand. It's postmarked Baudette. The picture on the front is the one Clint snapped of me holding my walleye. On the back, his messy script reads, *You won! Biggest catch of the season! You get your free week! See you next summer—Clint.*

"Man, you're so great," Brandon says. "Yes! This makes my year! Only ten more months till we can go back. The Bottom Dwellers reunion tour!" He races down the street, making *woo-hoo* noises all the way back to our house.

For a while, I can't quit staring at the postcard. When I finally do look up, I catch my reflection in the rearview mirror. I smile, liking what I see. I flip the visor down and slip Clint's postcard under the clip that holds my photo of the lady slipper. I smile at a couple of late bloomers who finally decided to open their petals.

"The heart is the truest compass," I mumble, staring at Clint's handwriting.

I touch my lips, feeling them curve into a smile, as I put the car in drive. Already I'm fantasizing about how Clint will look the next time I see him, sun dancing on the water as he steers his Lake of the Woods fishing boat toward the dock.

My whole body tingles with the kind of bubbly anticipation that I know even ten months won't be able to water down. I steer out of my neighborhood and down Old Mill Road, past White Sugar, past Hill Toppers', past all those businesses that keep reinventing themselves as the decades roll.

It really is true, I think as I stare at those ancient stone faces—history never leaves us. But it's not like it sticks around just to weigh us down, to taunt us, to torture us with what can never be again. History is who we are right *now*. I mean, just because a chapter of life is over, it isn't gone—basketball is still in my bones. And Clint is in my heart…

I accelerate onto the on-ramp, veering onto the highway that will take me to Springfield. I stretch my arm out the window. A wild screech of utter excitement fills the air as the odometer starts to add up the miles I'm putting between myself and my girlhood home.